Chapter One

Had a lit holiday with my fam! <3 feeling very blessed and looking forward to catching up with my mains xxx

Grace was having a shit holiday, not that she'd seen any of it. Even Mount Etna's volcanic ashes couldn't flick her Charlotte Tilbury Full Fat Lashes away from the Samsung Galaxy A9 Pro (with Infinity-O display, fingerprint sensor, and Bixby vision) during the two weeks she was kidnapped in club class to the *delicate and ethereal baroque town in Sicily* - an expenses paid endorsement by trustworthy Telegraph travel typist Zoe Madmarch-Hare - a woman of whom it could never be said did *not* resemble a maniacal horse with buttery baylayage pleased as punch with itself having looted Oliver Bonas in an equine revamping of the 2011 Mark Duggan riots.

OMG! I Soooooo love Solomon! She fawned over the Facebook wall of a classmate who was definitely ghosting her since she slipped the social noose. Solomon's online currency was strong having been on the London news speaking about moving from Sierra Leone to Putney with parents who run an online theatre project for digitally impoverished teens.

"What's his last name?" Dylan sprung up behind his sister's shoulder like a hack-in-the-box, holding an imaginary microphone "What are his greatest fears? What's the name of his first pet? Unravel for us some of the interpersonal dynamics which cemented this unbreakable tryst"

"WTAF!" Grace said the acronym which took the same number of syllables to say as the *actual* words and closed the door on her awkward, ugly, askhole brother. Her online activity was a delicately maintained political ecosystem and none of his business - human Candy Crush - a public display of affection for Solomon was worth three colour bombs on a wrap.

Grace had previously thought Sierra Leone was a car and gender fluid was the KY she'd found amongst their mum's Marie Kondo concertinaed knickers – it didn't spark joy but it did stop sparks flying - and she knew that proximity to Solomon was a point scorer. He had a definitive package - socially, if not in his trousers.

The cold leather of an armchair startled Dylan's sun-scorched limbs. *"Fam", "mains", what a colossal cucklord!* Sneering at her profile picture, he found himself missing the five-year-old sister who had helped him paint Tippex on snail shells so next time it rained they'd recognise individual characters, good old Snail Winton! - his favourite - Supermarket Snail was a childhood memory life could never wig snatch from him. The rules were simple, gather as many snails as possible in empty egg boxes and the loser had to leave them on a neighbour's doorstep, ring the bell, shout "SUPERMARKET SNAIL!" and run away. These adopted molluscs were instrumental in their parents' purchase of a puppy in the hope it would put their offspring off the snail trail.

Eleven years on, Grace had been replaced with a spectre - a hologram, floating through a virtual landscape to collect data and formulate an online approximation of vigour. Hair straightened so viciously it could advertise conversion therapy, eyebrows a kabuki actor would tone down, and contouring that would make Tony the Tiger feel like a flat-faced feline. But creepiest of all, the eyes. The lights were off and there was a pile up of un-opened mail.

Dylan felt a prick - of guilt - about his austere assessment when a new notification busy-bodied its way through the nosy inter-net curtains. *Grace Curtis likes the page You Were Born an Original, Don't Die a Copy!* His top lip snarled back so far you could see his gums which were inflamed courtesy of a crudely constructed toothbrush his mum had bought by the side of the road from a carefree nomad with a small pet monkey and no teeth, but plenty of enterprise – thanks to gap year Gabbys in hemp harem trousers and Sanskrit tattoos wanting selfies with him.

Ping, ping, ping. Half their mutuals also liked the page. Dylan knew that to jeer about any of this made you "negative". Some would call it a sleight of hand by a generation of risk-averse conformists trying to make pumpkin spice blusher the new punk rock. Dylan considered speaking his mind for a misguided moment, realising that this also would be considered a *rant* and so would writing that he acknowledged it would be considered a rant. And this, and this, and - looping endlessly with regularly repeating periods of expansion and contraction.

He closed the app, blue and white like sanctimonious toothpaste, Nurse Ratched with a balloon. The light faded, confronting him with his own face in the tyrannical time thief and he frowned at his reflection upon reflecting that the Bugsy Malone cheek of two summers ago had been evicted and his body was being squatted by Glenda Jackson bones and David Bowie teeth.

Dylan took a deep breath, felt sick in his throat, and coughed, making his eyes water. There was that smell again, tainted, stagnant, prickling the back of his nostrils. He hadn't even wanted this account. Dad had created one for him when he was twelve so that he could 'be involved' with a charity motorcycle ride he was planning with some of the other dads, a complete ersatz of the BBC 3 programme a few months earlier: "Three Amigos Magical Mystery Tour!". The three comedians were doughy, with podcasts, beards, cardigans, and autobiographies full of honest self-reflection about their patriarchal privilege. The TV series never seemed to end. Prime-time Michael Myers.

Three years had lapsed and Dylan had only used Facebook a couple of times. There was more on his page from his parents than from him. Once, in a mistaken moment of vulnerability, he'd chronicled how bored he was and, to his bewilderment, being five metres away at the time, it invited comments from both his Mum *and* Dad about how there was a "brill" Joy Division documentary on BBC4 prompting other parents to add their two pennies' worth. A bleak tragedy in which parents impale their offspring with The Cocteau Twins and garrotte them with Bauhaus. Dylan didn't write about being bored again.

"Dad, why?" without moving his lips, Dylan shifted long, insolent legs under the mock wood table in the airport departure lounge.

"Just one more!" Dad was positioning a glass of white wine so that he could take a picture of the glass - caption: 'be rude not to!' - his children behind it and, if he contorted his body and used landscape, an aeroplane through the window.

"Fucksake," Dylan mumbled through clenched teeth again. Dad was now lying on the ground as two French girls in skiing gear giggled at his ghostly arse crack escaping the top of his Levis. "Who's it even for?"

His protestations pissed into the wind as the pointless pictorial essay of Grace narrowing her eyes at Kylie Jenner's latest tweet, Mum frowning at an angry *rant* another mum had posted on the Neighbourhood App about fly-tipping, and Dylan scowling through a curtain of bony fingers and sun-bleached fringe was pissed into Instagram.

#holiday #children #wine #airport #travel #summer #flight #home #sicily #family #photography #travel #gratitude.

Time crawled on its belly until their people carrier crawled onto Magdalen Road. Dylan had been counting wicker hearts on doors and in windows since the M4. *3038.*

The family exited the Twickenham Tanker and walked single file up the garden path, each looking at their phones. From the back it would have looked like a family in mourning, heads bowed in silent private prayer. The procession was laced with terracotta pots, the pallbearers two fat, judgemental, bashed-in-the-face-with-frying-pan pedigree cats and the priest, a La Hacienda linea self-standing chiminea with sizable firebox and removable flue.

Chapter Two

"Helllooooooo! Hellllooo! Hello, you!"

Dylan voted Josh's "Hello" the most disingenuous due to his complete distraction by someone's adolescent daughter at the next table. Josh's wife, Sylvie, was at the stage where she almost encouraged it. It's what girls like that were for, flibbertigibbet distractions, and, correspondingly, Josh was treated like an incorrigible son.

Josh and Sylvie had blended into one gender with any primary sexual characteristics swaddled away in North Face Fleece.

Josh, Cecily, Sylvie, Eleanor, Dylan's Mum and Dad, and another man Dylan vaguely recognised sat around the large wooden table at the Vape and Pushchair, a pub with square plates and owl cushions frequented by Londoners with craggy but well-valeted faces courtesy of bespoke facials with a plant based holistic 360 approach to help you live your best life and try out your personality on Bulgarian beauty therapists who make you feel like the international metropolitan your 12-year-old self knew you could be. The tarmac tourists move back to the sweet bird song of the Home Counties before the children are of secondary school age or they turn into pumpkins, with a few anecdotes about pie and mash, burglary, and a homeless woman they saw eat a pigeon in front of Euston station.

Eleanor was best-of-a-bad-job blonde and had a habit of wearing a man's tie to pub outings, because someone had once told her she looked like Daryl Hannah in *Splash*. Coincidently, she also had a habit of pronouncing minutiae "my new tie", which made members of her Shoreditch book club want to strangle her with it.

London was the whore with a heart of mineable gold, long-suffering lovers left picking up the pancetta pieces till premature death them did part. They wore flip-flops and gilets in autumn, pashminas and other drapery depravities in winter. Their sentences were punctuated with "bit grim" and "quite fun". "Quite fun" for inanimate objects rather than something which might be quite fun, god forbid. Example: Someone admires a new path made using different coloured stones or a bunch of twigs wrapped in fairy lights stuck in a wooden bucket. The response, "Yes. I like it, actually! It's quite fun." On the other hand, "bit grim" can be anything from Covid-19 to their friends' relationships.

So, he said he just didn't feel happy all of a sudden and left 'Pip' or 'Frip' or whoever in St Albans and went on an ayuhuascha retreat in Peru with an asexual, fruitarian hypnotherapist who won't let anyone touch her face so. . . bit grim.

But all this was window dressing for the main event: *Their Children!* After years of taking a back seat to the class clown or office joker, a chance arose to showcase the sparkling wit the world had overlooked until now. Like Yorick's skull or an obnoxious puppet, we are all Ernie Wise now.

"Look! He's still got those gorgeous pre-Raphaelite curls!" Sylvie fondled the front of Dylan's hair, producing an uncomfortable smile. He thought Sylvie looked like a cross between the witch from "Chorlton and the Wheelies" and a blind nihilist with a Bon Marche gift voucher and personal vendetta against beauty.

Dylan knew what "Chorlton and the Wheelies" was because his parents had forced him to watch it on YouTube. This act of child abuse made 'A Boy Called It' read like a trip to Alton Towers and extended to "Hong Kong Phooey" "The Space Sentinels" and any other childhood memories they arrogantly assumed were important – including a Silvikrin advert featuring a girl that his Dad used to fancy.

Dylan's Dad and his friends were always talking about who they *used to fancy*. Toyah Wilcox, Moira Stuart, Mystic Meg, Ruth Madoc, a mouse ghost, a magic pea, a piece of wicker basket, a lesbian horse, an existential concept. Who they used to fancy quickly became a Top Trumps of who used to fancy the most inappropriate person, plant or thing.

"Life on Mars" by David Bowie played over the pub speakers. *It's a God-awful small affair, to the girl with the mousy hair.*

And it is also a God-awful small affair to the boy with the pre-Raphaelite curls, Dylan thought.

Cecily made the obligatory enquiry about Dylan's exams and what his plans were after leaving school. Dylan did have a five-point plan for leaving school:

1. Become incredibly rich in order to... (see number **2**)
2. Fund a reclusive lifestyle
3. Outlive everyone who would be upset if he died
4. Die of old age
5. Remember not to be reincarnated again

Dylan refrained from revealing his shrewd vocational proposal and, in any case, Cecily had that way of talking where before anyone finished saying whatever they were saying, she'd already nodded in agreement and said "Yes! Yes!" – constantly interjecting "Yes!" over the bit where the respondent was saying the important part.

"I congratulate you on your good taste!" Josh, a previously brown-haired, flat cap-wearing dynamics financial analyst, indicated Dylan's Ramones T-shirt.

"Well, I –" Dylan began, but his response was hijacked and the yawn chorus began.

"When we were in New York, we were at a loose end one night," the man Dylan vaguely recognised started with his story "and we got talking to this chap who worked in a delicatessen – actually he was a Russian cage fighter. And --"

"Well, of course", Josh interrupted, "that's what they do when they're not snapping each other's arms. They potter about with herbs and spices. Sage fighting!"

"Wouldn't sage fighting be where you beat up a clever old man?" said Dylan's Dad. The men went off on a 90s nostalgic Vic and Bob excursion, imagining the old man's name would be "Ian Hedgerow" and that the fictional character would have a long-standing feud with an enemy named "Brian Seven Hoods" and they wallowed in their uniquely surreal imaginations. The crowning glory was surmising there was something called "Mixed Herbs Martial Arts".

"Haaa," the Vaguely Recognisable Man snorted in counterfeit indignation, "As I was saying, this guy recommended the Ramones exhibition, which was being organised by a Dutch artist and you'll never guess who was there."

"Debbie Harry," someone guessed out loud. The name chimed a death knell in Dylan's head.

"Five points to you!" said Vaguely Recognised, "Got our picture taken with her. Look, it's my – ahem – Facebook cover photo!" He downplayed the words "Facebook cover photo" as if he wasn't - like all of them - hook, line, and blinker invested in his cyber second life.

"Used to fancy her," said Dylan's dad. His claim arrived with the dull algorithmic predictability of Rain Man watching "Wheel of Fortune". He'd never fancied Debbie Harry. He'd in fact, spent the years between eleven and fifteen clandestinely in love with David Sylvian from Japan.

“Oh no”, replied Vaguely Recognised. His quilted gilet strained around what he tongue-in-cheekily called his Dad Bod or Balcony Over the Toy Shop. Artisan, micro brewed craft ale gathered in his dry crunchy beard like Dutch elm disease in a neglected hedge and his abnormally long big toe wriggled in his sandals with the excitement of what he was about to say. “Debbie’s aged badly. Did you see her at the awards thing? She’s had a lot of work.” He made air quotes for work. Vaguely Recognised’s sausage meat lower lip hid itself in the turned-up collar of his £425 Harrington rain jacket.

“Yeah, it’s a shame, isn’t it?” Dylan’s Dad rubbed the top of his head and his fish eyes turned mistily nostalgic as if his 14-year-old self’s imaginary Debbie Harry erection deserved compensation.

“Well, I’m not overly familiar with their work,” Dylan dragged the festering conversation back from anecdote grave. “Dad got me the T-shirt. If I’m honest, I think they’re a bit overrated.”

“Blasphemy!” declared Josh, “How can you not have good taste in music with a name like Dylan?”

Christ, not again. Dylan sighed.

“We named him after the rabbit in ‘Magic Roundabout’, explained Dylan’s dad. There was a collective “ahhh!” of respect at this tired revelation.

“Used to fancy Florence,” Josh immediately regretted his cliched claim as questions about whether Florence was supposed to be a child hijacked his mind like paedophilic flash cards. Even the pop art Liz Taylor on a beer mat seemed to rolled her violet eyes.

“The rabbit was named after Bob Dylan,” sighed Dylan before his words were made redundant with the appearance of a young, slim, ponytailed waitress.

“Aren’t you cold?” one of the women asked, referring to the waitress’s H&M playsuit.

She read out the day’s specials, shrugging off the loaded question. “The soup of the day is butternut and sweet potato with croutons.” The waitress pronounced croutons the way it was spelt: *kraut ons.*

“Don’t tell the Germans,” Josh said to guilty sniggering as the waitress looked confused but forced a smile, took their orders, turned and walked back behind the bar. Dylan noticed each of the men – and some of the women, albeit for different reasons – follow her walk with twitchy, troubled eyes.

Dylan’s Mum leaned in to Josh, “You well and truly confused her!”

“Someone’s been Tangoed,” Josh replied, knowing they were all within the right age range to remember the popular advert.

“I know,” she returned. Few things animated her these days but the motif of fake tans did. “It’s like, you don’t *need* all that make-up.” Dylan’s mum pulled what she wanted to be a sad, kind, confused face.

Sitting around the table with their beards and osmosis-formed opinions, the men could have been a panel of talking heads on a Channel 5 “*100 Politically Incorrect 70s Sitcoms We Can’t Laugh At Anymore And This Is The Only Pretence Under Which We Can Sneak You The Footage”*. The new lads were old dads, with iPads.

Everyone went back to telling stories about different countries and different women the men *used to fancy.* The partners smiled, smugly safe in the knowledge that their surrogate sons only *used* to fancy people and found girls like the ponytailed plate-porter pitiable. Their men liked fleshy women in Italian wraps who smelt of dog and breast milk and hand sanitiser and had Storksak baby changing bags with insulated compartments for feeding bottles, organic aloe cleansing wipes, double foil-lined pouches, and room for a pony. They were fond of women who could answer a few questions at pub quizzes, the nice questions, ones about the Pennines and Sophie Ellis-Bextor.

The conversation blurred into a background murmur in Dylan's ears like the teacher in Charlie Brown, he only caught the occasional phrase.

Blah blah Tuscany, blah blah league table.

The smell of Sylvie's Crabtree and Evelyn award-winning Nantucket Briar Hand Therapy couldn't mask the yeasty smell of death which had followed Dylan all the way from Sicily to Cecily. He tried to stay awake by counting things in the room, dividing them up into colours and shapes and then adding up the resulting sub-categories.

Dylan excused himself and took his bag of sweet chilli and sour cream crisps outside and sat on the hot pavement. A tiny grey mouse, one which was really tiny – imagine an already small mouse, probably half that size – ran around the pub's air vent. After watching the rodent scuttle about, Dylan decided to name him Titus and smuggle him home. Was there life in bars, yes! Yes, there bloody was!

Chapter Three

The last time Dylan had got the bus to school he had been climbing the stairs when he was shunted to the left by a stampede of cacophonous shoes and faux hysteria. Five girls from his year pushed passed him, gurned, screeched, fell over, laughed a dry, tinny laugh and stamped their feet hard on the floor. This was all done with the lack of rhythm a group of friends tends to have when enjoying one another's company. No eye contact - that would break the spell as they opened their mouths wide to spill fizzy red powder accidently over a bystander's spaniel. "Sorry!" the fauxpology whined with full knowledge that it would be received as such. To convey legitimate regret would be *like OMG! shame*! The humour bar on the bus was low, lower than a podcast comedian limbo dancing under Richard Pryor's corpse. For Comic Relief, of course.

The hysteria reached an apex when an extraordinarily scarce dribble of content appeared on one of their phones from a classmate with eczema who had been named Mabel by thoughtful parents, thoughtfully choosing a classless name. This backfired, of course, because it immediately conjured up the image of thoughtful middle-class parents thoughtfully choosing a classless name, but never mind, because Mabel's insignificant others had given her the nickname "Lizard" in reference to her skin condition. At least now she had a *genuinely* classless name.

"What you gunna do when you leave schoo-oo-ool?" asked a girl who could have sprung from a How to Be an Average Teen YouTube tutorial. The word "school" was sung in three syllables: up – down – up, like a toddler with learning difficulties, or, indeed, someone presenting a YouTube tutorial.

"I want to work with special needs children," said Elspeth Roberts, who lived in hope of being asked. Though barely two years into menstruation, her global influencer game could rival Edelman. Most people take years to grasp a brief concept of using charity as both a weapon and a shield but Elspeth had inherited the instinct like a Deptford Dalai Lama.

Dylan supressed a laugh. *Haven't they been through enough? The Make a Wish Foundation would be making a wish for a tragic selfie accident before she has a chance to apply.*

After reclining for an apportioned time in the "ahhhs" of admiration for her future martyrdom, Elspeth and her Year 10 tentacles returned to the squawking and shrieking about Mabel and the few online traces of her they'd been able to find. They punctuated this every now and then with that spurious maternal concern girls have: *Worryingly thin, embracing her curves.*

"Shanika said that Jeanette said that Mabel come out with some whiny victim fuckery about *I don't feel comfortable in this class* when literally no one had said anything! She really needs to take responsibility for her feelings and stop blaming other people. She's only hurting herself with her behaviour," said a girl named Lauren who had two facial expressions: insincere and pious. Which makes one facial expression, really.

It was very nice of Lauren to use her after school time to be mindful about Mabel's lack of self-care. Dylan had hardly any extracurricular activities except karate, and that was more for the benefit of his Dad than him. The doublethink dribbled through needle-sharp Kaiser's incisors, rebranding the sheer joy of firing rounds at a walking target as a helpful life-coaching session.

Dylan went through the scenarios of what might happen if he spoke up. "Called them out on their bullshit," as Callum Best might have said on a reality show a few years ago after discovering someone had used his hairbrush. *Nah, I'd never hear the last of it. It would be outrageous. Besides, let them have their moment in the sun*, he relented. They were kings of their castles - if your castle was a Dax pomade-stinking double decker lost in London traffic and dreary drill - anonymous actors on a ghost ship playing to a captive TFL audience. This was as good as it was going to get for them before lanyards, double chins, and health scares. Dylan had a feeling that, for Mabel, it was going to be a terrible pilot sitcom never to be commissioned.

During the last summer term, Dylan had got into the habit of walking to and from school even though it took over an hour. He'd tried to make it fun by counting his footsteps. He was doing just that – *4008, 4009* – when chakra rupturing screams at a bus stop ahead jolted him from his mathematical meditation. Even adults were swerving the scene and two community policemen made a detour to Chicken Pickin, affectionately known as Salmonella Shack. Trying to remember where he was up to – *4005? 4007?* – the smell of hot rubbish was augmented by cross-strain weed. It was a heavy afternoon. When they say that on the 31st October the veils between the worlds are at their thinnest – well, it was the opposite of whatever "they" meant. The veils were brick walls. There was no doubt which world Dylan was in: the shit one.

Becoming aware of a mammoth circle of girls and a couple of boys encroaching on Mabel in her (fall-out) bus shelter, Dylan noticed the Visconti Tuscan Brown briefcase at her feet. The marauding mass were many and menacing and in too-big September uniforms and painful pumps. Her only friend, Amber, had been slowly inching away so that she was just a whisper closer to the others - she couldn't have been more obvious if she'd planted a flag in the ground.

Often, since starting secondary school, Dylan would be struck with an abysmal feeling halfway home that the house would be on fire. Or that everyone had been murdered, chosen indiscriminately. *Just one of those things.*

He'd force this thought into the forefront of his brain, repeating it over and over. His rationale was that things like that didn't happen: the supernatural, premonitions. It would be way too much of a coincidence.

"*Paradise Lost!* What is it? A porno?" Elspeth Roberts bellowed like a baby with croup and a fifty-a-day habit. *Her* uniform wasn't too big, in fact her Eddie Munster of a body gave it the look of a middle-aged woman with gynaecological problems stuffed into a fancy-dress costume for a hen night or fundraising fun run, or a last ditch cliched roleplay attempt eliciting a begrudging memory of an erection from a hated husband-in-a-bag named Paul. The words were said through the sound of hard red sweets rattling noisily in her quadrangled head as she brandished the book around Mabel's before throwing it to the mob, a "mob"! It was too formulaic. A bullying scene written by a failed novelist who'd never been bullied, been to a school or known a child, was made out of paper and lived inside a ship in a bottle containing an over-ambitious improv group.

"Give it back. My Dad gave it to me," Mabel protested, trying to smile and be in on the joke.

"Raah! Why's your old man giving you books about lost paradise? Pervert!" said Elspeth. One of the most depressing things about being bullied was, for Mabel, the inability to not be disappointed by the quality of the script.

"*Staggering dereliction of duty to the stage!*" "*The perpetrators failed to pick up on Mabel's slight speech impediment*" "*Being awkwardly tall for her age, the so-called bullies missed an obvious height-based reference by completely bypassing the potential nickname 'Tower of Mabel'*"

"See, I told you. All girls have tits," said a boy named McKenzie who moved in sudden jerks like a Pixar Polecat. His awareness wristbands slipped over his hand which was flat against

Mabel's chest. Green for bipolar, periwinkle for eating disorders, magenta for Mumbai wristband makers. He turned back to stare, wide-eyed, into her face. "Don't you speak?"

"She's autistic!" Elspeth spat, manic at her own wit and in the received pronunciation for conveying the mentally challenged.

"I'm not," Mabel retorted, "Autism is a neurodevelopmental spectrum condition. Many autistic people lack the ability to interpret facial expressions, tone of voice, jokes and sarcasm."

"Oh, my days!" Elspeth's eyes turned into bulging Halloween jelly sweets, "Did you hear? I swear that is soooo autistic!"

"Yes, that was the –" Mabel abandoned her explanation.

Their bus pulled in and everyone bundled up the stairs, barely able to contain their squawking glee. "*Paradise Lost.* Durrrrrrrr!" Elspeth threw the paperback from the top deck window and her audience squealed and yelped, safe in the knowledge that they were not bad people. They were spectators and would go on to have children and share Facebook links about random acts of kindness, Change.org petitions, recipes for cancer-curing drinks made from things you can find in a kitchen cupboard, and cat gifs. To sum up, they would adjust throughout their lives to the most acceptable and conforming way to behave. Right now, it was joining in with destroying Mabel.

The book flew through some scaffolding into a derelict building, disturbing a couple of pigeons. The bus party instinctively ducked down below the windows in case it hit someone who might retaliate.

When Dylan approached Mabel, she was still sitting at the bus stop trying to force a smile. She smelled of oats and ointment, which was different from the other girls who smelled of hot grease and spite.

“Okay?” asked Dylan.

“Yeah,” Mabel gulped down the word with a glass of denial and cocktail umbrella of shame.

Her face was hot and pink with indignity as the bus she should have been on barged its way in front of a Ford Fiesta.

“Where’d it go?” asked Dylan.

“What?” She knew what.

“The book,” Dylan pressed, “The book one of those trees with eyes threw.” Mabel just shrugged. “I mean, I’m not saying they’re morally bankrupt, just that they have more faces than Big Ben. I mean, each, not between them”

“Don’t matter!” she answered, almost smiling for real this time. Appropriating improper grammar happened more at times, a verbal manifestation of the trick vagina a duck has: *just swim up the wrong one and leave me alone*! “We always throw each other’s stuff.”

“Sounds fun,” he mocked “Is there, like, a league table or something? A premier division?”

“It doesn’t matter!” Mabel kicked her ethical shoes and licked her metaphorical wounds.

“Does,” said Dylan.

“Doesn’t.”

“Does!”

"It's there somewhere, don't matter!" Mabel waved dismissively towards the Victorian fire hazard and seemed to have waived her defences as Dylan walked in its direction, looking back once more with an auspicious eyebrow raise.

Passing a boarded-up Mecca Bingo, Dylan tried to gauge how easy it would be to scale a building with nothing to hold on to. Wrapping his school tie around his head, his hands felt slimy. "Anti-Climb Paint", the sign read, except someone had changed 'Climb' to 'Climax' via a sharpie. Rubbing some dirt from the grass verge on his palms – he'd seen it somewhere, a film maybe, one probably involving Tom Hardy – he shimmied up the pole of the scaffold. His fingers burned from the black grease, some substance they don't make anymore, something rank and nasty from the 70s like creosote or fibreglass or The Barron Knights. Something people used to feel nothing of throwing at neighbourhood cats. Throwing it at cats was practically a civic duty.

A couple of school kids shouted up non-specific things like "Huurrr!" and "Rudeboy!" and "Squad Goals!" and a "Da-da-da darrrr!" His heart beat heavy and hard and he felt nauseous. *Was this vertigo?*

Climbing higher and higher, he reached the tiniest platform and had to evict a moth-eaten pigeon. "He's been no-platformed!" he shouted to his bus stop judges, now with phones out knee-jerkingly filming the content, chips tumbling out of large, laughing mouths, still adjusting to alien adult teeth in the first flush of . . . tooth, as the pigeon flew off to start a YouTube channel about creeping McCarthyism. Dylan carefully navigated a semi-circle of wood big enough for maybe half a foot – one of his feet that is, not six inches – and had to shuffle himself around, clicking his clumpy school shoes at the heel like Dorothy longing for Kansas.

Once around the other side, he could climb through a tiny brick-framed hole. Another irate pigeon flew out close enough to his head to make it clear unscheduled visits were a social *faux pas* in the urbane code of pigeon etiquette. Reaching around in the darkness, his hand knocked into a book shape. "Sorry", he automatically apologised. Then, feeling farcical, he spun around, relieved to concentrate on his exit strategy. His heart jumped and his nerves filled with adrenaline when something grabbed at his ankle from the corner. The blood drained from his body, straight down to his feet, making them feel like phantom feet and paralysing him on the spot.

Trying to shake life back into his cold, oily hands, he could vaguely make out a homeless man – the U2 1995 tour T-Shirt gave it away - rudely awoken from beneath several issues of *London Style* magazine.

"Sorry to bother you. Forgot my book" Dylan motioned that he did indeed have a book in his hand and was not a burglar with a lackadaisical approach to wealth and affection for situational absurdity. He quickly realised he may as well have been holding an inflatable, clown, or Gemma Collins.

"Five equals nine – ha, ha, seven!" the vagrant computed, "Seven? Hmmm, I could have seven. Seven's alright. Three plus four. Neptune, Seven, Pisces, Bruce Forsyth. Nice to see you to see you. . ."

"Nice?" Dylan took a gamble.

"Aha!" the unsafe space squatter's eyes lit up. "He's got it. By George, he's got it! Yeah, he's alright. He's alright. Old blue eyes is back. Oh yeah, old blue eyes, he's alright. I'll kill you! You're alright. I'm not a paedophile. Who is? You murderer! That's alright. Nah, nah, we're all friends here! Zionist! Who?" He alternated between kind grinning, fierce rage and casual chitchat: "Lovely pub lunch, Hemel Hempstead. Agh ha! I'm a lamb, I am. I'm a lamb, too *fucking gentle* to live among *fucking wolves*!"

Dylan reversed out of the boarded-up building while the going was, good? retracing his steps until he hit the ground, dusted down his blazer, blew black soot from his hair and face and lifted the tie off his head. As he handed Mabel her book, she gave him a look he couldn't interpret. *Gratitude? Anger? Suspicion? Was it a smile?* he wondered, *It had ordered a smile online and was choosing which squares have a store front before payment can commence. What if someone runs a business from their front room?*

"You'd make a good soldier," Mabel said brightly, then opened the book to see someone had drawn a giant cock and customary asymmetrical balls all over the beautifully shaky 1950s pencil dedication her great-granddad had written to her granddad.

"Nah, khaki is so not my colour," Dylan replied in what he hoped was comedy camp, mock Gok. "Is it good? The book? I'm trying to read HP Lovecraft myself"

"*The oldest and strongest emotion of mankind is fear, and the oldest and strongest kind of fear is fear of the unknown,*" Mabel quoted, a little sanctimoniously. Maybe her persecutors had a point.

"Ed Sheeran?"

"I appreciate it. Really." Mabel raised the book a little and smiled a smile as enchanting as an enchanted elf in an enchanted castle in an enchanted forest, and kissed Dylan lightly on the cheek. He'd never seen her face do that before: the smiling thing.

"S'alright", Dylan said over his shoulder as he began to walk home without counting steps or anticipating any brutal massacres. *How novel.*

Dylan thought school was warped. Students had evolved to put up their hands during Media Social Science and Relationships Class and say things like "I don' fink dat anyone should be judged on what size dey are. All sizes are beautiful, yeah? And as long as da person has a positive attitude, den dare going to attract positivity into dare laaaaaaiiife." Peculiar little self-help gurus parroting the zeitgeist.

Boys knew they earned brown-nose points for nodding along with how "the objectification of women in society is problematic" and the teacher would praise them, pleased that 40-odd years of superficial pop psychology was now a default response. With the swipe of a thumb, they'd be back on the bus with the other jackals and snides, howling with laughter about how some poor unfortunate has a disabled mum and eats from food banks or how disgusting Jacob's porno footage of an elderly woman is. The amount of self-deception necessary to keep up this dual existence was impressively depressing.

Chapter Four

On the first day back after the holidays, Dylan left the house an hour earlier than last term to avoid the circus of the spineless on the imbecile express. There was going to be a 'special' assembly and even before his phone had started bleating with notifications of invitations to 'like' her tribute page, which had a cover photo of the palm of someone's hand with a hashtag and a heart drawn on it. Dylan had a feeling that Mabel had killed herself during the summer break. No long London days at Lidos or Westfield. Every hour had been a stomach-wrenching footstep on the Green Mile to 2nd September. The surprise seemed outlandish; it would have been more scandalous if Mabel *hadn't* done it by now. Bullying was an open all hour's business, a 24/7 service, the gift that kept giving, the city that never slept - it happened a lot.

Mabel had waited until Helena and Richard, her impossibly nice parents, were out on a picnic for the homeless before hacking at her wrists using a Gillette Venus Embrace *with protective ribbon of moisture for notably less irritation*. She'd bought it in August during a flash of foolish faith that there might be something worth shaving her underarms for soon. The last thing she'd seen was Emma Willis's sisterly smile on a money off voucher.

I'm proud to partner with the new 'USE YOUR AND' campaign, which aims to inspire and encourage women everywhere to celebrate all the different brilliant qualities that make them unique, the text read, next to a model with a rucksack made to look like a giant by adding miniature buildings for scale. Mabel had thought about those words as her radial artery haemorrhaged into the L'Occitane Neroli Milk Bath, turning it into a beautiful sea of rhubarb and custard. Lukas Graham's voice sang out from the television and she felt fleetingly guilty for not turning it off first. They never left televisions or lights on when they weren't being used.

“Think of the planet, Mabel Babel,” they would often say.

Once, I was 11-years-old. . . Graham sang on the tea-time television programme to an audience erupting into pleased recognition. Her final thoughts as she glided into the white noise of unconsciousness drifted from how she could “use her and” to where a giant would buy a rucksack to “Who on earth tells an 11-year-old to ‘get himself a wife?’”

Can’t believe I’ll never see your beautiful face again, began the tributes.

Your an angle in heven now

So traumatised by what has happened : (

I hope your at piece

You will be mist.

They were mostly giant yellow emojis with blue streams coming from the eyes. Some used emojis of other crying things, like cats and rabbits and non-specific generic animal-type animals. Someone, who must have been 3 gigabytes more upset than the others, posted a gif of a unicorn holding a bunch of flowers, then jumping into the air and turning into rainbow dust. Some students had tried to find pictures of themselves with her, but since Mabel was the social equivalent of toxic shock syndrome, there were none to be found. Still, you can’t say no to a 16-year-old – literally - it was banned in 2016 due to fears around the impact of negative reinforcement. Alternatives such as action words, motivators, positive redirections, and warning signals were allowed.

More and more of her grieving brostitutes were bypassing this awkward obstacle by taking selfies in front of Mabel’s tribute display on the school hall stage and uploading them to their various social media platforms.

Thick and fast came the inane prosaicisms. Banished was the Beano bully, the big bruiser who knew they were the villain, revelling in their Machiavellian spite. Mixed ability classes and awareness initiatives meant that the biggest bully in the school was more than likely to be overseeing an anti-bullying campaign. The subtle bully, the bully with cognitive dissonance and a Just Giving Page. We are all schizophrenics now. And Ernie Wise.

Fuck enduring this mass hypocrisy wank, spat Dylan, crossing the road, carefully avoiding his sister walking past a row of shops with her regular fremisis.

Glancing at a missing poster for a 12-year-old girl, one gone for three weeks now, Grace put her hand to her face as if in shock. "OMG! Bitch has a perfect jawline"

Dylan wandered lonely as a shroud for ten minutes, recognising the leisure centre and flats which looked out of place in the London suburbs, more like something from a seaside town – all white fasciae, balconies, plastic flowers and get well soon cards. He remembered them from the last time he'd bunked off with his best friend Liam, the only child at the Ofsted oilingly-outstanding Catholic infant school that was genuinely Catholic and who had relatives on a traveller site near there.

Like Mabel, Liam seemed to have been catapulted from another era, but unlike Mabel, in a way which worked. He rode a pushbike so old it had the faded remnants of a sticker for the TV show 'C.H.I.P.S' on the frame and rusty water would fly off if he peddled quickly. He was always eating an apple, including the core and pips. "A little bit of cyanide does you good!" Liam's aunty jabbed the wisdom at him with sovereign ringed and Sovereign smoking religious fervour. Liam wore a grey school jumper even in the evenings and at weekends, had eyes the colour of the translucent cola part of fizzy cola bottles and, like Mabel, didn't have any of the stuff kids were supposed to, but it never seemed to affect him. He didn't go to Dylan's big school, though. He was on probation.

Liam sometimes lived with Nanny Aideen in her council block behind some shops in town. The residents had slipped through the gentrification net due to it being so much of a death trap that it would have cost too much to develop. Instead, the council hired private contractors to plant huge trees concealing it from the powdery glances of the luxury flat dwellers in Elysium towers across the road in their JoJo Maman Bébé, bespoke cheese and naturopathic dog grooming Shangri-La. The council had added a few modern art sculptures, premeditated graffiti, and idiotically renamed it *Alleyway Square*.

Nanny Aideen had lived there since the 70s. Inside it was still the 70s. Paper doilies, sugar in a glass bowl, matey bubble bath and any guests who might drop by drip-fed repeats of "Minder" and "The Sweeney" on ITV4. The only signs it was the 21st century was a pink iPad upstanding on the sideboard with family photos as though it were an ornament, and a Hollyoaks calendar one of her sons had dropped off late last New Year's Eve. Sometimes, Liam stayed on the traveller site with his mum and sometimes with a man who might be his dad.

Dylan's parents often tried to drill him for information about Liam over dinner. He still remembered the capful of stingy Dettol in the bath whenever he'd been playing around his place and understood what their fascination with the other was about, the glamour, the same reason they watched programmes about "Gypsy Weddings" or "Brits Abroad" = people with the wrong hairstyles and mannerisms who were bred for circuses. *When was the last time a reality show featured people named Penny and Julian visiting a garden centre to pick out orchid plant food, occasionally making a tight-lipped, dry remark? Might as well watch Farrow and Ball paint dry.* Dylan protected his friend's sovereignty with his goat's cheese tartlet and saffron fennel-eating life.

The children of the travellers' site threw empty beer cans at each other. Two boys who had one pair of boxing gloves between them punched each other over and over, while some sociology graduates made a film about living "off grid". Inane, they had the fastest Wi-Fi in West London and more iPads than Boris Johnson's technology teacher. Dylan and Liam used these to watch YouTube videos of families challenging other families to bare knuckle fights, a jolly cock-smash of violent foreboding and friendly gossip.

Dylan hoped he could remember the way. Wandering past all the morning people rushing to work and school – skinny men with squeaky shoes, fisherman beards and WhatsApp concerns; women in tailored dresses and trainers, heels in rucksacks to change into at the office, all HD brows and iPhone jowls, earnest, desperate, frightened faces, stretched, eager necks from vicious yoga and chemical peels, worried, straightened hair and spreadsheet eyes, hanging on to 39 by shellac fingernails. Bridget Jones' picture in the attic. Johnny Vaughan's pillar of salt.

The smell of burning apple tree wood sparked a memory. It was what the day had smelled like last year. And as the September sun turned the bald head of a sex tourist golden, Dylan climbed a steep hill. Ragweed, nettles and dandelions sprawled around wild flowers that he didn't know the names of, except anemones. He knew them. Messy, like someone had filled them in with a too big paint brush going over all the lines and letting the colours bleed. They made the other flowers look either a bit civil servant, a bit wallpaper or like big, blousy suburban women in swimming hats with patio doors and rude gossip. You could rely on anemones to tell you the brutal truth. No one had told any of them summer was over. No back to school shoes for them, embers still burned and flew up in the air. *They couldn't have been moved on that long ago?*

It was eerily quiet. A broken xylophone sat next to a faded, plastic statue of Mary, eyes coloured in with green felt tip pen, making it look demonic. Some nightlights by a picture of Princess Diana and a gnome waving a flag with a sealion on it were next to a torn Man United shirt with some blood on it. A cultivated flower bed with a little gold urn like a genie's lamp was sectioned off by battered bunting and a make-shift tent was creatively erected from an old bobbly pink blanket thrown over some garden wire.

This must be where Mary Mary Quite Contrary had lived, too. Silver bells and cockle shells and a mobility scooter hosting a glow-in-the-dark Father Christmas, a Koala Bear puppet and a transparent envelope full of soaking wet birthday cards. A plastic watering can shaped like an elephant, the spout its trunk, had been dragged into the earth by wild vines. These were Dylan's favourite places, ones that look like ten years after human beings have been wiped out.

He lay down and played Rorschach with the clouds. A centipede elongated to become a crocodile. A skull morphed into a goat's head. Brian Blessed became a castle. A standard shrub waved in the breeze, smugly oblivious to the miserable complexity of teenage politics and online footprints. He really envied its simplicity. He wished he was that morphological beatnik.

Dylan thought about dead Mabel, who had never hurt anyone, whose only crime was to have the bare brass balls to annunciate correctly and play the clarinet. She just had the wrong coordinates. *Timing's everything. Why couldn't she see that?* wondered Dylan, *People should try to be incarnated into a time where the road rises to meet them and the wind is at their back.* Mabel's mother and father had globes of the night sky and *Reader's Digest* maps and thesauruses on the shelf. If it wasn't for their time-worn liberal guilt, they might have sent her to a private school where owning the complete works of Edgar Allan Poe and belonging to chess club were currency rather than being tagged in a photo with an auntie who's been on "Gogglebox" or a cousin in a grey prison tracksuit who sells Thai brick weed by the school gates. But these were the things which held credit in this state of idiocracy, this grave new world. Her only hope would have been to reincarnate in *this* same lifetime, like Terence Trent D'arby did. Dylan had seen it on a Sunday morning TV programme called "Walking about with God" or something.

He felt strange, like a stupid sad face emoji. He hadn't cried in years and felt he should be documenting such high emotion somewhere, considering it almost selfish or secretive to not share. He took his phone out of his blazer pocket hypnotically, and summoned Facebook. Elspeth Roberts, or as Dylan now thought of her; the nemesis of special needs children everywhere, had begun a status with the words:

Hey guys…

Always a bad sign.

. . .I know we're all feeling a little shaken up by the tragic news, if anyone's interested, I've written a little piece on my blog about how I feel regarding what's happened, there is a donate button at the bottom xxx

It had 1003 likes including three from teachers. In a way, it was genius. Genius, yet wretched. It's possible to be both, Dylan supposed. His tears turned a patch of his white school shirt transparent and sniffing them away, he fell asleep. The sunlight laughing through the trees brutalised his dreams with images of Mabel rattling a sabre at him which was actually the book, Paradise Lost, before pulling him into the ground which was suddenly a small basement underneath Halfords in somewhere, he thought was Southampton but could be South America. "none of this is real, all will pass" she stated – *bit cliché,* Dylan thought - cynicism, even in dream. The feeling of fear and pressure combined gave him one tenth of an erection – more death throe than death row - but he slept on, the breeze disturbing his hair just like the shrub he envied. Only occasional planes to and from Heathrow broke the honeysuckle and woodbine-scented silence, the smell of fabric conditioner in his clothes gradually out-fragranced by golden autumn air and musty earth.

Chapter Five

"Terrorise, threaten, and insult your own useless generation," Malcolm McLaren hissed from the 50-inch wall-mounted flat screen TV.

"What would be the point?" asked Dylan, "Someone would just turn it into a three second gif of a black woman flicking her hair and pulling a face, and anyway . . .HATE CRIME!"

"I'm so tweeting that! Perhaps without the race reference," Dad was very impressed with his son's response to Channel Four's Celebration of Punk screening of *The Great Rock 'n' Roll Swindle.* Dylan's was a nice household with intelligent parents, born in the 70s, who kept in touch with people they'd met at university despite having nothing in common with them anymore. If they watched "Britain's Got Talent" or "The Real Housewives of Atlanta", it was with a knowing sense of irony that it was trash, but that it was healthy to indulge in a bit of trash now and then. As long as they regularly made a disparaging comment to exhibit their superiority. Like a cheese burrito or pornography, it was okay as long as they were aware. It was ok for people like *them* - intelligent enough to treat things with irony - it was the poor who must embrace rigid lifestyle guidelines: halal meat, unisex toilets and green technology.

They had an archive of CDs and the obligatory Bill Hicks book on the shelf. They were modern parents with a Just Giving page and a Nutribullet pro. Dylan's Mum occasionally put a Manic Panic colour through her ever-so-slightly spiky hair or wore motorbike boots to Waitrose. They had been to see Radiohead when Dylan was a toddler. They'd sat in the bar beforehand and discussed his interaction with other children. Dylan, not Thom Yorke. Dylan's parents used the word "interaction" like something squirming in a petri dish.

Dylan's Mum and Dad liked Ray Mears and Romesh Ranganathan. They laughed at the humour which mocked their demographic. Sometimes they paid for it when they went to see a nice comedian who ridiculed his own situation which was similar, exorcising the need to change it - dark angry material about the school run and other parents. His Mum might tweet, *just watched two hours of love island #imsosad - just dropped off daughter at ballet had organic lowlights and an organic bagel #somiddleclass*

Reverse Schrodinger's cat. The cringe-fest *doesn't* exist as long as you *do* observe it happening. Schrodinger's cat's blog about daily life as a paradox.

Mum was finding it hard to concentrate on the article "Helicopter Parenting and the Infantilisation of Culture" because she was simultaneously monitoring an online conversation between Dylan and the mother of a girl in Dylan's class named Milan.

Milan's family were all female people who posted thousands of selfies, so photo-shopped that the nose blended into the face with only black dots for nostrils, spooky giant eyes and over-blackened pupils. They photo-shopped their own babies, too, adding little rabbit ears and twirly frames with hearts and teddy bears, sometimes making memes out of the best ones by adding the pre-emptive and confusing threat:

My Family Is My Everything So Mess With One You Mess With Us All!

Sometimes, they posted formless, illiterate assertions about how real men love real women: *with all their curves and moods and flaws* etc.

One of them, who had been to university, posted about how *Feminism hurts Everyone*! A guaranteed shortcut to procuring fandom from men enthralled with their culturally-expedient, outside-the-box analysis of post-modern neo-liberalism taken too far.

Milan lived in the part of town which dare not speak its name although it did dare have an "Invoke Article 50 Now!" poster peeling off the window of Age Concern. If it did dare speak its name, it would be The Downham.

There was a rumour that once, in the 80's, a mob - another mob! - got together to punish a local paedophile by pouring boiling water down his trousers. Dylan had wondered how they kept the water boiling. *Knock on his door holding the kettle? You'd want a camping kettle, wouldn't you? A Breville cordless compact travel one with adapter and cups. Perhaps they'd drunk tea on his driveway while they waited for the paedophile to put his cock away, delete his history, and come to the front door. Make a day of it.*

Another rumour was that there was a resident convinced he was living in medieval times. He could be seen in the main part of town in his cape and tunic, buying turnips and logs and once, in Scope, a James Whale autobiography. Mylene Klass had been visiting the community centre to usher in a short-lived scheme with a neurologic music therapist designed to get young troubled teens with mental health issues involved with music. Off-Key, an intern had enthusiastically named it, a decision later blamed for its failure. Well, that and the fact that the man who thought he was in medieval times believed Mylene was betrothed to him five hundred years ago. According to him, it had been written on an ancient stone - a piece of brick with some scratches - which he repeatedly tried to show her. The love-struck loon was squirreled away and put in Springfield Mental Hospital where he made all kinds of unreasonable demands like mint Club Biscuits and gender reassignment. *Who did he think he was? Motley Crüe? And how would he know what Club Biscuits were if he was living in medieval times?* Dylan's mind was awash with anomalies. *So many unanswered questions. If he thought he was in medieval times, what did he think cars were? Or planes, or Chicken Cottage? And why did he have a collection of DVDs labelled* Raw and Uncut Amateur Wives*?*

It was fair enough that Dylan's Mum was concerned her son was having a dialogue with Milan's Mum. Dylan's Mum knew her name was Milan, even without the lurking, because she had had it tattooed on her upper arm – Milan's Mum, not Dylan's Mum. That would be silly.

The radio rattled on in the kitchen:

Three teenagers have been stabbed to death outside a South London shopping centre, bringing this year's knife crime total to 33,278. And later on, Meghan Markle will be auctioning a thimble. Tell me why I'm wrong, 08709078658 is the number to call.

Ian Farrington's invitation to Londoners was a catch-22 since he had already branded anyone disagreeing with him a moron. To his frustration, there were no callers, so he moved on to his radio staple: Covid-19 - the new Brexit.

Chapter Six

Dylan walked into the kitchen and saw his dad sitting, one leg folded across the other, exposing the soles of his sports flip flops with the name Merrell etched into them. For a moment, he studied his father with the aloof neutrality which begins around the age of fourteen. Well, it did in the days before children were bought and paid for and knew on which side their bread was buttered. The Lots of Toys Forever side.

Standard dad issue combat shorts and Rage Against the Machine T-shirt, endlessly scrolling on the ever-present iPhone. Not so much raging against the machine as lethargically cradling the machine - impassively breastfeeding the machine while it sucks dry the dregs of your authenticity. But it was important to wrap yourself in the trinkets of yesterday's rebellion.

"You're wearing a Rage Against the Machine T-shirt and using an iPhone," observed Dylan, "Is that called irony?"

"That's a good question!" Dylan's mum smirked from behind the fridge door, making a mental note to tell the other mums her son's witty question. Her hand began to claw for her phone so she could write it on her friend Petra's *Kids Say the Funniest Things* blog.

"I'd be quiet if I were you," said Dylan's Dad, "Machines have paid for this house, your clothes, your karate lessons. Want me to go on?" Dylan's dad wasn't very funny. His second favorite joke was having an Apple sticker on the lid of his PC.

"No, dad. It's ok. You keep destroying the system from within." He made devil horns with his little finger and thumb and walked backwards out of the room. Dylan left the house and before the cock crowed thrice:

Son just asked if wearing a Rage against the Machine T-shirt whilst using an iPhone is ironic, I don't know where he gets it from….

Hilarious:)

The apple doesn't fall far from the tree!

Replies dripped in from assorted mums and dads with beardy little bios like *I once did a wee quite close to Brian Cant* and *I don't like wasps but I do like cheese*. They hash-tagged TOTP2 and adored Ziggy Stardust and Ollie Reed whilst limply adding their tiny kindling to the funeral pyre of all the conditions which created their dead heroes and removing the chance to allow their children the same un-plugged 20 years of life which they had enjoyed.

Dylan's Dad scrolled and scrolled with furrowed focus and his mouth made a twitching motion like a dog's arse about to have a shit or a camp character from a 70's sitcom who's been shocked yet aroused by a filthy double-entendre.

Dylan went for a walk around the block. It was rainy and, though sunlight was fighting against some black clouds, the rest of the sky was a big floaty cataract. The atmosphere had a second day in a new job feel - still uncomfortable but already dull. Smashed elderberries stained the pavement and, turning a corner, Dylan was confronted with a dad and his two boys in cagoules and bobble hats. Identical all three, they looked like an animated government advert for paying your taxes, washing your hands or downloading an App. A family@gov.uk.

Picking a snail up from the middle of the pavement and putting it on a wall for safety, a lifelong habit since his early Snail Winton patterning. Dylan noticed someone had stuck a flyer on a parking meter. He read the word "Offliners" next to a picture of an emoji bursting into flames and a mobile number.

WE ARE OFFLINERS! DON'T EXPECT US! DON'T CALL! DON'T TEXT! DON'T WHATSAPP US! WE'RE NOT IN

Another shit new retro club night. Bet no one turns up, Dylan thought about whatever it was. It would soon be turned into a Pure Gym anyway. He peeled off the promotional sticker, put it in his pocket and returned home.

Chapter Seven

RIP Grandma : (

The top post in Dylan's newsfeed tempted him with the offer *See more posts like this?* Maybe Grace had been hacked or his Grandma had been *hacked* – or maybe Grace was simply complicit with an 'in' joke?

A bit dark for her, though. Grace's favourite comedian was Maxi Hussain. He told jokes about funny things children say and then did half an hour on mental health. Well, Grace *said* Maxi was her favourite comedian, but she also had a T-shirt from Topshop that said Black Sabbath in lilac sequins and Dylan was sure she knew hardly any of the lyrics to "Isolated Man". So, it was anyone's guess. He refreshed the page in case it had been deleted.

"Mum?" asked Dylan.

"We've got some sad news. Sit down," her face was blotchy and wet. Like her parenting skills.

"Nan's dead?" The family hated him calling her "Nan".

"Nana has died yes, hypertrophic cardiomyopathy. Dad's at the hospital now."

"Sorry," he said, putting a hand on her shoulder. He wondered how long you had to keep your hand on someone's shoulder when their Mother-in-law had died. If he could type on his phone without being seen, he could Quora it. That was always guaranteed to garner professionally practical counsel. Dylan counted in his head *One, one thousand, two, one thousand, three, one. . .*

"It's okay," Mum allowed.

Exhaling, he went upstairs and opened his sister's bedroom door. Suddenly and without physically knocking, he shouted: "Knock knock!"

"Whoa!" Grace jumped up and slammed her laptop shut at the same time.

"Err, what's the matter?" asked Dylan.

"Have you heard of knocking? This is a safe space. You're bare trespassing."

"Bear trespassing?" asked Dylan, "Is that what Goldilocks did?" Grace had only recently begun saying "bare". This was almost as pathetic as last term's antiquated "mash-up". That had been "bare embarrassing", but not as embarrassing as when he'd overheard her talking to a Somalian traffic warden at the end of the street, punctuating her sentences with "bless up", "bumble cart", and "rice clock".

"You looked like you were editing something, photo shopping pictures, cropping and filtering. Pictures – pictures of you – you and Nan? What's the score, you look like Robin Williams in 24-hour photo."

"Get a life of your own, you howling munter. Stop being salty and sort your fauxhawk out -- srsly!" She flicked her ombre ironed curtain out of her eyes and, unplugging her laptop, knocked over several tubes of Nivea tinted lip balm and tripped over her own mint green glitter shoelaces. It was Chap stick slapstick. Balmagedden.

Dylan backed out of the room quickly. He knew all her log-in details, the div. One of her passwords was "mypassword". *The absolute wanksta.* It took him 56.3 seconds to find a series of photos uploaded to the Cloud of her with their Nan. First, Grace grinning, denim shorts (jorts), white H & M vest with lace inserts, head on one side, and Nan looking at her bewilderedly, leaning back, mouth open, with a creased brow as if saying something. Then there were several with Grace pulling at Nan's left arm as Nan's right arm was occupied clutching her heart. There were also a series of shots which began with Nan hunched over while Grace exuded for all her life was worth, Nan's head tipped right back in an endeavour to open her eyes like a Tiny Tears doll. Finally, there was an encore sequence with Nan suddenly wearing a pair of Grace's red rimmed heart-shaped Lolita inspired sunglasses. It began to look like an all-female remake of *Weekend at Bernie's.* (in the pipeline)

Having exhausted the arsenal of selfie possibilities, it was now socially lucrative to have a profile picture with an elderly relative, the older and iller the better. Bonus likes for a walking stick/hearing aid/pacemaker/tubes/oxygen mask/life threatening growth within view. It showed what an un-premeditating and authentic person you were. Dylan saved the evidence to a memory stick shaped like a tiny green ice cream.

The stupidest thing about Dylan's mum's helicopter parenting was that he'd learned early on how to perform just enough torment to allow her to feel special and competent whilst completely supressing his real feelings. Occasionally muttering something *about finding it hard to concentrate*, she'd look relieved – validated - with a project for the next few weeks, happily printing off articles and chatting along with Net Mums for the foreseeable. If he were honest, he'd tell her he felt nothing. Not depressed, not hyper not bipolar, just nothing. That everything was pointless: life, death, conversation, pointlessness.

It was hot the day of Nan's funeral. Dylan shuffled his size nines and glanced up to see Grace taking selfie after selfie with icy, robotic ambition. He logged into Facebook to see she'd settled on draft 57 of the statuses saved up for this occasion since Year 8.

Ahem.

Rip Grandma… today won't be easy but I know you'll be looking down on us all and keeping me safe throughout all my trials and tribulations. I'll miss your feisty attitude to life and am grateful for all you've taught me. XXX

All you've taught me? Feisty attitude? They'd met Nan maybe five times, ever. She lived in Cumbria. She wasn't feisty. The feistiest thing she'd ever done was return a Take a Break puzzle magazine with a bent staple. Dylan liked her, but she was mousy, not feisty. *Why does everyone have to be feisty?* he wondered. A homogenised type of bolshiness the evening news *love* when they challenge a politician at a community centre in their funny accent and haircut – ideally, a fat nurse from Hackney with a correct set of politics who runs a food bank from her own window box and works herself into an early grave. She'd be sassy. She'd be strong. She'd be dead by 50. A character "The One Show" would send a roving reporter to concern troll, with a proper reporter haircut and teeth. A reality show Christmas cracker beloved by the media until it's the *wrong* kind of feisty. (Jade Goody).

Outside the crematorium, Dylan stood in the burning sunshine, borrowed black suit absorbing the rays while Grace micromanaged the ends of her hair. Inside were flowers and brass fittings. Streaks of tiger stripe sun disclosed the dust in the air and the officiant read out an introduction while Dylan's Dad choked back tears. He was now an orphan! He felt dazed and dizzy as mousy Nan's life highlights were read out: Lancaster Grammar school, telephone operator, wedding day, meeting Derek Nimmo. His hand twitched in his pocket – Dylan's dad not Derek Nimmo.

There must be a tweet in this, he hoped, *something dark but comically tragic. Think, THINK!* Any residual resistance was defeated and out came the Tourette's tablet. Dylan's mum's glance at her husband was one-quarter frown, three-quarters each surprise, confusion and benign resignation. It was coming, it was coming.

At Mum's funeral, can't stop thinking the officiant looks like Inch High Private Eye

The officiant didn't. He was 5'7", but it was a good 70s children's TV reference combined with a dark situation and that was Twitter gold. Well, brass. Gold would be Katie Hopkins giving Gary Lineker heart-felt head with a grammatically incorrect caption and provocatively bold football result prediction. The phone was quickly put away, but by the time he was at the wake, Dylan's dad was happy to see he'd been retweeted six times.

#win!

He shook hands and accepted condolences from various friends and relatives, all the while struggling to dream up a continuity tweet. *Why couldn't someone else here look like someone or something?* Thought Dylan's dad, impatiently, *Why wasn't there an app for this?*

Back in his bedroom later that day, Dylan was spiritlessly flipping between YouTube channels.

*Incel Insurgence!

A very agitated man in a comedy beard offered the warm advice of a kindly aunt: *You must imagine that a woman is a sack of rotting faeces, every time you see one, instead of letting your natural impulses take over, concentrate on visualising what a…*

Dylan clicked on the next offering

*Alan Cartwright

that's right Michael, it doesn't matter left or right, black or white, male or female because we're all being played off against each other, and while we're at each other's throats we can't see the bigger picture where we're being worked like puppets, it's pathetic! Our level of consciousness is shocking. Now, Jews…

*Beta is Better

so called feminists could learn a thing or two from this 105-year-old great, great, great grandmother who just said on her death bed that she's not a feminist, and has devoted her life to looking after veterans, she's a real woman

Reply:

but Beta is Better- if I may call you that - you're always saying that women are best at communication and empathising and shouldn't try to compete or fight or have careers or be superheros or present sports programmes…so why do you do such a feminine job? sitting down and talking for a living, accepting donations and benefactors and being very passive and …well…by your own definition. . . girly? why aren't you in the ARMY?

Comments disabled.

*RadFem **2020**

And what's the elephant in the room about this latest terrorist attack? anyone? that's right! men! another man committing violence, men are only happy when they're destroying things, just as a sperm is an agitated parasite, not happy unless it's travelling in a pack, banging its sperm head against something, trying to get in, bothering people, men aren't happy unless they're burrowing, infecting, spreading, they can never just be content or self-contained. Valerie Solanas was right; life in this society being at best an utter bore, and no aspect of society being at all relevant to women… boring and literally, boring! it's ridiculous, we discuss all this shit on tv… rape, murder, religion, marriage, money, war…slavery, abuse, corruption, colonisation, we discuss it as though it's something we do all together as a human race! men invented all those things, all of them are down to half the population! every religion is a perfect mirror of a male's obsession with being in a gang and following rules, because they're WEAK, not content unless they have a bigger monkey to obey and God is the ultimate big monkey gang leader, why do we pretend we can't see it? can we talk about male violence please?

*ScalesofJustice (broletariot)

So, in this video I'm going to tell you why you HAVE to vote for Diesel Might in the Mayoral election, number one, he's a normal bloke, he's been in prison for 9 months for GBH and elder abuse and that gave him a unique insight, something which cannot be said for the other MK ultra-controlled candidates, he cares, he genuinely cares about the everyday man and woman because he is one! he's the only one who is going to undo the insidious right-wing tide that's flowing over us since Brexit. he's the only one who's going to stand up for the disabled, the disenfranchised, the minorities, the elderly –

*AutismWins

This 14-year-old girl has an IQ of 150, watch her do these maths equations…!

Comments:

@Overlordmatt *NOT HOT*

Reply: @warriorX *Was thinking that*

@Unnecessaryusername *Feminist propaganda! If it was a guy, they wouldn't be making a film about him and she's not even hot.*

Dylan continued scrolling through all the suggested videos. He wasn't old enough to vote, but if he was and there was an election tomorrow, he wouldn't have a clue. Whatever he wanted to believe, he could seek out a point of view or several, with convincing facts and data to back up the particular leaning, and he would be viewing life through the prism of that line of reasoning.

What was the answer? he wondered, *Watch all of it? Watch none of it? Watch all of it and then stand back and see what happens in real life to support what I've watched?* He remembered a book he had found on a wall in Acton which said something like this: "If you had a class full of students and asked them to describe the hall outside, quizzing them on all the details, someone would remember the colour of a tile, someone would remember how many doors there were, some would remember things which they hadn't seen, and some would remember things which resonated with their own memories. To get the best idea about the hall, if you hadn't seen it, you'd want to talk to the person who remembered the most things, correct things. So, should you try to find out the truth from the person who'd seen the most things? With the most panoramic, non-invested view? Who would that be? It won't be the person who thinks it's them."

Everyone was coming at life from a different angle, so how can anyone be right? Couldn't people see that? Dylan thought. It wasn't just a coincidence that people were making life better for the demographic that they happened to be, or overcompensating out of narcissistic guilt. Humans were like a parasitic worm burrowing into the ant and taking over its brain, forcing the ant to march headlong towards its death, hatching the parasite, and raining a million spawn into the fertile conditions below. They were all trying to make fertile conditions for themselves to spread. *How lazy. How cheap seats!* Dylan reflected with disappointment, *How can someone from Eton tell someone from Eltham that their view of the world is wrong and vice-versa?*

He switched it all off, the yapping voices and targeted ads designed to press his buttons, all claiming their version was the only one to be trusted. *There must be something new to watch. There must be other songs to sing.* Dylan's hand twitched and his foot tapped frantically with the exhausted mania of his overloaded hard drive, black floaters in his eyes, viscous, travelling cobwebs with little insects drifting in and out of view. It was all a drearily addictive

1980's video game with no off switch. He unplugged everything and went for another walk, taking Titus the mouse, with him.

Passing a floral tribute for a teen, stabbed to death over the holidays, Dylan was barely surprised to see two grief-stricken youths taking selfies in front of it, in between preening for the lens. He felt like a hater for thinking it was at all suspect. *Why can't I embrace it all and go with the urinal overflow?* Thoughts rattled around his head like Lego in a lunchbox.

He glanced at a mattress outside a nettle filled front garden with a note attached: *Free mattress. Dog gave birth on it.* A mum stopped and smiled indulgently at her little child's funny walk, stamping its feet, flapping its arms, and grimacing. The mother threw Dylan a knowing look, an "isn't my baby wonderful" look. Dylan manoeuvred around them stealthily. Later on, she would tweet:

young man spat and swore at me and my toddler this afternoon…

To which five people would reply: *#Brexit*

Seven would reply*: #leftwingantisemitism*

And one would reply*: #didnthappen*

Dylan knew something was wrong as soon as his mum shouted "Hello?" upon hearing him open the front door. It was a hollow hello, serious and strained. Making a U-turn on the stairs, he prepared himself for the concerned face that she kept in the drawer. Who is it for?

"Sorry about mouse Nan. I mean, Nan."

"Straight to the point, Dylan," she said, "I have a few issues to address with you." Her tone went from strained to firm - a newly-appointed assistant manager of a shoe shop about to lord it over some poor cow of a school-leaver apprentice named Kimi.

"I want to speak to my lawyer!" Dylan attempted to lighten the – whatever this was.

"Aha, very good. You weren't in school on Monday. Where were you?"

"The library?" Barely bothering to fashion a credible defence, he braced himself for the fall out.

"Why are you lying? Have you been eating junk food with Liam?" She opened his eyes between her thumb and forefinger as if she were going to see a tiny hologram of a cheeseburger and bottle of Mountain Dew. Everything was always explained in terms of nutrition. Dylan was still skinny and raw-boned from being put on a wheat and gluten free diet for the first seven years of his life until his mum finally found another hobbyhorse on which to project her Munchausen's-by-proxy.

"We've been doing so well."

We? thought Dylan.

"We've done a 360 since year eight. What's going on?" She tousled his pre-Raphaelite hair.

He'd been prescribed antidepressants in Year Eight. Duloxetine, a fittingly illustrative brand name. Dull and Teen, two birds, one stoned child. It all came about when he was late for class one day, "You're late" the teacher of the recently-added-to-the-curriculum Mindfulness and Identity class stated the obvious, presenting Dylan with the lead he'd been waiting for.

"That depends," he had replied, "If I hadn't turned up at all, this could be considered early!" He'd heard it in a Woody Allen film and had made a mental note to use it next time someone set out the stall by saying "You're late". Unfortunately, this homage had elicited an enquiry into his mental health.

What did he mean if he didn't turn up? Was he suicidal? Problems at home? Questioning his gender? In denial about questioning his gender? In denial about being in denial? Dylan could have explained about the film. But, you know, he was too depressed.

"Okay," said his mum, "we'll talk later. I've got Heart-Core Pilates at Canary Wharf, but for now – grounded."

Chapter Eight

Dylan didn't really go anywhere anyway, so he enjoyed the feeling of being grounded. It was vindicating.

He went to his room and opened the laptop. Dad must've been using it as his browser was opened on the podcast of a comedian that only someone as unaware as his dad could endure except their podcast was different because they didn't just talk, they "had a conversation" Dylan's dad's favourite joke was saying "Like Peckham on a Friday night!" in response to any on-screen depiction of turmoil. Sometimes Peckham was replaced with Penge, always a town beginning with P, though. Dylan's dad had never been to Peckham or Penge.

The familiar stench spread as the laptop lid lifted and flourished when the twitter feed ticker-taped at the bottom right. *Was the stale dirty mildew coming from the internet? Of course not.* Dylan snorted away the absurd notion.

Can't make up my mind, beef and tomato or chowmein #indecisive #libra someone had tweeted.

It could have been a 12-year-old girl with their first internet phone or a stay-at-home mum with nothing to break up the *Groundhog Day* of her life but pot noodle and a supernatural gift for astrology. But no, it was Miles Fernbridge, son of an entertainment agent. Another overfed face from the 90s turned pious, finger-wagging typist on temazepam. Except, recently, he'd been using expressions like "woke" "snowflake" and "safe space" which was a different kind of virtue signalling but just as dull. They were signalling their own sophistication about how they were intelligent enough to understand that aspects of left wing outrage trolling were ridiculous but it was one joke, one joke dragged out for all eternity, but, like in a class of twelve-year-olds, there are always the ones who are still rocking backwards and forwards talking about the time Mr. Miller fell off a chair 50 years later. Very recently, in fact, anyone who didn't find him funny (everyone) was suddenly a "snowflake".

Miles had been a controversial character in the early 2000s because of his jokes about things like missing children, dead babies, rape and any other low-hanging fruit. In fact, he had even used that in a joke:

People have accused me of only making fun of low hanging fruit...that's no way to talk about (insert any lower-class model or reality star's tits.)

Before becoming a born-again free speech advocate with the mischievous encouragement and publicity from a bunch of former Trotskyists posing as the best friends of Tory voting cab drivers, Miles had been online, raising awareness about racism, feminism and poverty. It was almost a cynical manoeuvre to put the public in its place by claiming his previously outraged audiences had no sense of perspective. Anonymous refugees seldom left them bad reviews on Chortle or tweeted them to *please fuck off the television* (give them time) But, the circle was complete. He was just replacing *ironically* cruel jokes with - cruel jokes.

It was a similar sleight of hand Alan Cartwright, conspiracy theorist/holocaust denier/anti-vaxxer, had skilfully employed when questioned about where all the money from a recent Kickstarter had gone:

to question where all the money has gone in a world where we're sleepwalking into an Orwellian nightmare is a sign of grave mental illness

"Sleepwalking into an Orwellian Nightmare" had become Alan's catchphrase. Miles Fernbridge had some catchphrases, too. One used to be "anal rape". Now it was "arse clown!" or other insulting invective plus knitted noun: "cock weasel", "cunt whistle", "fuck basket", each as twee and embarrassing as his tweed waistcoat.

Alan Cartwright was definitely Dylan's favourite conspiracy theorist. He'd been a game show host in the early 2000s when his father, a journalist, had died of a heart attack, which Alan believed the government had caused by rewiring the electrical appliances in his dad's house to disrupt his chakras. He also believed that most terrorist attacks were the government personally sending him a message. Apart from the ones in Paris. Those had been the brainchild of a trans-terrestrial messenger of the Fish Head God, Enki, and were also to send him a message, just – a different message. *Obviously*! He also thought words he used in his podcasts were put into soap operas to warn him that he was being listened to. It was a regular routine of Dylan's to log into Alan's website - Poking Beneath the Rabbit Hole - and access the chat forum.

Peacefullwarrior456 *another example of the illuminati pulling the wool over the sheeple's eyes*

Peacefullwarrior456 commented on the thread entitled NWO symbolism in the MSM

that's handy, since the sheeple are part wool already commented Dylan2456 (He had created his account in a hurry.)

Peacefullwarrior456 *laugh while you can ...you will soon be living in a global fascist dictatorship Orwellian nightmare, that's if you make it through the population cull, more and more symbolism is appearing in the media lately we just need to wake up and see it*

Dylan2456 *why are 'the illuminati' or whatever warning us about something that's supposed to be secret? how does that help them...I thought they were a secret organization anyway? Going to great lengths to keep their modus operandi covert, why blow it all and put a big freemasonic symbol in our faces basically saying ha-ha we're doing this lol"!?*

Peaceful Warrior posted three music videos: Rihanna, Brittney Spears and Dannii Minogue. Dylan sniggered to himself over the idea that anything as lame as Dannii Minogue could be representative of a Mengelesque agenda.

Peacefullwarrior456 *because they're psychopaths and they like to give us signs, it's all very OCD that's because they operate from the back of their brain, the reptilian stem, it's concerned with ritual, symbols, signs, hierarchy etc. It's a compulsion and it affects humanities frequency bringing it down and implanting ideas -- notice how they are all covering one eye in the videos at some point, symbolic of becoming a split personality, classic MK ultra-puppet symbolism*

Dylan2456 *...or really lazy and unimaginative art direction?* Dylan tried to be diplomatic.

Peacefullwarrior456 *the art direction will have been steered towards it, most of them will be puppets or handlers deeply entrenched and indoctrinated to the agenda -- notice how at 3.17 the mirror gets broken representing how the project monarch programming has shattered the personality into fragments*

Dylan2456 *...again, lazy stylists and directors? mirrors are used over and over in all art forms, I'm not saying you're not right peaceful warrior I just think you can never overestimate lack of ideas and lame copycat creativity bypasses, or do I mean underestimate?*

Dylan felt like a knob addressing someone as "Peaceful Warrior".

There was a long pause and Dylan wondered if Peaceful Warrior had retreated into his wigwam.

Peacefullwarrior456 *...notice how at 2.14 Rihanna puts the devil's horns on her head to indicate she has now completed her initiation and sold her soul to Satan*

Dylan2456 *I thought they were going for a kind of Viking look type thing? what if they're aware of all the conspiracy speculation and deliberately place these things in the videos to get more hits?*

Peacefullwarrior456 *"the best lies are the ones which are right in front of our faces"* He responded in quotation marks for emphasis.

Dylan2456 *who said that?* Dylan was suspicious that it sounded a bit halfhearted to be an actual quote.

Peacefullwarrior456 *that doesn't matter, it's true is the main thing*

Dylan2456 *but I thought they 'worked in the shadows.*

Dylan2456 *I thought you said these illuminati music videos were designed to tap into our subconscious.* Dylan recalled PW's quote from a month ago.

Peacefullwarrior456 *sometimes they do sometimes they don't*

Dylan2456 *convenient*

There was a six-minute gap before PW replied.

Peacefullwarrior456 *you can stick your head in the sand all you want but when you do your arse is exposed and it's going to get kicked*

Dylan knew this was one of Alan Cartwright's analogies, but also felt PW meant well.

Dylan2456 *so, what's the point in any of it? I mean, why are those people bothering with all of this, wont they suffer too? or their children, grandchildren?*

Dylan had been meaning to ask this for over a year, but always got distracted by the links on these sites. Usually memes of Donald Trump, clips of comedians, and mono-atomic gold powder for sale which increased the current carrying capacity of one's brain.

Peacefullwarrior456 *most of them are just puppets, the real ghouls are working them from behind the scenes, it's their agenda they are being worked to usher in*

Dylan2456 *ok, why do the 'ghouls in the shadows' want to usher this in, what's in it for them?*

Peacefullwarrior456 *oh…now you're asking!*

Dylan2456 *... yeah?*

Peacefullwarrior456 *how far down the rabbit hole do you want to go?*

Dylan laughed at the auspicious tone.

Dylan2456 *err…. all the way baby!* He smoked a fag out of his window and waited for the "truth". Dylan never got ID'd for cigarettes. In fact, he had to stoop to get through most shop doorways.

Peacefullwarrior456 *they want to keep us locked into a low vibrational prison of our own minds, it's been going on for thousands of years, there's lots of intergalactic wars of consciousness going on, this is the tip of the iceberg really. we've been in a low vibrational nightmare with only a tiny bandwidth available to access information, a tiny speck of visible light, man's consciousness has been kept in a prison, now that the solar rays are sending more information patterns, the internet and forums like this are a manifestation of that, we wouldn't be even having this conversation otherwise although it's run its course now, the internet not this conversation. ha-ha, the earth's heartbeat is quickening, the frequency of the planet is rising and it's causing people to wake up, soon we'll be able to speak to dolphins and communicate psychically with plants. When we all begin to wake up and raise our frequencies the vibration will be not conducive to the vibration of these dark entities so they will not be able to keep incarnating in this realm*

Dylan2456 *the internet's run its course?*

Peacefullwarrior456 *of course,*

Dylan2456 *ha-ha*

Peacefullwarrior456 *ha-ha*

Dylan2456 *will I be able to talk to a dolphin?*

Peacefullwarrior456 *why do you want to talk to a dolphin?*

Dylan2456 *I'm not sure*

Peacefullwarrior456 *this is another reason that they're trying to lower our consciousness and shut off our pineal glands*

Dylan2456 *the dolphins?*

Peacefullwarrior456 *no, the lower fourth dimension entities operating beyond our frequency range*

Dylan2456 *why do they care?! the lower dimensions or whatever? why don't they just fuck off somewhere else with a nice low frequency, you know, like wherever it is that Jimmy Savile is now with Myra Hindley and all the stars.*

Peacefullwarrior456 *Myra Hindley isn't dead*

Dylan2456 *never mind about that now!*

Peacefullwarrior456 *they're attached to us here, it's like having squatters, who have learnt how to get free energy*

Dylan2456 *cool!*

Peacefullwarrior456 *no, not cool! they like it here, as much as they ever like anything, they can feed off us, our fear our low consciousness, that's why they engineer horrific murders and disasters, they feed off our low energy, our fear, our grief, our confusion, they're parasites using us like a battery*

Dylan2456 *okay, I can get that but do you not think that humans are just ...a bit shit? just inherently weak by nature, grasping, cowardly, fearful, desperate, perhaps we wouldn't have been so malleable otherwise, because we're flawed, corrupt?*

Peacefullwarrior456 *but...we're infinite consciousness... we're all that ever has, is and ever will be, we're all one consciousness, I'm you and you are me, various aspects of the whole*

Dylan2456 *I don't believe that. I saw a man in the paper this morning who beat his dog to death. I'm not him, I'm nothing to do with him*

Peacefullwarrior456 *he's another expression of our collective consciousness, perhaps one you don't want to face*

Dylan2456 *nah, he's an abomination, he should have the plug pulled on his universal consciousness for what he did*

Peacefullwarrior456 *how will his consciousness increase in its frequency if we cannot recognize his aspect and offer forgiveness and compassion?*

Dylan2456 *I don't care, he's a cunt!*

Peacefullwarrior456 *your thinking is compartmentalized, it's your hive mind talking*

Dylan2456 *my what?*

Just then, an interloper posted a meme of a bumblebee that read: "Posh bees live in a behave"

Peacefullwarrior456 *a false reality created by our collective minds*

Dylan2456 *how does knowing any of this help me?*

Peacefullwarrior456 *how do you mean?*

Dylan2456 *okay, say I expand my consciousness or whatever or raise my frequency and blah blah and see the entire picture for what it is, just vibrating matter created by my own mind and that none of this is real and it's just a construct so there's no point in arguing or having an opinion because none of this is real and I cannot judge anyone because they are me and I am they, no ego, no conversations, no birth no death, everything is a false reality and meaningless*

Peacefullwarrior456 *...yes?*

Dylan2456 *well, what's the point? what am I supposed to do? It just makes the everyday world even more annoying and pointless and grey and people seem even more stupid and pointless and that there's even less for me to take part in or bother with, that's what I mean...what's the point?*

Peacefullwarrior456 *that's for you to work out*

Dylan2456 *aaaaaaaahhhhhhhh!*

Peacefullwarrior456 *you never hit me up for Xbox btw*

Dylan2456 *you forgot to give me your username*

Peacefullwarrior456 *PEACEFULWARRIOR5676T6*

Dylan2456 *cool*

Chapter Nine

Dylan felt light-headed and his eyes were broken from glaring at the screen. He went downstairs to the kitchen and opened the fridge door. It was one of those ones disguised as a cupboard because cupboard beats fridge! A wicker heart fell in the process and, perturbed with grappling it back onto the globule of glue, he threw it out of the window and onto the lawn where the dog, Michael Parkinson, merrily shredded it, distracted only when the doorbell sent the canine cliché galloping. His dad's intern, Shane, had come to help with an out-of-hours IT emergency which would no doubt provide lots of tweet-worthy material for later. Michael Parkinson lay at his feet in the hall.

Dylan's mum appeared, a caramel wigwam in brushed cotton. She smelt of wool and trail mix. "You're such a tart!" She rubbed the dog's stomach and he rolled around, joyfully naive of his owner's slut-shaming. Dylan was never comfortable with animals being called or 'tarts' for enjoying attention.

Shane was almost ten years older than Dylan and in the five weeks that Shane had added him on Facebook this was what Dylan had learned about him:

Shane was 25 and had a Barbour jacket. His mum had bought it with him. Shane had mustard coloured trousers, the ones that bunch up around your arse and look like you've shat into a pile of paper towels. He has a necklace with a tiny replica of a Topic chocolate bar on it and writes statuses about Cheryl Fernandez-Versini. Shane's friends share pictures of naked old women and shriek with laughter at an old vagina. Shane and his friends are outrageous.

Shane went to a "bad taste" party as Baby P. Shane's friends really push the boundaries. Shane and his mum don't like Cheryl Fernandez-Versini's hair. Shane's mum thinks Cheryl looks "tarty". Shane agrees with his mum. Shane's mum has been a mum and a dad to him – he repeats this whenever he hears the prompt. Shane's mum likes him to call her "Debbie".

Debbie is a baby boomer. Shane and Debbie read celebrity magazines together. Shane's mum thinks Kate Moss looks "ravaged" and Shane agrees with Debbie.

Shane is fashionable and he has a blog all about the aesthetic imperfections of various models and actresses and has a sick sense of humour. Shane's mum is paying for him to study photography. He took some photographs of a boy with an afro in front of some graffiti and some rubbish in a skip with a black-and-white grainy filter. Debbie paid a premium so that he could showcase his work in a Hoxton pub. Shane is outrageous.

Dylan tried to tune out Shane's excruciatingly high-pitched laugh and, refreshing the page, noticed his dad's email account was still open. He went to log out, but not before clicking on a new notification from a Stephanie Korovnik.

The paranoid solipsism of his 16-year-old mind kicked in. *It could be someone to do with the school,* he worried, *Perhaps a social worker, especially after the bunking off.* This had happened to Liam. A visit from a social worker was followed by a trip to the Maudsley Hospital where he tried to force triangle shapes into square holes for an hour. Suddenly after that, it was three terms at a residential school for statmented spectrum dwellers. *Better open it*, Dylan thought.

What he saw next could have curbed his pubescent progress more effectively than the hormone blockers thirteen teens in his year had been prescribed last term due to gender dysphoria and institutionalised child abuse. It was a topless selfie. It was more the surprise factor that had taken him aback. He could've limbered up to it, but there it was. Dylan wished he had one of those Lovecraftian time machines he'd been reading about in order to delete this latest mind file but there it was, burned forever into his psyche. Stephanie must have been at least forty, but she was wearing a Hello Kitty necklace – the waving paw suddenly seemed like a frantic call for assistance. She also had pink, synthetic knickers tied at the side, unreasonable bunting promoting a disappointing circus.

Stephanie was holding one of the plaits she had braided from the last few strands of her peri-menopausal hair. Her head was down and her eyes looked up in a strange, sultry pout which looked simply pissed off. Her come hither was withered mother.

Dylan would have dismissed it as spam from a barrel-scraping Eastern European sex trafficking ring if the subject hadn't been so specific.

Prince Albert on Thursday?, it read. *I'm second on the bill!! (lucky Bill) xx"*

The Prince Albert was a pub Dylan's dad frequented for the open-mic comedy he was always threatening to try his spazzy hand at. Either bottom-of-the-barrel Eastern European sex trafficking rings had really got their spamming trousers on or, more likely, his dad was soon going to be a weekend dad. A weakened dad.

Dylan knew that it was politically incorrect to not fancy a middle-aged woman. He'd learnt this in a long double-afternoon class last June called "The Male Gaze", which he'd found very hard to concentrate on due to being completely distracted by Miss Ashley's 38Ds. Not wishing to be guilty of toxically masculine age discrimination, Dylan felt very virtuous after a charity wank.

What a revelation, he thought to himself. Until today, his dad had been a one-dimensional entity, almost suspiciously normal. Dylan was right after all. No one's that dull! With a few clicks, Dylan instantly accessed Stephanie's entire social media history right up until seven minutes previously when she'd had a lethargically frosty exchange with a girl named Louise. Dylan resisted the urge to attach any soppy feelings to a million-mile-a-way avatar, but his curiosity was nevertheless ignited.

Also, Dylan tried not to imagine what stand-up comic Stephanie Korovnik would look like as a substitute for his Mum: telling jokes at the breakfast table, telling jokes in the bathroom, telling jokes on the end of his Dad's cock.

Chapter Ten

Stephanie Korovnik was a female comedian, something she was *not* happy about. As she made clear many times at her gigs. "I'm a *comedian* not a *WOMBedian"*. She had changed her given name of "Wheeler" to "Korovnik" after tracing her family tree back hundreds of years to associate herself with an interesting struggle or colourful peasant. "Korovnik" had been the surname of her great-great-great-great-great grandfather, a Russian cow dealer. She talked often of her immigrant status.

Stephanie's blog said she was a feminist, a special kind of feminist by all accounts – the kind who spends an extravagant amount of time discussing how other women (glamour models, reality stars, etcetera) look. This was all done through matronly concern, for their own good. Her act depicted women as a gaping wound of hormones and feebleness: A sort of little girl lost in the world who finds everything constantly confusing, especially sex. How impossible it is to eat cake without making your hips big; How men should give women wedding rings made from chocolate, right!? How funny it is when men and women don't understand each other because men are all practical and literal and women are all contradictory and mysterious. A typical opening would go something like this:

"Good evening! Sorry I'm late! My two-year-old decided to be sick all over the house, including on my husband's laptop (long pause). *I guess he won't be watching Redtube for a while.* (laugh of recognition about Redtube) *But it's not all bad. I got to try out my newly discovered twisted uterus.* (laughter at a woman talking about her uterus) *I used it as a Hoover attachment, great for getting into hard to reach places.* (From porn to uterus to housework. Breaking new ground in the taboo every Wednesday in Wandsworth) it was woman-face passed off as quirky empowerment and required no more than posters with a stupid facial expression, perhaps, hair in braids and holding a toy elephant but shaking a fist

in front of their pierced bottom lip – *I'm just a confused little girl in the world, but I might punch you . . . because I'm mad!*

I wish more girls were supporting the #losetheladsmags campaign She had tweeted halfheartedly, still hungover from a frenemies' birthday at a Shoreditch burlesque show. Austerity Measures the act was called. A fat goth with a demi wave and a nightie, really.

Why's that? asked Louise. The frosty exchange that Dylan would read a mere seven minutes later was about to kick off.

Louise was a post-millennial with a name given to her in tribute to her aunt, a heroin-addicted relative, recently self-identified as autistic, dyslexic, body dysmorphic, and anankastic. Louise's aunt had a blog explaining that last condition, and a Pinterest board! She suffered with adult onset diagnosis.

Louise often wondered if her life would have been a bit better had she been given one of the bright, optimistic, hamster-owning birthday present names from her class. Who knows how things would have turned out had she been a Hannah or a Chloe or an Ashleigh a Poppy or a Holly.

Why should you care about lad's mags? Stephanie had tweeted back; *do you care about the number of women who are raped and how the media influences societies' view of females?*

But isn't that just social Darwinism? responded Louise. She was part troll, part Billy Goat Gruff, trip-trapping over the bridge, looking for a greener pasture. *And didn't you used to strip?*

Whatever social Darwinism is I don't like the sound of it Stephanie was irked that her hashtag was being questioned when the idea was to soak in a validation bath with salted caramel conformation candles.

I mean, the kind of person who's easily influenced by images and takes it all seriously is going to be like that their whole life with everything, aren't they? Louise continued. *They probably believe in Mills and Boon novels, too! Think about it: 'lad's mags!' 'lads!' So 90s! Chris Evans in a duffle coat, idolising George Best and Jack Nicholson looking like his nan dressed him up to play in the snow…I mean, Chris Evans into George Best doesn't go, it's an… improper fraction or something.*

Louise's attempt at trolling was perfunctory as she was brain dead from a sedentary data entry job. Those were always more tiring. *Maybe I should try cleaning again*, she often thought. After an eight-hour shift cleaning, Louise always wanted to go home and, clean.

No such paradox existed for her recent evening enterprise. There were other ways to get money besides data entry and cleaning.

Stephanie took advantage of the block button after taking a screenshot of Louise's Chris Evans bit. She thought it could work at the Brighton Fringe. Then scrolled and scrolled – Twitter, Facebook, comedy reviews, dogging sites – until her battery - like her act - died. It was only then that she realised the awful clamor her 10-year-old daughter had been making on a keyboard had stopped some time ago.

"Molly?" Stephanie nervously looked around, "Molly?"

Oh fuck.

As Dylan's dad was still talking to Shane in the office room – which he had recently started referring to as his "Man Den" in a terrible Jamaican accent to sound like "Mandem" – Dylan scribbled down the mobile number Stephanie had added beneath her selfie just as a new email popped up from his dad's colleague:

Date with Amy tonight, lol!:) read an infantile emoji-splattered message from Adam Lastname. Well, that was his name in the email. Dylan's dad hadn't known Adam's surname when he had added him to his contacts, but was so anal about digital organisation he just had to input a lastname. Thus, Lastname it was. It was their little in-joke. Crazy!

Like Peckham on a Friday night.

Chapter Eleven

Adam Lastname and Amy met online. Of course.

Hey there :)

Hey :)

They were both approaching 45 but had assumed the cultural artillery of the younger generation to stay relevant. It had the opposite effect of course, of obliterating what crumbs of validity they had, oxidised by the osmosis of daily compromise. Amy was a trustafarian who had never had a job and stippled every sentence with "like".

"Shall we, like, do the eating thing?" she began.

They sat down, took out their phones and put them on the table. Amy checked a couple of emails. Adam Lastname clicked on a couple of messages, or at least pretended to. Two stupid birds tapping their beaks on a rock in a fruitless mating ritual.

The next day, Adam Lastname sat at his desk nursing a banana and mineral water, biding his time before the big lunchtime blow out, blueberries. He went home and watched lesbian porn. Sometimes he watched "Friends" or a Hollywood film and then went to sleep. He thought Imogen Poots was hot, especially after learning she had marched in peaceful protest at Trump's inauguration. He used the word "hot" like in a Hollywood film. He also subscribed to *Men's Health* and drank a power drink made from green powder and wh-hey!

He avoided carbs and ate clean and had some shoes that were just rubber socks with fingers to strengthen the arches in his feet that had been destroyed by third-wave feminism. He'd once had sex with a prostituted woman in Amsterdam. It was practice really, to become worldlier, like a man in a Hollywood film. It fleetingly occurred to him that he may have been sustaining and bolstering human trafficking, exploiting the disastrously plausible conclusions of abusive childhoods, drug-addicted refugees, under-age kidnap victims, paying to rape or at the very least, enabling a bad life 'choice'. However, it had been a fun and worldly experience for him. He suspected the prostituted woman hadn't been pretending with him and that, under different circumstances, he could have helped or befriended her and that she was just a "wrong side of the tracks" character with an interesting past. Just like in a Hollywood film!

Next to the hair loss prevention lotion and a copy of *GQ* was a length of rope. He had bought it when a woman he'd been talking to online expressed an interest in bondage. She had disappeared, though, like Houdini! He wondered if it would hold ten and a half stone.

Amy had a large flat in Islington and a Little Miss Naughty duvet cover – a funny and sweet self-referential joke if your idea of naughty is a recluse who sometimes exceeds the recommended daily dose of Wellwoman supplements. Well, 'recluse', apart from group therapy and the rare occasions when months of chatting online and selfie exchanges made it all the way to a real-life date. Her focal conundrum was that, having been very beautiful in her 20s, she'd acclimatised to having her turgid verbosity about how she "felt like an alien" or was "on her tenth incarnation" and "felt things more deeply than other people" indulged by men who hoped there was a honey pot of gold at the end of the rainbow where every colour was Amy coloured. Cruel, really. But don't feel too sorry for her. She was an unmitigated bitch in her 20s. She regularly faked *not* having an orgasm.

Amy was now a next generation mad cat lady – meaning she probably had an undiagnosed mental illness but had seen enough documentaries and memes about mad cat ladies to be able to make self-effacing jokes about being a mad cat lady, which cancels it out. In fact, she had so much toxoplasmosis in her muscles and brain that the parasites were doing her thinking for her. Luckily, in 2020, this did not really mark her out from larger society in any palpable way.

Amy's dad had emigrated to Thailand in 2002, buying a house and field and business for 26-year-old Boonsri, who proudly displayed the footage to her four thousand and fifty-five farang Facebook followers. Everyone said her dad was having a breakdown, except Amy's mum, who pointed out what a convenient form so many breakdowns take, recurrently necessitating the unbounded indulgence of one's most greed-driven, covetous, narcissistic, and socio-politically exploitative propensities. Rarely would they ever oblige the victim to work diligently for a hospice or relentlessly campaign for abandoned donkeys.

Amy's widowed uncle had also been hauled into the mess, being hooked up with a friend of Boonsri's. Dinner in Pinner now resembled a Bangkok backpacker bar in decline. Empty eyes and long silences broken up every so often with "Go on! Say 'cheeky bugger!'" subtext: *in your funny accent, you vapid, cheddar weaseling, blingsexual currency draining coronavirus.* Meanwhile, the photo of Amy's dead auntie saw everything, staring down with poker faced grace.

Marlena on the ball, her "mac and smile" says it all. Amy had misheard the lyrics as a child. *Must be some mac! An Aquascutum perhaps.*

When the date was finished, Amy and Adam Lastname decided not to see each other again but agreed to be friends, like the oxymorons they were.

Home for Adam Lastname was a new build home-buy near MI6, the ones by the Thames with the huge billboards on the side with blonde women in yoga clothes holding croissants and smirking sideways – exposing colossal canines because they've scored such a terrific place to live.

Adam sat up in bed and opened his laptop to RedTube. Two young women with nonspecific faces greeted his sticky eyes. One couldn't really tell if they were attractive or not because they were an equation, an equivalence. The eyebrows stenciled perfectly, a teacher's tick on your homework face. *Eyes – yes, two of them – legs – check – teeth – at least an A1 on the shade parade.* The faces made the best of themselves for the job they had to do. The women weren't skinny or fat, just bodies the colour of caramac bars, uniformly sprayed like they'd been done at a garage to pass the MOT. Oh, and requisite belly button stud above the orthodox bald genitals.

"Caramac bodies and licorice hair", that's what Adam's Nan called it. Not referring to girls on RedTube. She wasn't *that* type of Nan! She wasn't a NILF. No.

News readers, TV presenters, singers, etcetera – "They all have the same licorice hair", Adam's Nan would observe, puzzled. She meant dyed deep brown or black and ironed and serumed into a limp-ended helmet, which is what Adam Lastname held in his desk-jockey-soft-as-a-princess hand.

No curls, no shades of ash or ginger. Just caramac bodies and licorice hair. A banal box of wholesale confectionary. No Curly Wurly? No Star bar?

There was no undressing, no materiel, fabric or substance to the hardcore clip. One girl sat on a showroom looking kitchen's worktop, because kitchens are sexy and where most lesbian encounters take place. The other knelt in front of her, rubbing the worktop one's tuppence ha'penny with two fingers and every few seconds looking up with a weirdly wonky, cockeyed smile. The kind of smile the duty manager of a sports centre might give whilst negotiating a refund for a pushy mother because the pool was closed. Caramac bodies like corpses on a slab, iron-on, ironed-out, peel-off transfer versions of sexuality – replete with sporadic, semi-animated jerks, flashes of pierced belly button, and fuchsia nails. But there is no fuchsia in England's dreaming!

Adam Lastname tried not to be distracted or disgusted by a wisp of hair the razor clearly missed or the dark curled lip which looked as dry and shriveled as a dead snail dropped under your mum's washing line by a slack-jawed jackdaw. He bravely soldiered on wanking. Rub, rub, sexy smile, rub, went the pair of half-wit-looking stooges. But not as half-wit-looking as Adam right now. The recipient, every few beats, touched one of her own tits. Always the same one. Could've been a pre-dementia businessman on a bus who's forgotten his wallet then remembers it's in his top pocket. *Still, they really are lesbians*, Adam remained convinced.

For a second, he noticed a small Donald Duck figure on a shelf behind them that had a knitted pink scarf around its neck. *Who had put it there?* he wondered, *The scarf hadn't come with the toy. Hold on. More crocheted than knitted. Someone's put effort into this. Donald Duck wouldn't be seen dead wearing that effeminate woolen boa! He even looks like he's embarrassed and hopes no one will see him. He's in the wrong bloody place then, isn't he?*

Adam tried to think about his co-worker Anita, tried to merge the image of her with the women on screen. *Women,* he persisted, *dirty slags, love being fucked. They love it. Dirty slags all love being fucked.* It wasn't working, though. It was no longer enough.

Try and think of taboo things, things I'm not supposed to think. The things themselves didn't particularly turn him on anymore, the accessibility of porn had exhausted every fetish, it was like a Hungry House menu you'd tried every dish from and were still hungry for a flavor you couldn't name. More the idea of the act itself, was the pull, the act of finally giving in to something, being helpless, giving in, removing the mind policeman, and seeing the most tarnished and tawdry parts of his psyche.

Although Officer Anxious arrived on time for work in a yellow hi-vis, holding a torch against the caution tape of his mind, back to the caramac bodies and licorice hair, the lifeless chicken factory flesh of no music. All that remained on the soundtrack was the dead air of an empty kitchen and rubbing the dead curled snail that's so dry her partner in mime must spit on it to avoid starting a fire. *That's okay. The spitting is SEXY and SPON – TANEOUS!*

Adam Lastname wanked his cock as the two girls rubbed their matching fannies, two girls in a kitchen, two girls there was nothing out of the ordinary about. *Phwoarrr!* Not *arf!* We are all reader's wives now, and . . .

Adam Lastname wiped his hand and logged into "World of Warcraft".

What a time to be alive!

Chapter Twelve

"Didn't think they'd shit so much," Amy said out loud to herself, mopping up the pile of rectum warriors exactly the colour and consistency of the chocolate power bombs she saved in her fridge for what she still called "the munchies". She'd bought the mother with four Labrador cross puppies – crossed with another other dog, not dogs that were bad-tempered – from a small ads website. Amy had managed, bravely, to put aside her semi-reclusiveness and social anxiety long enough to scurry to a horrid North London pub under cover of night where, wrapped in a headscarf and massive shades, she handed over £750 for the lot.

"Where are you going?" she'd say every time she put one back in its basket only to have it crawl away again just like a living creature. *And why wasn't the mum showing any interest in bringing them back?* she'd wonder. After all, this was the whole point.

The mother dog licked her arse nonchalantly, oblivious to her brood. *Didn't she have any maternal feelings*? Amy thought. *Wasn't this shit instinctive?*

The next day at about 4pm, wearing a headscarf over her nose and mouth – although the odour of puppy shit that now filled her flat wasn't that much more unpleasant than the strawberry incense she'd been buying since 1993 – Amy drove the puppy party to a reservoir.

A guy she'd met on "Guardian Soulmates" once took her out there for a 40-minute awkward silence interrupted intermittently with self-help affirmations. *I'm still finding myself spiritually, and that's okay. One thing I've learned to accept is that I'm on a journey.* She was pleasantly reassured when his lunge at her mouth was sticky and uncoordinated. Post-date autopsies with the online avatars she called friends, were infinitely sexier than anything physical.

He had been the first person she had heard, or rather, seen use the expression "my bad." She had stared at the screen for several minutes trying to decipher what it could mean. *My bad what?* He had sent it in response to her pointing out his last message had been blank. *I know my bad.* With no comma.

"I know my bad?" she thought at the time, *Do you? Like knowing your prog rock or early Marx?* It put her off him for a while. "My bad" it sounded, toddler-ish.

It grew into a joke, though, and she eventually delighted in any conversational openers in which she could use it. "My bad!" she'd reply in quotation marks when he corrected her on what day of the week it was. And he would often reply with an eyeroll emoji. She obviously couldn't see the moment when he began rolling his eyes in real life.

Eventually, he stopped getting back to her. Ghosting, it was called, even by fully grown adults. Of course, this is a misnomer since ghosts are always clamoring to get people's attention and people often go to very extreme lengths to find ghosts as well! In fact, Amy's entire online existence was a desert lately. Online activity was her heroin and she needed to smack that bitch up.

Unfortunately, the canine bitch in her car was still worryingly apathetic about her babies.

She lugged the metal carrier up the stone steps and surveyed her backdrop. *Not a bad set,* she concluded, *Could do with a sunset or some photogenic minorities or something, but it will have to do.* Taking the puppies out and putting them on one side of the water, she noticed a rubbish tip had been slowly turned into a rubbish island made from broken pipes, a golf buggy, pizza delivery bike, some hearing aids, copper tubing, paper towels, Roy "Chubby" Brown DVDs, milk cartons, "Blue Peter" videos (the Mark Curry years), nappies, razors, chicken bones and a government USB containing millions of people's personal data.

The puppies yelped, played and tumbled in a viral internet gif of cute - h*opefully*. She pulled the mother by the haphazard rope lead and put her on the other side of the reservoir so that it would mean she'd have to swim to the other end to rescue her offspring.

"Look! look!" Amy tried to draw attention to the puppy pile, but mum had other ideas. Instead, she barked happily, wagged her tail, cocked her leg, and did a wee against a bush. Then she sniffed around a bin, jumped in the air, got down low on the ground, dug up a daisy and barked at a duck.

Meanwhile, one of the puppies was getting progressively closer to the edge of Rubbish Island. Amy ran back and forth, phone hanging from the sleeve where it had been attached like a five-year-old girl's mitten, ready to film at a moment's notice. Her cast, however, were unruly B-listers. As the sky turned darker, panic set in.

This wasn't going to work. The plan had been hatched under a deadly codeine plus self-hatred combo. Amy had been watching the episode of "Some Mother's Do 'Ave 'Em" where the psychiatrist concedes in the end that Frank is indeed a failure – thinking – as she did with everything – *that's about me!* She had wanted to film the dog's mother swimming to retrieve her pups. That being done, she could upload it with a caption like:

Aww, can't believe what I saw earlier! was going to call the RSPCA but she had it covered!

Or perhaps she could write *but THIS feisty mama had it covered,* adding a degree of sass in the process. It was perfectly customary online to use expressions you never would in real life such as "feisty mama". It was also normal to talk in "whoo hoo!" high energy exclamations like Nicole Scherzinger sing-songingly appraising a ballad by a skinny young Irish girl.

Whoo hoo you just rocked my world and you know what? you GO girl!

Or possibly, if it had been a particularly politics heavy day, Amy could dictate in words which would, if translated into a human voice, be an insipid, sanctimonious preachy whine:

We could all learn a lot from the unconditional devotion I witnessed today.

That'd be sure to get at least forty likes, wouldn't it? Amy calculated. *Who could not like it? It would be like saying you were an unkind person.* And if the post didn't get enough feedback, she could always add an "R.I.P".

We could all learn a lot from the unconditional devotion I witnessed today, which reminded me of my Aunt who died on this day 17 years ago R.I.P

Amy realised with a heavy heart and heavy period that it wasn't going to happen. Mum dog was running in circles, high on her childless freedom, the very embodiment of a dog poster for 90's Girl Power!

"But, your puppies!" Amy pleaded as she made some desperate yelping sounds and pointed to Rubbish Island. "Over there!"

As she turned sideways, she became aware of a presence behind her. Then, she heard a noise as well as a presence, definitely something, a human something. *Could be a sheep though,* Amy thought, *They can sound like people, can't they? Sheeple. You know, those ones that sound like the House of Commons.*

There it was again, whispering this time. *Sheep don't whisper do they?* she panicked, *Not even when one of them has been entertaining cultural pretentions beyond their class bracket, smoking French cigarettes, going to see experimental theatre, and describing the last film they saw as "Two hours of exquisitely filmed alienation".* Amy zoomed in on the direction of the voices with a military precision absolutely wasted on her life of idle ineffectiveness. She saw a couple of women holding up their hideously cased – *what were they? Kitten's heads in purple diamante?* – phones.

This is not good, Amy thought. *This was "totes awks, dude".* Although, despite the impending disaster, she couldn't help thinking how fearsomely common the women looked. These were the kinds of horrid humans which her reclusiveness was all about avoiding. One of the phone-holders had sunburnt pink skin, rotund arms like pork sausages in a faded lilac vest, and no bra. Her light brown hair was pulled back in a ponytail and looked like it had never even been dyed. *How do they get through life with these strange 70s ashy hair colours?* Amy asked herself, *No deep chocolate or rich mahogany? No Ombre T-sections?*

The interloper's wide face was all scrubbed and pink and open, while her friend – accomplice? – did have dyed hair. In fact, it was fried and bleached – freached, if you will – and cut in a heavy fringe and basin. In keeping with their meat-themed union, this one had arms like roast chicken drumsticks, over-tanned from years of Spanish holidays, patio sun loungers, and casual racism – she expected. They were all crumpled and bony. Dark glasses covered most of her face, which wasn't hard because her face was pretty much a nose and chin which had finally fulfilled their lifetime ambition of being within kissing distance. There was just a sniff of a Rizla between the two. How those years of straining to look up or down at each other must have ached. The friend looked like one of The Muppets, one of the background ones with a name nobody knows, one of those instrument-playing muppets.

Amy waved weakly at the retired dinner lady looking pair. They scared her, especially their faces, which showed every thought drifting in and out of their Brexit-voting Wetherspoons heads.

These people were constantly reacting, thought Amy, *like animals, really, to what they thought seemed to be immediately manifest. Terrifying.*

The two women said something to each other and moved towards the stone steps. Amy couldn't get to her car without passing them and the puppies yelped while their mum pulled on the rope. Amy quickly tied it around a post. Picking up into a sprint, she headed in the opposite direction. *Fucking hell, it will take ages to get home now.* Amy didn't *do* public transport.

Chapter Thirteen

Dylan's mum actually did have a job. Not that they needed the money, but she needed to feel active - actively taking the job of someone who needed one. She worked part-time as a museum curator. The art history she studied at university had led to a series of wearisome secretarial roles unconnected to her studies and so, this had seemed refreshing at first. She was, in fact, much more stupid than the school-leaver single mum down the road they gossiped about, the one who'd started taking Poundland multivitamins and attending a night class that provoked her network of dendrites and glial cells to grow by the day.

"We thought about all this at college!" was the unspoken consensus of the educated. Now was the time to show your maturity and talk about house prices, garden decking and how the latest Disney children's film is "actually really well done and there's a lot of subtle adult humour slipped in. Really quite clever!" They also enjoyed: 'Drunken History, Stupid Shakespeare and Dickhead Dickens'. Hilarious downgrading of culture for guilty graduates who've been there, done that. So, Dylan's mum made the most of the few blood circulation prompters which helped her feel less like a stagnant slug in a slurry of salt.

One of those prompters was Gabriel Cohen. He did digital marketing for the museum, among other duties. She could exchange knowing sarcastic eyerolls with him. Gabriel had also shown an impressive amount of pop music knowledge at the occasional pub quizzes they'd been to while her husband slumped at home reading yet another novel about medieval chariots flying through space in the future.

Gabriel was tall with intelligent features and a hilarious Twitter feed. He wore glasses and posted footage of himself teaching his three-year-old daughter, whom he saw at weekends, an unspecified martial art. He also had his own media communications agency called NRTV, which was short for Narrative but was also shorthand for Near TV – a double-edged sword which was even more exemplative of his luminosity and acumen.

Dylan's mum found it hard not to find it sexy when Gabriel got very angry about bigotry, whenever he really lost his rag and wrote something controversial like *Why on earth has Julia Hartley-Brewer got a radio show?* This made her feel like she was back at university in a secret drinking club where no one else quite understood how farcical the rest of the world was.

Today wasn't one of her work days and so, she was at home, looking after Michael Parkinson. The poor dog had been ill for six weeks now, something to do with his kidneys. The vet had advised the family to monitor his behaviour and bring him back if he still seemed under the weather.

Dylan's mum's Twitter feed was filled with reactions to a terrorist attack in London the previous week.

The amount of coverage on this is INSANE! where was it when Eric Bristow was being homophobic? one little news item, racist much? Gabriel had tweeted.

Dylan's mum felt a mixture of excitement, veneration, and universal love for the entire world. She "hearted" his tweet and quickly tried to think of something to mirror his selfless resolve. Michael Parkinson walked past her lethargically, glancing up a couple of times while she scanned her brain for an authentic opinion.

Funny how no one refers to CHARLES MANSON as a 'terrorist'.... she wrote, leaving the dots as thought provokers.

Aha! she reflected, smugly, *think on! dot dot dot.* She waited. Gabriel would be sure to pick up on this. She sat patiently by the social quagmire, a content-providing fisherman waiting for someone to bite her newsworthy rod.

You do know that Charles Manson didn't actually kill anyone, don't you? a woman with the username @MayaofLondon77 tweeted back at her.

Er…are we talking about the same Charles Manson? beard? swastika on forehead? bit murdery? Dylan's mum responded.

Yeah, didn't kill anyone, not saying I'd invite him to my two-year old's pirate party but maybe research before jumping on the blandwagon #blandwagon

The nerve! she thought. Dylan's mum looked at Michael Parkinson for backup, but the dog was sprawled in the corner, nose buried in his tail. *Who was this annoying little bastard?* She tapped back to Gabriel's feed. He was busy exchanging politically-expedient witticisms with a whole bevvy of forty-somethings who understood references about everything from *The Mayor of Casterbridge* to Anthrax's cover of Alice Cooper's "Eighteen" to Matt Bianco being prank called on "Saturday Superstore". Dylan's mum threw down her tablet, picked up the laundry basket and, admitting defeat, continued with less pressing matters like washing and ironing – instead of moshing and irony.

The radio on the kitchen window sill blasted out songs from her youth. Prefab Sprout, Deacon Blue, and Echo and the Bunnymen filled the air. She wondered if Gabriel liked Echo and the Bunnymen. She sang along, happily forgetting about the Twitter B-words. Since she had become a mother, she said "B-word" instead of "Bastard" or "Bollocks".

"April Skies" was faded down and regular programming was interrupted with breaking news. There was a high school shooting in California. Dylan's mum retrieved her tablet and checked what people were saying. Of course, there were lots of *why isn't this story being covered more?* and plenty of *imagine what they'd be saying if this were a 'person of colour'* mostly from white people whose social circles were so white, moths flew at them thinking it was the moon. Her brain went into overdrive. It was like Benedict Cumberbatch's Sherlock Holmes where he moves ideas about in the air with his hand, discarding each one when it doesn't quite fit. *What did he call it? His brain hat?*

"Got it!" she exclaimed, heart racing. She typed the pearl of wisdom, the gem of genius, the cubic zirconia of circumspection:

Perhaps we should ransack this boy's home and see if we can find a CHRISTIAN BIBLE?

Michael Parkinson was making whimpering sounds just like when he was a puppy. "No, Michael!" she shouted at the barking dog, tapping frantically to see whether her clever comparison had been picked up. "Silly boy!" she chided.

Result! Gabriel Cohen retweeted her straightaway and even replied with a smiley face. *Bless his socially-conscious heart,* she thought. Gabriel was followed by lots of people, not necessarily celebrities, but people on the periphery of celebrity – comedy writers and producers and people named 'Nick'.

Scroll, scroll, scroll, tap, tap tap. How life affirming to suddenly be included in conversations with people, clever people, people like Quentin and Arabella. It really is like being a student again! Dylan's mum tucked her charcoal Uniqlo legginged legs up under her on the sofa, forgetting that she usually hated how this position shoved all her cellulite together in a large loaf of arse Braille. It was suddenly voluptuous, Rubenesque and continental.

"Might even crack open one of those tiny German beers," she said in a celebratory smile, unaware all the while of Michael Parkinson's convulsions on the kitchen floor. The neglected canine was drooling and his nose and tongue had turned very pale.

backs out of room whistling she replied to Robin Ince. Robin Ince!

Dylan's mum walked around the room with her Amazon Fire, glancing at her reflection in the mirror which, like her son, she usually avoided. She didn't look that bad, really. Not that different from when she was in her 20s. There was still a hint of when she was in her 20s or early 30s. Her 20s were trying to send her a smoke signal, in a badly rolled red rizla.

She'd only just noticed it now. Pulling the skin on her face back and pushing her nose up, she ruminated that she could definitely do a blog which could lead to a *Huff Post* article. With a network of people like these, she could even make middle-age work for her. She could re-invent herself. Dylan's mum illicitly imagined herself newly single and drinking too much coffee with Konnie Huq and Sue Perkins outside a Notting Hill café while they discussed ideas for a BBC4 show where regulars from QI have to drink ale, on roller skates whilst only using Shakespearean language to the tune of Africa by TOTO.

Perhaps they'd be joined by that woman who won the Edinburgh fringe with that groundbreaking two hours of material about the perils of periods and being a "terrible" feminist, which involved such shame-faced hedonism as attending a "Dismantling Harmful Beauty Standards" gallery and accidently admiring your own reflection in the glass cabinets containing a belief-challenging display of used sanitary products.

Some sparkly purple Barry M eye shadow she'd bought at a boot sale and had thrown into a basket of toiletries that never got used started calling to Dylan's mum's psyche. The neglected cosmetic became interdimensional space dust, a time-travelling portal-raiding sulphur dioxide gatekeeper to her new life.

Perhaps she'd wear it to the next pub quiz with Gabriel and that guy he knows who worked on a Blur album.

Dylan's mum liked her new friends, Konnie Huq and Robin Ince. She'd probably become friends with other media people, too. They'd all live in Shoreditch or Crouch End or Islington or Stokey. She would probably start calling Stoke Newington "Stokey" and Crouch End "Crouchy" and Shoreditch – they'd come back to that one. And the trio would always remember to make self-referential remarks about living in "middle metropolitan leftard cardigan elite bubbles".

They might want to borrow her Barry M eyeshadow, Huq and 'Kins. They'd think it was funky, like something Kate Bush would have worn on an album cover. *Ooh!* she fantasised, *they could talk about Kate Bush. Well, no, not Kate Bush. She endorsed Theresa May, didn't she?*

Dylan's mum had seen all the clever, feminist men tweeting about how they used to want to come on Kate's tits, but not anymore. *Who then?* she wondered, *Siouxsie Sioux?* Well, she'd research her views on Palestine before dropping a makeup-based reference into the convo wouldn't she.

They'd all probably Zoom, or Skype or perhaps do Google Hangouts? And they'd all love Dylan's mum because she'd be more trustworthy than others who were "in the business". They'd cherish her tales from civilian life and ask permission to use extracts from her stories in articles and stand-up routines. They'd tell her they envied her experiences. They would find her useful. After all, those quotidian things seldom happen to them anymore. There might be some tricky social politics to maneuver. *What if Tim Minchin hates Eddie Izzard? What if Richard Herring can't abide Owen Jones?*

Dylan's mum could definitely help with those sorts of predicaments. They'd probably seek her input out first. She could prudently instruct them that, in the great scheme of things, they were incredibly blessed and how she'd been reading about the plight of Benghazi women and found it hard to take petty gossip seriously and they would all say, “My god! You’re right! What were we thinking? We’re so glad we know you, Dylan’s mum – who we all secretly fancy.”

Michael Parkinson lay still in a pool of saliva with legs as stiff as Meg Ryan’s conversation with his namesake. His chat show days were over.

Chapter Fourteen

"I've got some sad news." His mum sat Dylan down in his dad's gaming seat after school. "Michael Parkinson's passed away."

"You mean –"

"The dog, yeah" She was mentally designing the RIP meme she would post later. "He'd been poorly for a while, hadn't he? It just became too much for him this afternoon. I'm sorry, mate." She rearranged his fringe and he shook it back, trying to wriggle away from scrutiny.

"But I thought the vet said just to watch him and, you know, monitor his behavior and that," said Dylan.

"Just one of those things, mate. Aw, I know he was your friend, wasn't he? He was a good friend. I'm sorry, mate."

Dylan wasn't falling for this chummy mummy bullshit. "Just wanna be by myself for a bit," he muttered.

"That's fine, mate." She reached for her tablet to tweet before his body had turned the corner.

Aww son's upset about the dog dying, it helped a lot with his autism and his toxic relationships

Lots of people replied and she got three new follows from autism accounts and one from a pet crematorium in Luton. *#win.*

Dylan put the radio on in his room to hear Ian Farrington.

"Why is it such a taboo for men to talk about their mental health?" asked Ian. "*Is it that old macho thing, you know, stiff upper lip, don't show any weakness, be the man of the house?*

Well, perhaps today we can break the stigma. My show seems to have a history of men being able to open up. I've no idea why! So, here goes. . .first caller, you're on the air"

"I was wondering how much Shakespeare and all that lot - the ones who had their missus's locked up for picking violets at sunset or eating two helpings of gruel in a petticoat or wearing a bonnet to girdle a swine on St Cygnet's Day - thought up - and how much was them earwigging their wives and daughters, barmaids and prostitutes, whipping their feathers out every time they heard a tasty one-liner and taking all the credit"

Ian put the last call down to rare case of someone with an *actual* mental illness as the phone lines became jammed with people wanting to talk about how they're not allowed to talk about their mental illness. Dylan looked at his mum's Twitter account. Apart from finding out he was apparently autistic now, he also found out that she'd been on Twitter for the entire afternoon. *She was supposed to be looking after Michael Parkinson. Was it even worth bringing it up?* he wondered. *Would my reaction just be more evidence of my autism and more fodder for her social media feed? Do not feed the beast,* he thought, *do not feed the rabid beast.*

Chapter Fifteen

Stephanie Korovnik had immediately taken to social media when she realised her daughter was missing. Her husband, a writer, was on a book signing/brothel tour in Germany. It was day three when she tweeted:

Oh God, just realized I had a hair appointment booked for today, I can't possibly go. I keep breaking down whenever I realise how normal everything was a week ago

You should go darling, doing something normal everyday will calm you, don't neglect yourself, Molly wouldn't want that, a celebrity, so far below 'Z' list you had to use the Cambodian alphabet to find him, wisely opined.

Do you think? Stephanie replied with her left hand as she was already opening her car door.

I do; besides, you can put a missing poster up in the window

Ok, I'll go, if Molly saw the state of my barnet right now she'd run screaming for the door.... Stephanie could never resist performing. Even at the expense of her, potentially raped and murdered child.

Fifteen minutes later, she sat in a chair by the hairdresser's window as Italian Claudio fussed over her.

"She'll be back," he said, "She's probably just gone on an adventure. Oh! Have you read that story? Oh, my *god*. She is so *brave*!" Claudio was indicating a piece in the magazine on Stephanie's spindly lap about a woman who was forced into a marriage in Bangladesh. When the woman ran away, she was captured, gang raped and subjected to an acid attack which left her scarred for life. She now devoted her life to protecting women and girls, speaking with politicians on legislation, and guest lecturing at colleges and women's' groups.

Stephanie looked at the photo above the article. The woman in the picture looked directly into the camera with a determined, serene expression. She wore a crisp white vest and blue jeans. Such nobility, such incredible poise and strength, such poignantly inspirational, majestic, thought-provokingly, resilient determination and tenacity. Stephanie pointed at the picture sedately and asked, "Do you think my hair would take that colour?"

Chapter Sixteen

Amy had returned to the reservoir later that night and picked up her car, clattering around in massive Sophia Loren sunglasses and more scarves than Tower Hamlets' busiest launderette. The puppies and their mum were gone from Rubbish Island and their smell pretty much gone from her flat. She felt silly but relaxed upon coming back home. Stretching out on her enormous L-shaped sofa bed, she ate another Belgian chocolate, held her phone over her head and took a few selfies. *Life was okay. Who needed to have footage of a mother dog saving her puppies in order to feel loved?*

She felt warm, as though she'd learnt something about herself. Sometimes you need to have a wake-up call, a near miss, to make you realise what you have. This experience would help her become a stronger and more spiritual person. She uploaded her image to Facebook with the nauseatingly transparent caption *I think I might actually like myself, is that ok!?*

Amy was cynically aware that women had to support anything related to liking or not liking oneself as if everyone were suddenly harbouring the legacy of some Elizabeth Fritzel level PTSD requiring industrial levels of therapy and self-love and that, by showing some support or approval, they vicariously gained caring girl points. Amy lay back and waited.

Ping! Ping! went her phone. She ate more chocolate and popped a codeine. *Ping! Ping! Ping!* the phone persisted. Her post was even more popular than she'd anticipated, she bathed in connection, life-affirming and familiar. She decided to let a few more build up so there would be a surplus to enjoy. The crescendo was almost sexual. Withhold, withhold, withhold --- then give in. It was edging for dopamine-dependent approval addicts. *Ping! Ping! Ping! Ping! Ping! Ping!*

No longer able to resist, she clicked on the F icon, feeling her blood rise. Amy was bathed in happy sedation. Everything was alright. She was warm and her cyber avatar was being fed serotonin up its arse.

Notifications: 1087.

A titanic flurry of stimulation was being rimmed by apprehension. A shaky feeling. A feeling ex-pubic schoolboy frequently pay hard, inherited money for.

You were tagged in a post with Sheila Leyton with Metropolitan Police and 4 other people;

Dear Metropolitan Police can you please arrest this ignorant criminal?

Three thousand and seventeen comments.

Watch this evil cow try to drown innocent and beautiful puppies

Views 678k

Amy, it's Rosalie, get in touch, it's not you in the video, is it? DM me.

At last! Amy was trending.

Her heart raced, battling the codeine as she marched up and down. Eventually, she rang her mother, whom she regularly barely bothered with, despite being completely funded by her savings. They quickly decided on a flight to get her out of town. Berlin, perhaps. She spoke German. Or maybe she could go to Rome. She'd been there during her gap year, which had, so far, lasted twenty-seven years.

But time was of the essence and the police were making their way up the mountainous steps to the front porch.

Despite her internal panic, the middle-class autopilot took the controls and she was polite and co-pilot-operative. After an hour of questioning - mostly about where and from whom she had purchased the animals - she offered, "He did look the type to have been involved in other shady ventures. He had that sort of 'Essex look'. Tracksuit and gold chains."

"I'm from Essex," an exhausted interviewing officer exhaled, burned out from a lifetime of pedestrian Essex jokes.

"Oh, of course. But there's Essex and then there's Essex-Essex," she babbled.

The officer nodded, "I'm from Essex-Essex."

Oh dear, thought Amy, *My bad.*

Chapter Seventeen

Ian Farrington had been given an agenda for his phone-in, which meant that he had to read up on trans issues, something he knew nothing about.

Trawling the internet, Ian washed up on the shore of an extremely long comments section on someone's blog.

After editing his notes, Ian Farrington adjusted his mic and began his three-hour discussion. *Another seven knife crime incidents in the last week. That's one a day. More on that later, but what I want to talk about now is trans people. If you're a trans person, I'd love to hear from you. Perhaps your son or daughter or mum or dad or sister or uncle or cousin or neighbor is a trans person? Give me a call. I'm fairly intelligent. I like to think I can put myself in most people's shoes, high heeled or otherwise, but this one's really stumped me. Give me a call and tell me what it's like. Hello, Susan. You're on the air.*

Hello Ian, she growled.

Chapter Eighteen

Apart from school, Dylan's existence had been entirely online since being grounded. By now, the novelty had worn off and he was stir crazy. The more his real life shrank, the more he craved escapism.

On Wednesday night at 9pm, Dylan was logged in and waiting for the live streaming of a talk about how everything is an illusion. It was presented by a retired professor trying to flog his books.

"Derp!" Grace shouted as he closed the door on her River Island face. Opening all his windows first, he picked up Titus the Mouse, lit a bent Sovereign, and put his feet up. *Buffering. 3-2-1…*

And we're extremely honoured to introduce to this year's Thinkers of the New Millennium Society esteemed panel member, committee contributor, author of sixteen books, including Here We Go Round the Mulberry Universe, The Secret Codes of the Universe and How to Unlock Them, Avatar Existence, Groundhog Man, *and the book that launched many a Reddit thread* (laughter from the audience), Your Life is a Computer Game but Who's Holding the Console? *Astrophysicist, philosopher, owner of an extremely comprehensive collection of 1970s prog rock* (laughter again). *We're extremely lucky to have him as he's about to jump on a plane and fly to Berlin for the Dissecting the Paradigm Festival. A very warm welcome please for Professor Lawrence Kinney!* (Applause)

Hello, Dr. Kinney began, *You know it's great to be back in London. In fact, earlier today, I was browsing around some of the many esoteric book shops as I always do and was extremely agitated to see one of my books placed in the Mind-Body-Spirit section. Now, you might think this is an overreaction, but I work extremely hard on my research and to see myself relegated to such flimsy conjecture as angel cards for everyday decisions* (laughter) *or witchcraft for beginners* (laughter) *was frustrating, to say the least. Those of you who have bothered to read my material, which I might add, I produce at great personal expense, financial and emotional, will know that I deal in hard facts. All the science is there. It's been checked, cross examined, and re-examined. But I don't want this to turn into a rant. I'll get back to the point of all this and what I've been studying for twenty-five – in fact, more than twenty-five years.*

Dylan puffed away, absent-mindedly listening.

Dr. Kinney continued, *One of my favorite recording artists, David Bowie, once sang "It's a god-awful small affair to the girl with the mousy hair" Well, science now agrees that it could well also be a god-awful small affair for us, as we're only seeing what we call reality with a tiny fraction of visible light at the back of our brains which then decodes it into signals depending on what we're expecting to see. This is how hypnosis works. This is how someone can be hypnotised to not see the person standing in front of them. In fact, if the entire spectrum of what's possible, the data potentially accessible to us, were measured in terms of actual mass, what we see could be compared to a few drops in the Atlantic Ocean. We are, in effect, spiritually blind.*

Tapping the tiny top of Titus, the Mouse, Dylan concentrated. Or, at least, the avatar controlled by his future simulation builders, appeared to express concentration.

So, back to why you're all here, said Dr. Kinney, It is my assertion that reality is not what we think it is. I mean, he held aloft his plastic coffee cup in the studio, *we can all agree that this is a brown coffee cup. A very nice coffee cup in fact* (laughter), *but if I were to bring a bat into this room, the bat would decode it by converting the echo spectrum back into the echo time separation.*

Here, a woman in the studio audience raised her hand.

Yes, lady with the glasses and – no, no, on the right – the lady in a sort of mauve cardigan.

Well I just –, the 57-year-old woman hazarded, wondering how anyone could think her violet ballet wrap was a mauve cardigan. Kinney's tiny fraction of visible light must have been off.

We usually ask people to say who they're with, admonished Dr. Kinney.

Oh, I'm on my own. Billy No Mates! She tried to put laughter into her voice.

No, we mean who you're affiliated with, a panel member said bleakly.

I'm affiliated with the college. A dinner lady. I'm Jean, said Jean.

Ah, one of our free ticket holders, returned Dr. Kinney with a gentle sneer, *Well, that's fine. Just remember there's merchandise for sale by the bar if you want to contribute later* (laughter) *What was your question?*

Thank you, Jean whispered as an aide scrambled up the aisle to get a microphone to her. *I was just wondering, does – does it matter if an owl* (her voice hit the microphone, suddenly rendering her words loud and static) *could see it diff—* (more feedback and pops) – **erently***?*

A bat, Kinney corrected sternly.

A bat, yes, sorry. Or does it take on a meaning of its own based on how we all see it? Aren't we supposed to see, I mean like a mouse, for instance –

Okay, interrupted Kinney, *Now, I'm glad Jane –*

Jean, it was now her turn to correct, but the mic wasn't picking up her voice.

--brought up this question of consensual reality, because in a way, yes, and in a way, no. Let me explain. So, you think you're having an experience as Joan the cleaner?

It's Jean and, well –

But who are all the other people? continued Kinney, *They're also you!*

So, you're me? Jean looked puzzled.

Precisely. Although I think you wear that cardigan better than me! (laughter. The crowd really liked that.)

But you're not me, countered Jean, *I'm going home to my flat in Streatham and you're flying off to Belgium for your Unraveling the Parameters meeting.*

Dissecting the Paradigm. In Berlin, Lawrence tersely interjected.

Yes. So, you're definitely not me.

Let me explain, Dr. Kinney formed a bony shipwreck with his long knotty fingers, *Your body is the vehicle. Your mind is the steering wheel. But it's being driven by your infinite consciousness. which we all share. We're all everything, every one, every moment that ever has, ever is, or ever will happen.*

There was a round of applause and a "whoop-whoop" from a young man in a beany hat and a *Zeitgeist: The Movie* T-shirt.

Well, no – Jean stated, matter-of-factly. The noise died down surprisingly fast. *I mean, that's like saying you have a tree over here and a bit of the tree falls off and plants itself in the ground over there and turns into another little tree and years later people are admiring it and then you come along and say, "Oh no no, there's no point looking at that. It's just part of that one over there", almost as if you're calling the people idiots or something!*

I don't think I've called anyone an idiot! Dr. Kinney manufactured a humble smile and scanned the room. Many people had turned to face Jean, something that would usually make her self-conscious. But Jean was lost in her own curiosity.

I've got a small carved marble swan at home on my mantelpiece, she responded.

I suppose there's no accounting for taste. Dr. Kinney threw his bait to the cheap seats, but no one was biting this time.

Now when my nephew visits, Jean continued, *he always admires it. Named him Simon, Simon Swan. Anyway, what if I say to him, "Stop being silly. It's not Simon Swan. It's just a part of a mass of marble it once belonged to."*

Yes? Dr. Kinney's expression was pained now.

Well, there'd be nothing, would there? No art, no objects, no books. We'd constantly be contemplating what it's not, lest someone like you implies we're somehow missing the point.

Ah no, returned Dr. Kinney, *it doesn't mean that one cannot appreciate our individual expressions of the whole, just that we become aware that it is an illusion.*

But it's not, is it? It's not an illusion at the time, is it? And what if your infinite consciousness is just a part of some other massive thing that hasn't even been discovered yet?

Yes?

Well, you're going to feel a right 'nana, aren't you? When the hysterics her bluntness elicited finally died down, Jean continued, *It's like hitting a mouse over the head and saying "No, no! Stop being a mouse. There's more to life than scuttling around and squeaking, you know? What about the Sport's Centre and Wednesday and creeping Sharia and pillow cases and Marginalisation?"*

Dylan covered the delicate ears of Titus the Mouse.

But, dear lady, Dr. Kinney knitted his brows together. The furrows were burrows. *If we thought like that, well, we'd never had made any of the discoveries of the 20th Century. We'd have just put our feet up and watched "Coronation Street".*

Oh, perhaps, Jean shrugged, *and it's only my opinion, but I just think that once you realise that you're not what you think you are, then you have to come back to what you think you seem to be and stop worrying about it.*

Dr. Kinney pretended to be making some notes, but was violently scribbling out a drawing he'd been scrawling of a bat with a woman's face flying into the Twin Towers. *Die! Die! Die!* he thought. The pencil broke through the paper and marked the vibrating atoms that had been slowed down to a frequency which made them appear solid, somewhat like a wooden table.

Chapter Nineteen

Dylan wasn't lying when the next morning he said he felt as if his head was exploding and his heart was beating through his eyeballs. He *did* feel like that - every time he imagined what was happening in the class beigely named Vocation and Community. A geography teacher, who'd taken online courses in counselling, DJ skills, and ethnic jewelry making, was going to take today focusing on how the students could grieve positively for their fallen classmate Mabel.

Dylan, though, was at home watching "Loose Women" which hosted the usual line-up of a recently transitioned London gangster being congratulated on their bravery, a Northern soap actress dropping anecdotes emblematic of how down to earth and stupid and common she still is – *And so, I ended up in the cleaning cupboard all night thinking it was the bloody vestibule!* – and a reality star currently playing one of the weasels in a new production of *Wind in the Willows*. There was also a woman who'd had £60,000 worth of plastic surgery to look like a cartoon drawing of herself. She was explaining it away with matter-of-fact therapy language whilst the others looked concerned but accepting of her preoccupation.

Most importantly, Stephanie Korovnik was there, surprisingly refreshed and plugging her latest show. *I understand why some people have said it's a bizarre thing to do but it's my coping mechanism*, Stephanie offered. *I have always dealt with things through laughter. It's in my DNA. I come from an extensive line of feisty immigrants who --*

Dylan nodded off and was only jerked awake when the soap star said, *And join us after the break when we'll be talking social mobility with Russell Kane.* He genuinely thought he was watching Alan Partridge.

After Russell's insights and a song about Brexit played on banjo by a man named Jeremy in yellow trousers and a flat cap, they returned to Stephanie and her missing daughter. Stephanie tried hard to frown, but her latest career injection had called for some forehead injections. She'd been studying Kate McCann circa 2008 and was concerned that Dr Raj had been so syringe happy, except she couldn't show it. She wanted to look young and grieving, but still sexy. Sexy grieving.

Suddenly, upon seeing Stephanie Korovnik, Dylan faintly remembered her conversation with the girl named Louise. He tried to find her profile. Every trace was gone, though. Louise was what you might call off-radar.

And the rent was due.

Chapter Twenty

Louise plucked the final pubic hair from her 'bikini area', doubt from her mind and left the Crystal Palace bed and breakfast her last key worker had shoved her in. She'd tweezed every single wispy traitor whilst watching "Penguin A & E" with Lorraine Kelly. Not literally *with* her. Lorraine would have probably advised against it. *Och noooo hen. Grow yourrr weee bush ooot. Ya shouldnae haveteh confirmtah oppressive beauty standards. Beseeds, it's yourrr crloooooning glooooooolry.*

"Smile, beautiful", an unhappy-looking man with a pink Pringle jumper demanded of her as his pink Pringle face folded in on itself like a paper fortune teller from a 1970's classroom. *Pick a colour – pink. Pick a number – four. An imbecile in a jumper will squeak a cliché at you.* Not a fortune as such, more a dull, time-travelling inevitability.

Louise ran through the options. The easiest one was to smile, to the response:

"That's better," There was now an 85 percent chance of a follow-up remark. Alternatively, she could answer back, blowing open the entire social dynamic which had just happened, one that turned a prying eye to the hypocritical landscape which meant that old women didn't tell young men to smile.

So, insipid smile it would be. Besides, she was running late and blood was dripping down her leg.

"That's better," he stated, "looks more pretty. And thanks for accepting that. A lot of girls these days. . ."

Louise had a stark suspicion that this kind of incident had mutated the 1950s-man wolf-whistling at a stocking-clad secretary into a faint, fickle fraud.

These men weren't Sid James, having an eye for a pretty ankle burned into their DNA. They were beaky, tweety birdies. Over-feminised by xeno-oestrogens in plastic packaging, digitally addicted baseball caps, subscribing to old men's podcasts who insist women are happier being ultra-feminine 1950s homemakers but offering nothing in the way of, *man.* They were performing male drag. And what a drag it was.

There were some days when, in the fifteen minutes it took her to walk to the library, depending on her responses, she might be bestowed with the appraisals "beautiful", "gorgeous", "cunt", "bitch", "sexy", "ugly", and "slag" – which is sure to be a porno version of *Snow White.*

Some consistency would be nice, she thought. It was dull. Dull as dishwater, almost as if they wanted a row. Anything, just human communication. Hungry ghosts floating about in their oblong bodies which were mutating into the shape of iPhones and laptops.

She hurried past a row of shops, eyes burning with hay fever, her charity shop jeans held up with a dressing gown cord, waist-length hair separated into a million flamin' hot sauce ringlets, and not even extensions.

"I've got a naaaiice big cock for you, y'know," she suddenly heard.

Louise looked around and gathered the information was indeed intended for her, despite the lack of a formal introduction. A car full of overgrown toddlers with stubble were giggling like convent schoolgirls in a gender-neutral changing room.

"I'm a lesbian," Louise settled on immediately before regretting giving them anything at all.

"That cos you're so ugly?" they sniggered. The giggling became fey, faux laughter.

"Yes, that's right," she returned. "Incidentally, why did you bother to offer such a repugnant vision this information about the size of your cock?"

Louise strode right over to the car and looked inside at the collection of awkward man-children: *never had a fist fight in your lives,* she thought. There was a pickled onion Monster Munch 12 pack on the floor and some pointless grime whining out of someone's device.

"Incidentally!" echoed Frankenstein's sheep in the passenger seat.

"Incidentally!" a couple of the others chimed in, as if she were using outlandishly obsolete jargon. They repeated the word amid embarrassed laughter, trying to will it into being funny. If they could make it funny, then it wouldn't be embarrassing.

"No?" asked Louise. "Okay, bye then!" She concluded the exchange cheerfully to laughing but clingy and wistful looks as she walked briskly away. They had got one: a real-life exchange with the opposite sex. The mileage in this was inordinate. They would talk of this day and whip each other up into a feverish frenzy often, especially when there was a lull in the conversation. (often)

Someone soliciting for charity allowed eight men to walk past un-accosted whilst balancing a clipboard on his head. He pulled a stupid face and tried to high-five Louise, exclaiming, "You look friendly!"

He must care very much for the cause he's working for this week, she thought.

After running home to change into leggings and put talcum powder on the underarms of her T-shirt, she travelled halfway across London with the Oyster card she had found in a bin with an alarm clock and a peach soap dish.

Reaching the toffee-nosed Hampstead address that she had scribbled on a Co-Op receipt; she pressed the buzzer five times. Just as she was turning to walk away, the door was opened by a man with the face of a tea-stained matinee idol haunted by asbestos and molded over the years into the shape of *What the Fuck Now?* He had a can in his hand, a cigarette hanging out of his mouth, and a testicle visible at the side of his burgundy knickers. The overall vision reminded Louise of a pork-in-breadcrumb appetizer which had been spilt onto her bipolar Auntie's special festive tablecloth. It happened the same night her mum had got very drunk and demanded to know where the canteen of cutlery their Nan had won at a 1975 Tombola had disappeared to. That Christmas had *not* ended well. Her auntie still had a horizontal scar above her top lip giving her the look of a cute bipolar rabbit.

The man upstairs, a prime-time television personality with a family in Buckinghamshire and this work-related 'base' in London, had booked an escort instead of a taxi, which he usually did the other way around, and, in a fog of Zopiclone and pizza, he wasn't answering. Now, Louise would have to go all the way home. *Bloody typical*, Louise fumed.

And the papers are always saying young British people don't *want* to work.

Chapter Twenty-One

Steven Starkey wasn't good with elephants in rooms and this elephant had an erection, a marching band, was wearing a lavender cravat and shouting, *Cooooo-eeeee! It's me, the Elephant in the Room. It's rude to ignore people, you know.*

"Do you like being an escort?" he asked Louise.

"What makes you think I'm an escort?"

"Sorry," he mock stammered, "You're quite right. Do you like being the unlikely young acquaintance of the most odious cretin on television, renowned for hiring escorts and performing hospitalisationly mortifying acts of spite on them? That is, when he's not tweeting about toxic masculinity and climate change."

"This is my first job," she lied. It was actually her third, but she'd been told to always say first.

"Oh, Christ," answered Steven, "You drew the short straw."

"What?" Louise looked at her plastic Pokémon watch. Maybe she could draw out the chit-chat for a couple of hours, cover her expenses, miss rush hour, and get paid for her time.

"Short straw, luvvie, you know," Steven started speaking as though she were deaf. "You pulled your New Look leggings out of the laundry bag for nothing. Anyway, he's a..." he sang in a high-pitched choir boy voice, pointing at the ceiling where the passed-out pork-puller slept, "Men-tal pa—tient!"

"Out on a limb," Louise said, "Wouldn't that be most clients?"

"Oh, they've sent a *character*," said Steven, "Go on, fuck off home, love. You're not safe. I'll get you a cab." He took a twenty pound note out of a little china box shaped like a shell and waved it at her as he clicked his uber app in front of a framed poster for the film *Vertigo*.

"Is this where you tell me he's a cannibal?" she asked.

"Worse."

"A cannibal with one of those novelty doormats that says, '*strangers welcome, family by appointment only'?"*

He sighed, "Are you sure you weren't en route to audition for an all-female BBC4 sketch show?"

"I'm tired. Come on, a sit-down at least?" Louise said.

Steven put the phone down. "Sure?"

"Yeah," she grinned, covering up her nerves which she realised were stronger than she'd been feeling in anticipation of sex with a strange man who was obviously the kind of man who pays for sex with a much younger, impoverished woman. "You're not mental, are you?"

Steven turned on the stairs which smelled like Fresh Linen Air Wick and Mr. Sheen and pulled a lizard face. "I'm not mental if you're not a crackhead."

Louise rolled her eyes back in her head, slackened her jaw impersonating a Tarantino version of a crackhead, and followed him up to his flat.

"Gosh," he said, "this is just like *True Romance*, isn't it?"

"I hope not. I'm not in the mood for Gary Oldman in a bad wig."

Steven frowned; he knew a lot of comedians so wasn't used to people being funny. He fell on the floor and waved his cigarette about. "Well, what shall we do? I don't have any Pokémons or tracksuits or whatever you're all dancing to these days"

"Whatever you want," Louise sat down. "I've got time to kill."

"Do an impression of John Le Mesurier apprehending Snoop Dog for bombing in the pool. Or a short lecture on Bronze Age mystics." Steven turned suddenly, stared, then went back to talking at the ceiling. "So, you're a. . ."

"I'm a what?"

"You're a twat?" he misheard.

"No," she laughed, "Are you deaf?"

"A bit, yeah."

"You were saying I'm a – something." Louise picked up the can of warm Kestrel he'd abandoned..

"Oh," Steven held his arms up as if measuring her aura and spat tobacco at a plant. "They've sold you the idea you're an empowered woman in charge of your sexuality and fate like a cool chick in a Hollywood film who's *sexy* and *dangerous*. And that your life will make a remarkable story one day when a predatory women's magazine comes to interview you about how you escorted your way to a law degree or shark taming certificate or pilot license." Steven fell asleep for a few seconds and snorted awake, picking up his monologue where he left off. "But fate is conspiring in your favour. Besides, Impotent Wanker upstairs is dead today. No different than any other bottom-feeding mouth breather with a tattoo of The Little Mermaid and bodies in the wall."

Louise looked sideways at the walls. “Yes, I can see you’re normal. Nothing wrong with you.”

Steven feigned a twitch and a Tourette’s “c-c-cunt.”

“Please don't say 'cool chick' again," she implored.

"Coooool chick," he affected in an exaggerated nerdish monotone.

"And isn't Impotent Wanker an oxymoron?"

"Fuck off," smiled Steven. They maintained eye contact for a friendly amount of time. Three seconds.

Louise took off her coat. Steven looked up and put the ring pull from his can in his eye socket like a monocle and let it fall out in a Lesley Phillips-kind of way.

"I once shoplifted a bag specifically for shoplifting," she offered.

"Ha!” he laughed, “We're bonding!" Faux theatricals slid back to his regular coffin faced gargoyle.

"Can I say something?” Louise asked. “Well, it's an opinion, so it's an IMO."

"Yes. Don't forget the obligatory disclaimer. God forbid anyone suspects you were making a statement."

Louise ventured anyway, “Well. IMO, you really shouldn't be drinking and smoking so much in the day. You seem too nice."

“Haha,” he mocked, “Listen to me, carefully. If I were an HIV-addled, smacked-up piss-pot, pulling my flaccid meat piece to CBeebies like shit parade upstairs, at least my intentions would be straightforward and honest."

"Are you saying you're not interested in sex?" she asked. They maintained eye contact for five and a half seconds this time. "What do you think about when you wank?"

“I can't think now that you've asked,” Steven wasn’t fazed. He was good friends with the woman who wrote *The Vagina Monologues*. Nevertheless, he tried to deflect. “All the images springing to mind are stolen things, like that clip of the 1960s with that man doing that stupid dance on acid with the purple bandana. The 60s! Five people in London who took the wrong cough medicine while the rest of the country were still in twin set and pearls, watching ‘Coronation Street’. Cut to Granny Takes a Trip and then Mary Quant and then –”

"You think too much!" she interrupted with a flinch, “Did you hear something?”

“Just the emaciated reverb of your shallow squawk. Well, what do you think about?"

"Unlike you, I know exactly what I think about." Louise continued.

Steven glanced at his phone for the first time since his offer of a cab. Feigning disinterest, he rattled off the headlines. "Another three stabbings outside a South-East London college and teenagers to be given compulsory B6 injections to ward off depression epidemic caused by Covid-19 vaccine. Oh, and Meghan Markle is on a raw food diet. Do go on. You were saying my sexuality is soooo interesting.” Steven yawned a mime artist’s exaggerated yawn.

"I imagine the sorts of things that men think about and then I think about how ridiculous and easily programmed men are and get turned on by that, sort of “she explained, “Sort of, the predictability of it, the easiness. A kind of depression really. I put myself in the head of a man and get turned on by how stupid they are and what a terrible world it is. It’s like giving in. Yes, I give in to how shit the world is and have an earth crushing orgasm. Probably because there’s not really porn for women, is there? So, I’ve turned men’s weakness for porn into my own porn. Which makes me better than them because I’m one layer ahead!”

"You're even more pretentious than me," Steven said. "What's your opinion of men? And generalise or we'll be here all fucking day"

"They're all right. They'd behave better if women acted in a more authentic way. But then, women would act in a more authentic way if men behaved better, chicken egg sort of thing" Louise was pleased with her summery whilst also wondering if it was a trap to get her to be derogatory about men so that Steven could kill her. Perhaps he was a PIGTOE or whatever they're called.

"What do you mean, *authentic*?" Steven was far too apathetic, and arthritic to think about murder.

"Most women are a culmination of characters they've seen in films and tried to imitate" she went on. "The result being, each one in the mix is so watered down and faint it's a weaker personality than they started with, plus the exhaustion of constant acting makes them dull, Camile Paglia says that men are more at the extremes of the intelligence spectrum, more retarded people and more geniuses but women hang around the middle. Of course, she puts herself at the genius end, you'd think she could stop saying 'okay' so much if she's such a bloody genius, 'okay'" Louise impersonated a particularly grating Noo Yawk accent.

"Ah, except you, of course, you're the different type of girl" Steven called her bluff. Which was rude because her name was Louise.

"Yeah, which is another role to play. Good that you're perfect though. How do you support yourself?" she enquired.

"Like this," he leant up against a cabinet.

"You're used to people thinking things like that are funny"

A faint tension crossed over Steven's brow. "Men are more visual than women though, aren't they, hence the porn"

"Myth" Louise seemed sure, "Several scientific studies have proven that when they wire men and women up with electrodes, without the social conditioning and restraints, their brains react exactly the same to visual stimulation, it's a beta male argument. Women see a wider spectrum of colours too, so, if anything, we're *more* visual. The beta male world has had to invent these inversions because they are small with no bright colours or huge antlers. Convince everyone that women need to stick feathers in their arse and lipstick on their tits. Don't look at us, girls, keep occupied bouffanting your minge. You never answered, how do you support yourself?"

"I get commissions and people donate money so I can make podcasts and things, and I also do satire, a lost art. And people pay me" He was processing the minge bit, trying to turn it into the kind of BBC4 sketch he was derogatory about upon her arrival.

"What people?" she narrowed her eyes like a Siamese rat.

"Good people. People with good taste."

"People like this?" Louise picked up a card containing a cheque for £1000 inscribed with the good wishes *Nice one for Friday, Steve. Keep up the good work and do more jokes about raping feminists! And hijabs! Great stuff! Free Tommy! And if you're ever in Thailand ...Know what I mean!!! - Brian.* At the bottom of the card, which featured a picture of a young girl sitting on Pinocchio's face with the caption "Tell me more lies", was a babyishly scrawled Union Jack

"Who satirises you?"

"No one. You can't satirise a satirist. It's what's known as an objective truth, a universal law of nature!"

Louise thought for a second, she was allergic to 'can't' She was can't-phobic, on the spectrum; "You cannot satirise a satirist . . .said the satirist, wielding the pitchfork of truth he used to puncture holes in society's pompous hypocrites. A pitchfork bought and paid for by pompous hypocrites on the condition that they poke holes in SPECIFIC pompous hypocrites. I.E not them"

Steven shook his head. "Gotta earn a living. And that's parody, not satire"

Louise had another go. *"Oh, la-di-da, you cannot satirise a satirist, it's what's known as an OBECTIVE TRUTH* - explained the satirist, patronisingly, whist working on a sketch cleverly satirising the corrupt and exploitative glove puppet industry and simultaneously accepting a much needed (if friction-ful) blow job from an under-aged, trafficked glove puppet which had been sent to them by a 'patron'. *But that's not a glove puppet, it's a hand rod puppet!* The very clever satirist explained. *The puppeteer's dominant hand goes into the head of the puppet, operating the mouth, and at times, facial features. The puppeteer's less dominant hand controls the arm rods, thin rods connected to the puppet's hand or arms. And also, what you're doing is parody, not satire"*

Steven looked as though he had, what young people refer to as 'a sad boner' so she cheerily distracted.

"What's this?" She pointed to a folder full of half-scribbled paper.

"It's a new and exciting sitcom, exactly like 'Fleabag' but called 'Nut Case', it's got hilarious to-camera internal dialogues said by a posh lady with the time, money and resources to --"

“Oh, shut up,” she exhaled, “You’re just jealous. You’re what my Nan would call ‘a headache.’”

“Well, let’s face it, it wouldn’t be ‘your Nan’ without her phenomenal gift for observing a train of thought and interpreting it with miles and miles of colourful metaphor and creative analogy,” Steven feigned familial figment about Louise’s Nan, for comedic purposes. Louise was a much tougher audience than the girlfriendless gimps he had become used to telling him he was a ‘genius’ every time he mentioned Schubert or Pratchett. Speaking of which.

“Stop being so ratchet,” she demanded.

“So – what?”

“Ratchet” she repeated.

“Batshit?”

“Ratchet,” she corrected.

“Who’s Rashid?” asked Steven.

“Never mind” Louise gave up as Steven lit another cigarette from a lighter shaped like a lung, “Seriously, those papers, what are they?”

“Just work,” he said, “It’s bullshit.”

"Oh. It’s made up?"

"Well, no,” he stammered, “yes, no, it's lazy and possibly wrong. But I'm going to make it right!"

"What for?"

"It's something to do,” Steven answered. “It's nice and neat and tied with a bow and I’ll get paid and can be like piss-pot upstairs and hire escorts with perfume that smells of a pensioner's perm solution. Or is that sperm solution?" Steven coughed away the insult, feeling a pang of pity.

"I'll sum it up" he said as he threw the papers about, "Blah, blah, blah *American Psycho*, but with Cockneys and tinned peaches, splattered with descriptions of things which sound dark and vicious. 'Her disgusting tits like two Hackney recycling sacks filled with three-day old porridge'. Or, 'he mumbled like a stroke sufferer munching on a 15-year-old whore's muff', etcetera, etcetera." He slammed a random book against his forehead. "It's lazy and the metaphors make no sense but it's what people want. My agent will reject the first three drafts for relying too heavily on wry social observation to the detriment of the story. He'll email that to me as he pulls at the grey in his wispy beard, he grew to disguise the weakness of his jaw. Then he'll swivel in the ugly walnut Queen Anne spoon back chair his lesbian sister bought him as a wedding gift long before his wife left him for the actor who plays the barman in those drink driving ads. Hitherto, the fine upholstery will be forever stained by the bleachy spunk he donated in lonesome response to crass Hentai via 4Chan. Finally, he'll update his blog with a black-and-white picture of some skateboarders in New York and a poem by a refugee named. . . Rani."

Louise had long ago stopped listening, but continued to nod as she looked at a black-and-white framed picture of Steven shaking hands with a bookish-looking woman with dangly earrings and too many teeth. "What was that picture for?" She freed one of her can-clutching fingers to point at it.

"I'm a judge on a novel writing competition. It's my penance."

"My Nan writes things," said Louise, "Short stories to magazines and stuff like that." Suddenly, she brightened up. "When's the next one?"

“Don’t wear out her rheumatic wrists, dear. People like that don’t win. It’ll be won by an English Lit graduate named Pippa Elizabeth Hat who lived in Mumbai for five years and, inspired by the culture, was compelled to write a story about a young boy at the turn of the century who only has a bicycle for company and starts to believe it’s his father. Hey!” he snapped in an instant, “That’s quite a good idea.” Steven grabbed a pen and paper,

“Aren’t there any competitions for diverse background-type people?” asked Louise.

“Well,” he said, “you’re the wrong kind of diverse, you and your *Nan*. They’ll throw you and your –” he frowned at her feet, “– Air *Mikes*? – under the bus as soon as look at you. Not only do they not want to help you, your very existence calls theirs into question. If your Nan could create anything on her, no doubt, non-existent rations of financial, artistic and emotional support, what the fuck is their excuse? Not posh enough to be all warm, familiar and harmless and not the kind of demographic that makes them feel enriched yet benevolent and vicariously cool.” Steven retched up that last word and shivered in disgust. “What they really want is a brown version of them.” He squinted at her complexion. “And you’re not even white. You’re. . . translucent. I can see your lilac blood.”

“That’s not fair,” she protested.

“Moo, I know, never mind. There are no great movements or generations anymore, anyway. Everything’s finished. Literature’s dead. Adults are infants. Scooby Doo advertises banks. I mean, millennials. Not really a generation at all, is it? More a barely sentient surveillance system.”

“Well, what can we do?" Louise really didn’t care about the answer. She kicked a pair of hairdressing scissors under a chair. Steven cut his hair himself and performed his own dentistry.

"What?" Steven sniffed; eyes still closed. "I've depressed you. Better get your B6 injection." *snore, snort, jerk, awake again.* "Nothing. It's over. There'll never be a youth movement ever again. We've had the last generation. It's not a *thing* anymore. They've been bought and sold, paid for and invoiced – owned, as you young people say."

Louise laughed into her can.

"I mean look," Steven violently tapped his phone until Facebook appeared, cold and blue and clinical, like a "Blue Peter" badge or a Suzanne Vega song. "Rob Meuheux likes Women's March. In the 90s he called all women skank whores. Even his mum. *Especially* his mum."

"Well maybe he's grown up?" Louise offered, "People can change."

"Pfhhnnn!" Steven snorted roughly and then said in his standard clipped nasal impression of Anthony Hopkins, "First principles, Clarisse."

"Stop messing about," she played, "I love Kenneth Williams, too."

Steven narrowed his eyes and slowly shook his head. Louise was glad that these were the kind of conversations they were going to have. She'd often wondered where intellectual life lived and it lived here, with one bollock out, insulting all its friends

"What was I saying?" asked Steven, "Change, yes. But how funny, how con-ven-i-ent," he stretched out the word, sounding like a piglet, "that people always change in a way which is going to make life more convenient at the time. Do a hashtag women's march when you're twenty-five and virile and sexy and you risk something. With your peers taking the piss and even women your age thinking you're a bit creepy, even a bit fey. But do it when you've something to lose and it's controversial. Not to please your Wellingtons-wearing wife who's suddenly a feminist and because your disproportionate-to-your-talent ego is now invested, indeed incarnated in your female child. It's all so convenient and can't be trusted because they'll be the first to jump ship as soon as the land is safe for them again. And on the other side, meanwhile, there will be endless jokes about safe spaces and trigger warnings, and people laughing at their own sophistication every time a performer says "SJW" or thinks that satire is saying "It's so toxic that John Cleese hasn't died again today – *NOT*!" A Wayne's World trope stretched for eternity like a pair of Vanessa Feltz's tights. They're all so behind the times. I mean, hurry up. Dear God, *hurry up*."

Louise rested assured that Steven well and truly did *not* like convenience. She opened her mouth, thinking he'd finished, but he hadn't. The tirade continued. "Oh, suddenly he wants women to be taken seriously. Well, I'm sorry, dear, no. Jesus retched. Ours was the last generation and they've been got at. It's the end. There's no more. No more flowers to smell."

"You don't strike me as someone who uses Facebook," observed Louise.

Everyone's turned into a cross between 'Rumpole of the Bailey' and the 'News at Ten'. *Ad hominim* this, strawman that. The lying, disingenuous bastards. Cardboard cut-out cants."

"Is everything that hopeless?" Louise asked, "I mean, if a generation was to rebel, properly rebel, what would that look like?" She retrieved the scissors from under the chair and put them in the inside pocket of the coat she was clutching. She was enjoying her afternoon, but was aware it could also turn very bad at any moment. This was most afternoons, mind you. She'd had more scrapes than a cervical smear nurse.

Steven made chattering motions with both hands while he thought, as if somehow rocking the ideas into existence. It seemed like a long time. At one point he tapped his temple with his nails. It was all very, insect. He went over to the window and opened it a little. The room was filling up with spiraling smoke. "It would be complete rejection of everything, but not in a way which just puts you into another group -- conspiracy theorists, social justice warriors, parodies of social justice warriors, parodies of parodies of social justice warriors. Boring,

boring, boring. A rejection of all of it. Messy and noble, not in a punk way. That's been done anyway, obviously. It was too aesthetic, really. 'Ooh, poor me. I've got to spend all my Baby Boomer money on drugs and brothel creepers and houses and forty years of counselling in LA. And not traditionalism, trilbys and newspapers. That's too hipster. It would look like – like –" he struggled to find the right term, "feral children. Now, that would terrify those keyboard wizards."

"Warriors," Louise helpfully helped.

"Wild, dirty-faced, tree-swinging, fire-building, physical, frenzied, emotionally-robust, anti-health and safety, confrontational, non-conforming, super-resilient, non-nanny state, un-digital, un-plugged, live show, here and now, in the moment, fuckers!"

"Grace Kelly. . .Roland Rat. . .We didn't start the fi-yah!" Louise sang merrily.

"You're too young to know Roland Rat, or Billy Joel" Steven calculated.

"We did it in school. 80's pop culture. It was the head of year's idea." She explained.

"How renegade of them to make their teaching job all about their own cosy nostalgia" He took a long drag on a Gauloise and at the same time Louise felt a breeze through the window on her crotch where her leggings were threadbare. She was cognizant of her cold, hairless genitalia and what she had been primed for when she'd turned up. It all seemed very wrong now, perverted even, now that she was in the company of someone she actually liked.

"It's usually people who had Nannies who don't like the Nanny state" She said, smooth and custardly, the devil's advocaat.

Steven came alive again and went straight to a specific place on one of the book shelves his flat was furnished with. "Wild boys and feral girls, like this." He waved the book around

Louise's face so fast she couldn't see any of its pictures of crazy-eyed, dirty-haired children who lived in forests and wastelands.

"That's just homelessness that never goes out of fashion."

"No," Steven disagreed, "These poor bastards didn't know they were wild, did they? They had no choice. I'm just showing you this is what it might *look* like, the opposite of a culture encouraging, indeed rewarding, narcissism. It would look wild. It would be dirty. Just look at everything being thrown at you and do the opposite. That would be a start."

"Like Amish."

"No, not like fucking Amish, you pointless prick! They're just another niche, another trap, another glitch, another set of rules. Messy, noble, frighteningly clever. What are we constantly told? We're dumbing down. Read. Think. Reject. Ignore. FOMO? Miss out! Think, study deeply, refuse the hijack. Gen Xrs and Boomers have had a lifetime of raw polaroid photos in pubs and clubs, landlines and real time experiences to create their characters so they may as well embrace the last 20 years of their lives with technology, it's a novelty for many of them. Their successors are smothered in the cot with thin, painful tinny curation by buzzing, constant, neurotic swipe. Create a live show and smash the phones that are your jailers. Disaffected youth? Disinfected youth, more like! Even if someone wrote all this down, it would just be another thing to like on social media, another string to your profile, a personality add-on, a nod to your so-called rebellious nature, a box ticked in small, bite-size digestible pieces. Safe, risk-less, sheltered, caged, pointless, empty, castrated, and impotent. You're not educating yourselves. You're drowning in your own reflections like Narcissus."

"The rapper?"

"There's a rapper named Narcissus," he sighed dejectedly, "Why am I surprised? "

"Well," Louise said, "the whole thing sounds great. I just need to win the lottery so I can live off-grid. You've got no idea how much it's going to cost to live without money." She wondered if Steven was going to say "messy" and "noble" again soon.

"Where did you get the idea this involves living without money?" asked Steven. "Money is fine. Money's magnificent. It's just that you've been using it to laser your eyebrows and Botox your muff."

"Do I look like I Botox my muff?".

"Of course, you do. You all do."

Chapter Twenty-Two

Three cans of Kestrel and a migraine later, Louise left Steven to sleep off his opinions, which is exactly what she did when she nodded off sporadically throughout her bus ride home. A man with a mental disorder and lots of carrier bags sat opposite her, diligently diagnosing his fork collection and muttering to himself about the Home Guards, a tribunal and Whitney Houston. Every now and then, he would say "slag" or "whore", turning his head closer to Louise and changing his tone from muttering to angry. At one point, he began shouting, "suck my dick, suck my dick" Then, looking to the side, he grinned at his own brilliance to invisible admirers. The passengers on the bus carried on, chatting on phones and reading about Cara Delevingne's new mental health tattoo in the *Metro.*

It was clearly Tourette's or something, thought Louise. Although, when a tall and muscular thirty-something-year-old man came and sat next to the poor unfortunate, he managed to keep completely silent. *Selective Tourette's! Who'd have – cunt, shit – thought it?*

Louise scanned over the usual graffiti on the bus seats – "Korrup", "Krimnal", "Kake Dekorata" – to find a crumpled flyer that had been stuffed down the side with a chicken bone and Ribena carton. "Offliners" it read boldly, alongside a picture of the Facebook logo sitting in a dog food bowl filled with liking thumbs. Next to this was a mobile number. *Must be some pretentious new club night,* she sniffed, *It's probably in Hoxton, probably has a Facebook page. It'll be a Pure Gym soon anyway.*

Jumping off the bus near home, Louise popped into Costa to pocket 10 sachets of brown sugar, enough for two cups of tea. A radio phone-in could vaguely be heard above the mechanical bubbling of the coffee machines:

The gloomy fact of the matter is that my daughter, who's at uni at the moment, working incredibly hard, will probably not be able to afford her own home until she's well into her thirties.

Louise shuffled the fifteen pence in her pocket and wondered if mackerel in tomato sauce was still reduced at Lidl. Her aquatic musings were interrupted when a member of the mum-and-giant-pushchair relay race attempted solidarity in contempt about a teenager wearing a very short dress and thigh boots. It was that look where one is supposed to maintain eye contact for an extra heartbeat, signaling that you're a co-conspirator in judgement of another woman's inappropriateness. Louise enjoyed messing up the chain of events by staring blankly at the woman she was supposed to be in cahoots with. If they'd been laying it on thick, she could raise her eyebrows and ask "What?" With a shake of her head and a shrug, she could really throw a spanner in the works of society.

"Oh, no, it's fine, I have enough!" Louise annunciated clearly with an upper-class Joanna Lumley accent, teeth together. She warmly-smiled confidence to a barista with a treble clef tattoo and a topknot he was insufficiently embarrassed about. Excuse me, excuse me," he had chided nasally in reference to her condiment pilfering.

Stuffing the lovely brown sachets into her jeans, Louise scampered off to sit by the canal and think. Being so far below the poverty line, flat earthers asked her if she could see boats disappearing over the side. She wondered what life was like for that dad on the radio's daughter at uni who'd be able to buy a house in her thirties. Louise wondered if she'd even make it to her thirties. Or mid-twenties, for that matter. Before her eyes, three magpies dived in and out of trees. "One for sorrow, two for joy, three for a girl – oh, no thanks. Can't I have the gold, please? Where's all your mates?".

Chapter Twenty-Three

"Ok, I'll come to you then." Louise's Mum didn't hear her because the moment her daughter spoke, she spoke over her. It was like a callous deviation of the "Yes/No" game that no one had told Louise she was supposed to be playing. "And do you know," her mother continued, "I could feel quite suicidal when I look at the garden. Really, I've got so much to sort out. It's not easy, you know, on my own. The roof needs doing. Not that bloody Pete next door could give a shit. I think his wife's left. Don't blame her. He's got bipolar. So has the builder who's supposed to be coming around next week. Not that he will. Something not right there if you ask me. And I need to get some more plant food for the begonias and go to the bank. Ah, nice chap in the bank I speak to. He's got bipolar. I could get really bloody depressed about the garden. I could. I really could if I thought about it. It never bloody ends," she ended with a heavy sigh.

Louise punctuated her mum's sentences with noises to show she was listening. She was trying to hurry the conversation up because she only had 49 pence left on her pay-and-go phone and the people in the room next door were shouting so loudly that the Rizla-thin walls vibrated. She had concluded the shouting wasn't a row. It was just the way they had conversations. Louise was going to be evicted again in a matter of days. She had £16,000 worth of debt she'd clocked up solely on living expenses. A fact which she didn't mention to anyone. She also had an inflamed lower spine, unexplained crippling headaches, and gum disease she couldn't afford to have remedied.

"You'll know what it's like one day," her mum rattled on, "when you're old like me. Not easy, you know. I could really bloody well go to sleep and never wake up when I think about the amount of work that needs doing to the spare room."

"So," Louise confirmed, "Thursday, then. 4ish?"

"Yeah, s'pose so" Louise's mum sighed.

"Ok, bye. Love you."

"Don't be daft!" she brushed off her daughter's attempt at warmth, dismissing it, as she always did, as saccharine sentimentality.

Louise was the post-1980s underclass, born into a house filled with cultural norms which had worked perfectly for generations before but were less than useless to her. In fact, they were a hindrance. She would find herself lumbered with memories and social sensibilities she didn't know what to do with. None of it worked for the life she had been thrown into. She'd set her family's living standard back to the time of her great-great-great-Grandma, and she'd had six stillborn babies and been blown up in a wool factory.

Two hours and thirty-seven minutes Louise spent getting ready. *Hair up, hair down? Too much lipstick, not enough? Perfume? Nah. Fitted top? Oversize sweatshirt?* She was looking for the version of herself her Mum wanted or liked or even wasn't repulsed by. She thought that she hated show-offy women. She always had something to say about *that* kind of "broad". *Blousy, up themselves, daring-to-enjoy-attention types.* So, last time she'd worn a grey jumper and no makeup. She'd approached her with as big a smile as possible and tried to embrace her, but her mum's body was as limp as lettuce.

Her Mum had laughed in a high-pitched twittering way like a hedge full of judgmental sparrows. "What?" asked Louise.

"You look like the man who used to deliver my Nan's fruit and veg! Thicky Norman we used to call him. He wasn't right in the –" She twirled her finger around her temple in the universal mime for mental and moved on to her conversational staple, "Shame Woolworths went"

Louise decided this time to put her hair up and wear a sort of blouse and lipstick - look like someone coping with life. She saw her mum coming out of the station and psyched herself up. *Be kind. Be happy.* Louise practiced the smile long before she could see her. She'd even written down a few subjects to talk about on a crumpled piece of paper torn from a red council tax warning. This time she'd thought of everything and nothing was going to go wrong.

Walking up to her, arms out for a hug, Louise's mum's body was flaccid and her cold limbs raised a tiny bit together, like a puppet in a raincoat. She smelled of throat pastilles and dust. Louise kissed her on the cheek and asked with disguised dread "How are you?"

Her mum only laughed.

"What's the matter?"

"What do you look like?" she sniggered, "I'm trying to think. Wait a minute!" A businessman walked past and smiled at Louise while her mum tried to remember who her daughter reminded her of. Suddenly, it hit her. "Olive from 'On the Busses'! All drippy with your hair like that. Oh, I loved that series. Bloody Drippy Dora, you look like! Ha! Get dressed in the dark, did you, Drippy Dora? Ha! Or Mrs. Doyle! Would you loike a cup of tea, father? Ha!"

"How've you been? You look well!" Louise smiled, trying to pattern onto what she thought a normal family might be like and re-capture her optimism, but it was gone.

Mum didn't answer her. "Yeah, just looking at this," she felt the sleeve of Louise's blouse. "Makes me think of some old curtains we had when I lived in Victoria years ago. They were slightly green, though. Not green-green. Bluey-green, kingfisher-green. Not turquoise. Funny old flat that was. And do you know what was nice? Every one of the girls I shared the flat with recently got in touch with me to tell me how much they liked me and said that they always knew they could talk to me and how thoughtful I always was. They all said I was one of the kindest people they'd ever met! Isn't that nice?" Louise's mum affected a humble titter. "Is there an M&Co here? Got to return a peacock feather broach."

"Would you like to get a coffee?" Louise asked, trying to make eye contact, although her Mum didn't seem to be able to reciprocate. In fact, she didn't answer her the first five times. "Mum, would you like to get a coffee or a tea?"

"Yeah, s'pose," she finally acknowledged, "Not bothered. Need to sit down, though. I've got terrible pain in this arm."

"Let me carry your bag."

"No, don't be silly." Louise's mum clutched her bag close to her body as though it contained stolen celebrity glove puppets "Ow, ouch"

"Please, mum," Louise persisted, "Let me take it. Come on."

"No no," she responded, "It's fine. Ooh, ouch."

"Anywhere in particular you'd like to get a drink?" asked Louise.

"No, I'm easy. You know me!" she beamed, "Just thinking, they'll think you're looking for a sailor dressed like that!"

"How about here?" Louise suggested as they happened upon a pretty Italian coffee shop,

"Yeah, s'pose," she agreed, "Not looking for anything special, are we?" Louise's mum began to cough uncontrollably.

"Ooh, mum, are you ok?"

Her coughs continued to punctuate her words, "Just – that – dog," Louise's mum motioned towards a little puppy drinking a bowl of water at the feet of a plump Italian woman dressed all in black with large sunglasses.

"You are allergic to my dog?" the stranger asked in a very friendly and confident manner.

"No, no," said Louise's Mum, "Well, sometimes I am. He's smaller than a mouse, isn't he? I love your sunglasses!" She said this in the strange foreign accent that she did when speaking to foreigners – sort of a non-specific, one-size-fits-all caveman speak. *I go here, yes?*

"Oh, thank you!" exuded the stranger. "Well, we are leaving now, so you can stop coughing!" The woman put her hand on Louise's mum's arm reassuringly.

"Don't worry," said Louise's mum. "We're not stopping. I was just saying, if we sit here people will think she's trying to pick up a sailor!"

The stranger looked confused but smiled politely at them both. As she passed Louise, she said, "She's very beautiful, *molto bello* we say in my country."

Louise's mum didn't reply. In fact, she seemed to pretend she hadn't heard. "This one ok?" Louise asked, referring to some empty seats. She was determined to remain cheerful.

"Yeah, no," waffled Louise's mum. "A bit small. It's just I've got this heavy bag. Wasn't she funny what was she saying? Molton Berry! What's that, a smoothie?"

They continued along the road, coming to another eatery. "This one ok?" asked Louise.

"Yeah, why not? Any old hovel will do, won't it?"

They entered and Louise ordered coffee for the both of them and, after an exhausting negotiation, a small piece of banana bread. Once that was achieved, they sat down. "I've been thinking of doing a training course in –" Louise started.

"Oh, look! It's so tiny!" Her mum was looking past her at another mum with a new baby.

"There's a course in mid-wifery and –" Louise continued, but her mum was now blinking and smiling at the Nappy Valley cherub. "– and I thought that might be something I could –"

"Oooh, ow! Ow!" her mum interrupted.

"Are you ok?"

"No, I'm bloody not. My arm is in agony from carrying that bloody bag."

"I wondered what you thought about –" she noticed her mum frowning and frantically scratching her sepia age-spots, as speckly as ignorance - as absent as mindedness "What's the matter?"

"I can't wear wool," she confessed.

"Then why – Mum! I've been wanting –"

"It's want, want, want with you. You're the most wanton person I've ever met."

"That's not what wanton me . . ."

"These bloody, sodding glasses," Louise's mum continued, "Honestly, I don't ask much in life, but I need a good pair of glasses and the man I saw, I didn't like him. I remember him from before. Used to work in the chemists near your infant school. You remember him."

"No," exhaled Louise.

"Yes," persisted her mother, "you do. You do. Oh, yes you do. Piggy face, gay mouth, and he talked me into getting new frames. Well, I know what frames I like. I should do by now. And it's an important thing, your glasses. You don't know. You're lucky. You'll know one day. Anyway, they're not right, you know. They sit awkwardly on the bridge of my nose. Hurts a lot."

A woman from Malta who lived in Louise's street recognized her. "Hello, Louise!"

"How are you?" Louise asked and got up and hugged the neighbour very tightly. A hug that a Chilean miner might have given the cave rescue team. Did you find out about that course?" asked the Maltesian woman. "You promised you'd let me know."

"Got a phone conversation with the providers on Monday and I have to put my forms in the post by 5'o'clock tomorrow," answered Louise.

"If you want some stamps, I have some." The woman rummaged in her battered leather purse. "And is this your Mum?"

"Yes, this is my mum, Dawn."

"Let me hug you!" The neighbour hugged the head of a sitting Louise's mum, stiff as a corpse and just as musty. "I need to tell you; you have a lovely daughter!"

Louise's mum simply tittered. "I was just wondering whether I could take her back to the hospital and get a refund! Exchange it! Get some peanuts instead or a budgie! Haha. You never see rainbows on the ground anymore, do you"

Louise smiled along, embarrassed. Her Maltesian friend smiled in confusion. "What?"

"From petrol - your eyeshadow - made me think of the rainbows petrol used to make on the road, dead rainbows we used to call them. I'd exchange this nuisance for a dead rainbow any day!"

No! She is lovely! I wish I have a daughter like this!"

"Be careful what you wish for," mocked Louise's mum.

"See you later and good luck with course," said the neighbor.

"She was funny, wasn't she?" said Louise's mum. "Maybe she'd confused you with someone else!"

Louise tried again. "I had a hospital appointment the other day. They –" But her mum wasn't listening. Instead, she started smiling and blinking at the baby again. Louise decided to continue anyway. "They said I've got an inflamed spine and I need an MRI scan because of the headaches –"

Now staring into the distance with her hand on her chest, her mum complained, "I can't eat banana bread." Nonetheless, she proceeded to smear the delicacy with a sachet of margarine she kept in her handbag with the platoon of precious puppets.

"Mum!" exclaimed Louise.

"Oh, tell me about it," said her mum, "There's not a day goes by that I'm not crippled up in pain. I struggle with it, I really do. I remember the day that I first noticed it because it was cousin Michelle's birthday and she – listen to this, bloody typical this is – she rang me and asked if I had the plates that she left with me after Harry died. Why, I don't know. I'm supposed to have everything. Muggins here, oh, don't worry. She'll do it. So, she rang me and –"

"Mum," Louise had absent mindedly been sprinkling sugar on the table and was making a crisscross pattern in it, like prison bars. "I saw this course. It's a course I could do."

"Ooh," continued her mum, "I meant to say I met the loveliest girl the other day, just on the corner of Churchfield Street. Beautiful girl, you know, just had that way about her. Natural, pretty –" Louise's mum went misty-eyed with the romance of it all. "— and she asked me where the prison was. I reckon she had a relative banged up or something. Maybe her dad, yeah. And we had a chat and she goes to the college. Catering and Business Studies. Said she wants to open a restaurant. And do you know what? She'll do it. She had that air about her, you know. Just lovely. Such a pretty face. And we chatted for ever such a long time. She said, 'You're lovely, you are. I wish you were my mum!' Isn't that funny? Maybe, you know, maybe her own mum's a bit useless. Well, you just don't know, do you? I gave her twenty quid, she said; *you're the most generous person I've ever met*"

"Bye Mum," said Louise dejectedly "It's been lovely to see you." A distant church bell rang as they stood up as if heralding their exit; *bring out your dead.*

"Well, I won't be able to move at all tomorrow."

"I'm sorry," offered Louise, "We could have met closer to you. I did ask you."

"Too late now," Louise's mum snapped, tutting at the melted jelly sweet under her savage shoe. "Don't worry about it. Be dead soon anyway."

Once more, Louise tried to hug her mum, but was greeted with another, "Ow!" the warm banana breath caught Louise's cheek and, for a second, she closed her eyes and imagined it might feel something like love.

"Sorry."

"Go on! Send me home in bits, why don't you!"

Louise didn't have any money left on her Oyster card. So, she walked the eight miles back to her B & B, wondering if her mum would like her if she enjoyed Beryl Cook pictures, Catherine-bloody-Cookson or Toby Jugs. Louise wondered if there was a coat, haircut, liver cleanse, shoe or chakra which would crack the code and invoke a warm reaction. Her mind scuttled: *Was there a way of speaking, a mannerism, an occupation, a walk, an eyebrow shape, an accent, a duvet cover, a bracelet, a hobby, a brain transplant, a perfume, murder, mobile phone contract, a Peace Prize, a Damehood, disease or death that would invite a flicker of interest? Or was it as she suspected, that she was just . . .unlovable?* She sniffed a big strong sniff and shook her head and shoulders and core personality away, replacing it with one of the other layers, not the top one but a gatekeeper one, an *ooh look at me being a little bit authentic,* one. *As if.*

Chapter Twenty-Four

Dylan paced up and down in his room. "Bored, bored, bored. Something has to happen. Something has to *happen*" he rambled to himself until he caught a glimpse in the wardrobe mirror and realised he looked like the man outside the post office with the cassette recorder that played religious music. The one who barked at traffic and tried to bite his own ear off.

He decided to call the number on the "Offliners" flyer. *What was the worst that could happen?* Tapping in the digits quickly before he could change his mind, Dylan waited and listened as the phone rang twice and then clicked onto a recorded message in a not-too-unsexy woman's robot voice. That is, if you find robots sexy, which Dylan definitely *did not.*

"Welcome and congratulations," said the woman's voice. *No!* thought Dylan. *It was one of those "you've won a competition" scams.* The voice continued. "You've reached Offliners. Please have a pencil and paper ready if you can still use your limp, spoiled little mitts for anything other than tapping and fapping?"

He had to call it a couple more times to catch the address in time to write it all down. *Dickhead,* he thought. *Probably been hacked. A black hat – or was it grey hat? IP is probably now linked to a Nigerian bank account.*

Ping! His phone whined to tell him his old man had tagged him in a photo from karate. Dad was wearing sunglasses and a T-shirt that read "Sarcastic Comment Loading". The caption underneath the post read: *Son had another #amazing morning with me at #karate #Saturday #fatherandson.*

Fucking hell, thought Dylan, *We'd barely spoken that day!* On the day in question, his dad had been glued to his phone for so long that his face, chin, and neck had all blended into one melted white chocolate fountain.

Dylan switched his own phone off at that moment, but its presence still bothered him. He gouged out the sim card and threw it into a drawer. With that, he felt a little bit better. And it also solidified his decision to meet up with the Offliners.

Later, Dylan listened to everyone going to bed and realised he hadn't thought this through at all. He got dressed in front of the mirror, as usual avoiding looking at himself. He had some nice shirts, some button-down ones, shirts he'd bought with his own money. But Dylan thought he made everything look wrong, like making a cake with all the wrong ingredients. A white T-shirt would evoke images of Hannibal Lecter; a denim jacket would call forth Robin Asquith, all confused at being catapulted into the future. *Confessions of a Time Traveler* – not that he knew who Robin Asquith was - but he knew he looked like the 1970s. Dylan was always wrong, always awkward, always at odds. Regardless, he got dressed. He opted for jeans and an unbranded sweatshirt. Once dressed, he opened his bedroom window. Dylan had absorbed by osmosis every American high school film and British sitcom where people climbed out of bedroom windows. There was always a drainpipe. So, Dylan expected a drainpipe. *Where was the fucking drainpipe?*

Plan B involved the bathroom window. He crept along the landing past the massive black-and-white framed picture of him and Grace from ages seven and nine, holding their chins in their hands. He winced every time he saw it as he remembered the photographer insisting they adopt this popular pose so that his parents could tick another "Doing Family Right' box. Once inside the bathroom, he cursed the hoarder-level amount of bottles and jars on the windowsill. *Cinnamon and snail mucus skin restorer? Magnesium oil? Dr Hauschka's entire laboratory? And cultured stem cell and fish enzyme pore tightener? No wonder there was something fishy about my mum. She sells fish cells by the sea shore.*

Dylan stifled a self-aware laugh at doing something so clichéd as being a teenager sneaking out of a house at night. He maneuvered through the window and realised he could jump onto the garage roof, but would have to land quietly.

Taking in a deep breath, he noticed the stars. Orion's belt was looking particularly glam rock as Dylan defied the suburban stalemate and cleared the leap effortlessly. Cogitating briefly over a career in burglary, he walked quickly towards the train station. His excitement was only dampened by the notion that if he were to be spotted by any of the neighbors, it would be game over for him and a Munchausen's upgrade for the old dear. This was unlikely, as it was a dormitory town where everything shut at 6pm, creating a middle-class Marie Celeste while "Great British Bake-Off "shone from cosy televisions. If you heard a child having his or her hair washed from a tiny bathroom window whilst simultaneously smelling lemon shampoo foam in their drain – well, that was the closest thing to a feeling of community for this suburban citizenry. But wary was Dylan of any potential interlocutors still. Adopting the gait of a much older person, Dylan imagined being cocky and depressed at the same time. This worked a treat.

Dylan felt much more relaxed when he was on the train to Hounslow. He sat in the part of the train with the two long seats facing each other. Five other humans sat in their assorted padded jackets slumped over phones.

One woman chatted on her phone in a long, loud complaint splattered with pseudo-legalese. Another invertebrate brushed his head fiercely with what was definitely a clothes brush and, when he wasn't brushing, tapped certain points on his skull. The tannoy announcement poured like cold disinfectant over fat, sleeping rats. "If you see anything unusual, please tell a member of staff." *How would we know any more?* wondered Dylan.

He had to ask for directions upon arriving at Hounslow, showing the address to a cab driver who looked and sounded like dead comedian Mike Reid. ~~He~~The cabbie's arms were garlanded with tattoos of sentiment – West Ham, a generic sexy lady and 'Kai' his baby son who died after being dropped on his head in a drunken gloom after West Ham had lost 4-1 to Spurs. Dylan was directed to a narrow alleyway and told to cross the road and go straight up a hill. "An' keep your 'and on yer a'penny!" the cabbie shouted, laughing at his own foreboding advice. It sounded like a thousand cigarettes in an acetone fire, crackling away, all warm~~ and~~, ashy and asthmatic.

Dylan felt a rush of expectation as he climbed the hill. He was sure he could hear distant voices. He smelled a bonfire, too.

Could it be true? Dylan dared to hope, *this was going to be the live performance? Fuck your talent show bullshit! parents in floods of tears jumping up and down with a 19-year-old they vicariously live through. Fuck YouTube wars and 'calling each other out' on pitiably, babyish beefs. Fuck parents tagging you in pictures to compete with their fake friends. Culture wars, screen eyed oblongs re-enacting their playground paranoia with sock accounts sponsored by think tanks funded by fraud, all old, all of them, telling us what to do. Vampiric old bastards hijacking youth, cluttering up all our platforms and turning up at festivals, refusing to carve out an adult life of their own. Fuck off. Hurry up and die and let kids be young again you baby snatching sad sacks, you pied pipers of piss. All the generations are now sewn together in a giant, patchwork body bag made out of fat, flaccid, family flesh in cartoon onesies and animal slippers and it needs its stitches ripping out, suddenly, bloodily and as a matter of medical emergency. This is it. This is really happening!*

The first youth movement since new wave, rave, grunge – does grunge count? – anyway, whatever it was, was definitely happening. *The older generation could never understand why they couldn't erase the Gap by wearing us like a skin suit,* thought Dylan. *Forget Generation Gap. We are about to create a void, a cavern, a ravine, an abyss, a flume, a gulch, a gully, a glen* – there would be a culture divide.

Dylan reached the top of the grassy knoll, or whatever it was, to see eight or nine clean teens in Jack Wills hoodies, all looking at their phones and milling about shiftily.

Suddenly, he felt the anticlimax. *Jesus*, he sighed to himself, *is this it? What a weird little place. Completely hidden, even though it's surrounded by high rise flats.* The area was pitch black. Only a single streetlamp showed the green amongst the silhouetted trees. There was a lake with a little island in the middle which hosted a few ducks the town had forgotten about for so long they refused to accept bread anymore and ate only weeds and fish. Not tonight, though. All the pesco-vegetarian pond life had been scared off by human voices.

"Hello," said a short fellow with glasses and a Friji milkshake in his stubby hand.

"Alright?" replied Dylan, tracking his way in by stepping on milk crates that had been put in the water to make a path. Soaking the bottoms of his jeans with stagnant brown toad water, like Hansel counting breadcrumbs, Dylan memorized each step so he could make a quick getaway if things turned a bit *Wicker Man.*

"Have a seat," implored a long streak of piss with a sunny expression, who motioned to another milk crate.

What's with all the milk crates? wondered Dylan, *Was this event organised by a disgruntled milkman on the verge of extinction due to EU quota regulations? Probably. We are all no doubt going to be murdered. "Last Round for Brexit Milkman"* The Express *headline would read. Or "Put Out to Pasture: How the Brutal Bloodbath that Skimmed the Cream of a Generation Could have Been Avoided*".

"Take that one," said an impeccably groomed young man in a clip-clop horsey voice who made sitting on a milk crate look like a task from "The Apprentice".

"What are we doing?" Dylan asked, trying to sound casual. He sat awkwardly feeling like a lamb to the water.

Another boy with so many layers of sarcasm that he could have gone full circle and meant it, responded coolly, "Rebelling."

"Reveling," contradicted a posh-looking blonde boy in a marble-mouthed, patronising drawl without even looking up from his iPhone.

"We're rebels" squeaked an embarrassed 18-year-old in a flatly knowing voice.

"This is exactly the problem," said a fuck-haired boy with glasses and a teen activist set of clothing, replete with anarchy badge, body odour, and beanie hat. His Che Guevara T-shirt had been on a 90-degree wash once too often and the eyebrows and moustache had faded, making the proletariat pinup look more like an angry Frank Spencer. Which if you think about it, is much more alarming. "When in the history of young people have they ever gotten together and made a self-aware declaration on the act of rebellion? Culture is eating itself."

"You keep saying that, Elliot," reminded a girl in a green hoodie. Her sleeves had been rolled up just enough to reveal the stars and planets tattooed on her hands and forearms.

"And you keep saying that," replied Elliot.

"Off topic!" said another girl, who resembled a young Yvette Fielding. The girl looked like she'd just seen a ghost.

“Someone’s all tarted up, hoping to meet some hot men,” squealed a mincing boy named Lennon who was camper than a world war and just as bitchy.

“I’m wearing a cagoule and jeans,” responded the Yvette look-alike with measured bafflement.

“I know,” agreed Lennon, who’d grown up used to getting away with being a vicious little cockless recreant, as the children of policeman are prone, “but, anyway – filthy bitch! I’m only joking, can’t you take a joke, I love you, you’re adorable, that’s just my sense of humour, ask anyone, that’s who I am, oh my god, I can’t believe you think I’m serious…”

Dylan looked around, wondering if it would be noticed if he just wandered off.

"Why don't we start with what we're against?" muttered a mindful minor from Mile End, swigging from an ethically-sourced bottle of apple and kiwi-flavoured oxygen water.

"I’m against this tree", said one.

"I hate my parents," piped up Elliot. This elicited some sudden interest from the phone gazers.

“Uh oh, serial killer alert!” said the green hoodied, star-handed girl. She then gestured in Dylan’s direction with her Saturn-scrawled, scribbly shaft-shaker. “What about you?”

"I hate his parents,” said Dylan. Everyone looked downwards and laughed in an embarrassed-to-be-laughing way.

"My dad's a giant toddler,” Elliot continued, “He and my mum copy things off the TV. They made me go to see Marcus Brigstocke."

"Who?" they responded in unison.

The girl in the green hoodie looked at Dylan like a micro biologist who'd found a sexy new virus. "Seriously, though, what about you?".

For fuck's sake. What was her problem? Dylan thought. *Why am I here?*

"This is, like, group therapy or something!" Elliot shouted. Dylan suspected that would be a familiar scenario to him.

"Yeah, like, hold the squeaky Mr. Happy toy when it's your turn to speak!" sneered the kid with the squeaky voice. He did indeed have a dirt covered, dog-chewed Mr. Happy toy in his hand. This peculiarity, it was clear, had already been addressed before Dylan's arrival. Dylan was an outsider to the joke.

Perhaps Offliners would eventually have two factions, pre-and post-Mr. Happy.

The squeaky-voiced kid offered his toy to Dylan, which everyone found pleasingly absurd.

"I don't know. I –" Dylan inadvertently squeezed Mr. Happy, which forced out a defeated squeak. Actually, it was more of a sigh. "I didn't ask you" Dylan said to Mr. Happy's happy face amidst classroom sniggering. "I haven't really got any reason to be pissed off. There are loads of people worse off than me. It's just something's missing. Something's not there."

"Like a splinter in your mind!" said a spiky-haired blonde boy with an American accent. Everyone laughed apart from Elliot, who wished he'd said it first.

Dylan felt self-conscious, so he pretended to examine a tree. which led to scratching off its skin. The pretending soon became utter absorption, though. Leaving Mr. Happy on the ground, and scattering the peeled bark from the ~~poor~~ abused #treetoo on the ground, he began to clamber up its rough, scaly trunk. The smarting of palms pressed against the stoic stalk presented him a flash card of déjà vu back to the anti-climb paint he'd braved to retrieve dead Mabel's book. By the time he got to the third branch, he felt confident enough to say, matter-of-factly, "I... just. . .don't feel…" Suddenly, possessed by the night or the moon or the weirdness of it all -- or, for that matter, sixteen years of stifling, suburban, hothouse, battery hen, techno soup boredom, he shouted:

"Alive!! Alive!! Alive!!! I JUST DON'T FEEL ALIVE!!!!"

"Shush!" whispered a new arrival, "That's all very moving, but let's not give away our location, yes?" This latest addition had arrived with a military air and seemed to know a little bit more about this event than the others. After whispering something in Elliot's ear, she addressed the small crowd. "Did you all leave your phones at home?"

"Yeah, Madison," said a few of them, who somehow knew her name.

"Yeah," said some others.

Elliot clawed at his inside pocket with his immaculate fingernails, "Er, yeah."

"I've just realised, if my parents wake up and see I'm gone, they're going to go fucking mental! They'll think I'm being bummed by some MP in Dolphin Square," Dylan said. He climbed down quickly, looked at Flynn's watch, and felt reality suddenly kick him in the balls.

"That's, like, homophobic?" said a strange little goblin girl who knew only that she should say it because it's something that's there, like pavement or marriage or triangles.

"Kek!" said Elliot "Anyone got a charger?" *Who says kek anymore*? Wondered practically everyone.

"Of course, no one's got a charger," chided Madison, "The whole point of this is not to have a charger. Not having a charger would be on the first page of our manifesto, if we had one. I think we should, by the way." She was only partly feigning exasperation.

"Look, I've got to go," Yvette Fielding's spooky sister looked worried, "I've come from Southampton and I need to get the Mega Bus."

"Me too," shouted some of the pubescent partiers, "Me too. Yeah, hashtag MeToo –"

Suddenly, the group devolved into disorganised chatter, "I'll send you that link, the troll to end all trolls!" erupted one of them. Instinctually, they were now en masse exchanging Snapchats and WhatsApps.

"No!" Madison hissed in a pronounced stage whisper, "No links! We're offline! Offline! Don't you understand?"

The midnight mischief-makers sniggered at being told off again. Without warning, it looked like the awkward party was breaking up.

"Okay," Madison continued, "It's not exactly been *Lord of the Flies* meets *Game of Thrones*, but it's a start"

"Lord of the what?" asked a kid in an Adidas hoodie, scrunching his nose curiously.

"Michael Flatley, innit?" said Dylan, acting as cultural attaché.

Dylan got a warm feeling from Madison, the only one who seemed to know what she was doing and what this was supposed to be about. She had those ears that stood slightly away from her head, which always made people look like intelligent animals listening out for information. She opened a brown hold all filled with flyers. It was one of those holdases from those films about guns and money. Madison encouraged every attendee to take a load to distribute in advance of the next event.

Chapter Twenty-Five

What the fuck just happened? Dylan thought over the events of the evening on the night bus back home. He felt as though he should have a feeling of disenfranchised time theft, but in fact, he felt okay.

Opening a window above his seat and breathing in the night air, he searched for the rotting smell. It didn't come. The vague worry on the way home that someone had got up to use the bathroom and had closed the window was as much exhilarating as it was nerve-wracking. But nobody had.

Swinging up onto the roof, holding onto a hanging basket, he was soon home and dry. Then, he crept back to bed, as quiet as a mouse monk, wearing felt slippers to church, slippers which mouse monks don't have because everyone knows how poor they are.

At the next Offliners event, nearly forty teenagers turned up. Gallows humour alternated with rampant emotionality and possession of incredible amounts of information about certain things and total ignorance about others. Jake knew twenty-five Bukowski poems by heart, although he had to ask what "left wing" and "right wing" meant. Poppy could give extremely thorough monologues about neuropsychology thanks to Ted Talks, but she struggled to navigate the 24-hour clock. Tamsin knew the entire history of the NHS with a computer-like ability to recall names and dates, and yet she was surprised when someone mentioned the French Revolution "They didn't!" she howled, eyes widening and spitting out her Petits Filous. Internet teens. They spelled weird "wierd" and you're "your". They wanted cool without discomfort and a Fujifilm Instax.

Deactivate. Madison, the default leader for now, clicked on the most subversive word of the 21st Century, followed by Flynn, then Noah, and then Isiah. Like an avalanche of 100 monkey syndrome, others in huge chunks of the suburbs did likewise, from sons in bedrooms on privet-lined avenues, daughters in Zone Two flats with takeaway window views. From cottages to Chicken Cottages, patchwork hills to William Hills, they were tuning in, turning off, and logging out.

The Offliner events initially were monthly with more people joining each time. Soon, there was a style developing which made one recognizable as an Offliner. It was unfashionable, a little like a Christian youth group three weeks into their desert island plane crash when they begin to question their faith in God and the extent of their shampoo rations.

By the fifth meeting, the Offliners were finally getting organised. All the previous get-togethers had been an experimental mess. There had been symbolic destruction of phones – symbolic because only cheap ones were destroyed. There had also been taking of drugs, legal highs, mostly, as well as some sexual trysts once they got their leg over the whole consent issue. Of course, these were all the usual young person activities once upon a time, but these post-millennial postiters were haunted by an unsatisfactory feeling in the night mist that they needed to be more. That everything had been done before. It was going to be a long, hard road out of 5G hell.

"How can I rebel when my mum has fucking blue hair, sleeve tattoos, and a drug-fueled past she's confronted and come to terms with? And she's always happy to discuss anything with me because she's my friend as well as my mum," some poor little novitiate had asked.

"All hail the Offliners!" Elliot tried to add a solemnity to his tone that befitted the auspicious nature of the proceedings. However, his laughter choked his final two words and the plastic Tesco bag on his head fell off in the process.

There was also some sniggering from the congregation, but they regained composure in time for the opening prayer.

"Our Father – or Mother – we're not assuming Your gender/Who art offline/Hallowed be thy name – What's Hallowed?/SSSHHh/Thy kingdom come thy will be done/Offline as it is in Heaven/Give us this day our real life/Forgive us our statuses/As we forgive those who status against us/Lead us not into Playstations/And deliver us from our chargers/For thine is the offline kingdom/The power down and the glory/For ethernet and ethernet /Offline."

It was clumsy, but they were going to refine it to keep it more on message.

"I renounce the internet," repeated each teenager, as they placed one hand on a copy of *1984* and had their other hand slit with a Gillette Fusion Five by an acolyte called Owen. Owen was an attention-deficient boy from Plumstead with pin eyes that were hard to ignore as they were harrowingly like John Venables.

Everybody joined in except for Elliot, who was haemophobic or some such thing. The participants mixed their blood, pressing palms together and smearing it around with the icy autumn rain which helped numb their skin. After this, they rubbed them all over the Penguin Classics book cover. Next, they chanted – or rather, haphazardly stuttered over each other, failing to suppress their laughter in places – the following words: "It didn't come in grey overalls and gin, but bright screaming primary colours and green smoothies and a million diverse ways to showcase your unique personality, etcetera." This extract had been Flynn's idea. He promised to edit it and make it rhyme somehow. Make it more chanty. Write something witchy.

A few days after this swearing-in ceremony, Dylan approached Grace, "Need you to do a little favour for me," he asked his sister as he plugged in the memory stick containing Grace's gallery of geriatric genocide. The look travelling between the two siblings knew its destination and had printed its boarding pass.

"K," said Grace.

“These are my log-in details,” Dylan said, “Everything’s there, Faceache, InstantGran, the lot. Every six hours, sign in and write something believably bland. Now, Grace,” his sister glared suspiciously at his hand on her shoulder, “this is a role which I have absolute confidence in you fulfilling, indeed excelling at!”

A skeptical frown interrupted her proud smile, “Er, I’m not sure –”

“It’s okay,” reassured Dylan, “It’s an experiment.”

Dylan lied to his parents with the old staple about having an induction for a Duke of Edinburgh Award in order to attend the sixth meeting of the Offliners. ‘Duke of Edinburgh Award’ was a magical incantation casting a spell of compliance over passive parents the UK over.

LOL look at this chick’s reaction to seeing her bf’s tattoo! his reassuringly brainless Facebook status was up, thanks to Grace. His dad, in response to the post, pressed the “Ha-Ha” emoji. If anything, Grace was overqualified. But she would definitely keep Dylan’s parents off his scent for a while.

He located the coordinates for the ensuing gathering using an actual map and compass. It turned out to be in the underground passage of a restored Gothic castle near Strawberry Hill. There, Dylan walked into an atmosphere of Clinton’s Cards on a Thursday afternoon on a cloudy day in Bromley with Whigfield playing over the speakers.

“Studies show that our generation are more like a cross between yuppies and hippies,” said a girl in thick-rimmed glasses and an unbranded and oversized sweatshirt, “Our ambition is apparently to travel the world, working our own hours, doing something childish and free like making eco-friendly sandals from recycled rice and calling it the Cheeky Dancing Monkey Company. Hmm, I wonder if the domain is free?” Sophia’s commitment to neo-luddism was questionable.

"Sounds great," said Dylan, finding a place to sit, adjusting to the strange, damp smell.

"Studies show, studies show, says the human graph – and, by the way, where were you last Wednesday?" a boy named Lucas sniped. This was surprising, given that he was generally a friendly child from Chalk Farm who always brought Oreos and looked too young to be out late at night alone.

"You know where I was," returned Sophia, "I had that little interview at *Huff Post*. It's better the media hear it from us directly or they'll just go and make up shit and we'll be hunted down and shot or something. Anyway, I was saying, people move differently. Something's changed. Something funny's going on. We all know it. Everyone can feel it. People shuffle close to you, phones in their hands, sneaking furtive and serious glances, approaching real life like a selfie backdrop. Why? Because they're looking at life through a YouTube screen, searching for a glimpse of scenery they can nail, post, and bask in recognition for. They look at each other through dating app eyes, swipe to the left or swipe to the right whilst every now and then sharing a post or gif mocking the very thing they're doing. We've been given a way to feel we're constantly off the hook. They don't have to let anything emotionally hurt them enough to snap out of it or to make a change. Satire cannot work because people no longer feel shame, or at least, they're able to log out of shame and into their alter online ego. The self-referential nods to how sad it is gives us a little valve to open and feel as though we've touched base, kissed the earth, and found authenticity again. But it's a cycle. The attempts to show how somebody might be doing the internet differently or how we understand the pathetic aspects of it clearly enough that it doesn't apply to us – all these just make it easier to carry on and continue being a non-person. A person-dot-net. A thinned-down, calved-up, one-dimensional, third-generation cassette recording echo of a person. We're bubble gum with all the flavour chewed out. I mean, have you been to a shopping centre recently? It's the zombie apocalypse with lightweight embroidered bomber jackets and high impact slogan tees, vaccine tattoos and temperature taking cameras. Communism on a skateboard. Let's face it, something is rotten in the state of Primark."

Everyone fell silent following Sophia's soliloquy. The rest were seemingly in the grip of a dreary depression, not to mention suspicion about Sophia's recent journalistic collaboration.

"Well, we can't go back," Poppy counselled wisely, "We are what we are, for better or worse."

"Till death do us part!" said some vociferous revelers, lowering the conversation with an injection of Christmas cracker humour.

"We should, like, sacrifice some chickens or something," suggested Owen.

"Touch any animals and I'll sacrifice your micro-penis over this fire, you stupid little scrote," Sophia countered.

"For fuck's sake, I was only joking," Owen mumbled. *How did she know?*

"Shut up" chastised a posh girl named Kaia who sometimes dropped her H's and sometimes added them in the wrong places, as in, *would anyone like some K Heff C?* She was wearing a Wham! sweatshirt, which could have been ironic or vintage chic or, long shot, she could have just liked Wham! Whatever the reason, Kaia continued, "And I notice you weren't here last Saturday either. You're deffo still online. You even talk in memes. You are a meme."

"We had a meeting with Sadiq Khan, didn't we, Kayak?" said Elliot, "It was kray! They're starting a youth board, advising teens about the dangers of too much screen time."

Elliot is kray alright, thought Dylan, *St. Mary's Kray, in Orpington.*

"'Ow did you get h-in touch with 'is people?" asked Kaia.

“There was a tweet, wasn’t there?” Elliot reminded her, “We want to hear from you if you’re a teen who doesn’t use the internet.”

“’Ow would a teen who doesn’t h-use the internet see a tweet?” she queried.

“Uh,” Elliot hesitated nervously, “my sister told me about it. My dad came with me.”

“Your dad!?” Kaia gasped.

“They’ll just get some imposter otherwise,” said Elliot, “and – what she said” He pointed at Madison as Kaia shook her head.

Kaia continued, “We can’t go back and be carefree teens dancing in a 1950s coffee shop in Soho. We’re the first generation to have had internet our entire lives. When’s the last time you saw a teen dressed eccentrically?” All eyes then shifted to Caleb, a delicate boy with heavy make-up on one eye and an asymmetrical purple mohawk. This he kept dry on damp days with an old lady’s rain hat from Savers.

A plump-faced boy Dylan hadn’t seen before with some bad tattoos of angels and people’s names began circling anyone who was talking. When he wasn’t doing that, he was shadow boxing. Later, Dylan discovered his name was Andrew, although he insisted on being called Andre. No one knew why. Andre was a Michael Jackson music video idea of a rough and ready street hooligan. *Don’t mess with me, I’ll enigmatically glower you to death.* Andre was the sort of young man who demonstrated how hard and grown-up and connected he was by shaking the hand of the security guard in Londis and asking, “Alright boss?”

By the seventh meeting of the Offliners, the milling about and shuffling had stopped. A generation hailed as being the laziest and most infantile in history was beginning to militarise.

Dylan was covering miles after school, putting flyers in places one would only see if one was looking up from – and not down at – a phone. Sometimes he would leave a trail of clues leading to a flyer, a treasure hunt to hone down the curious. Of course, he made sure he left one in a spoke of Liam's bike. If nothing else, the flyer would make a cool sound.

Chapter Twenty-Six

It was at the fourteenth meet of the Offliners that Dylan finally saw her for the first time. She had pale skin and freckles which seen together reminded him of Twiglets – and he didn't usually like Twiglets. Her hair was even more pre-Raphaelite than his.

He quickly discovered that her name was Louise and he was glad that she didn't have one of those birthday-present-hamster-owning girl's names. Louise had arrived at the event, thinking it was some kind of outreach programme, as if the Hare Krishnas might be there with the pasta and mint tea and milk jelly stuff they make in Camden.

Louise wasn't really one for joining movements, too used, as she was, to looking for the best survival route. She was like the cat in the beginning of *Animal Farm* who votes on both motions. At least, that's as far as she had got with the dog-eared library book. *So gloomy!*

Now, however, Louise found herself at the actual event. She thought she'd better say something. Perhaps she would just plagiarize Steven Starkey. *He wouldn't mind,* she convinced herself, *He'd be proud, anyway. Where else would I have been on a Friday night? Penge?*

Eventually, Louise decided to take an oratorical gamble. "We need an income source if we're going to keep this thing going," she began, "The most essential element in what's going on outside of these events is that we've been bought and paid for, cuckolded and owned. We need larger locations, with uncensored speakers, before people lose interest. We need to print more flyers and hire venues where we don't have to hide and can stop creeping about and worrying. We need to up the ante more than any movement in the past because we're dealing with more legislation, don't you think?

"I'd like to up your ante!" shouted an almost refreshingly 1980's throwback of a boy.

“Trust me - you wouldn’t” Louise continued, shuddering at the thought of what her auntie’s laundry list of mental health conditions would do to an involuntarily celibate virgin. “I mean, they’re giving the first babies microchips for fuck’s sake. It’s in the paper every day, ‘specially since that stupid comedian’s child has gone missing. They’re blatantly using it to usher this in. It’s not good enough to like George Orwell on Facebook. That doesn’t get you off the hook! George ‘Oh Well’, more like! Box ticked! Carry on! Some people genuinely believe that Western humans reached a peak in the 60s and have been sliding backwards ever since, dumbing down and conforming. Look at our music, our comedy. If there’s going to be a revolution, it needs to be a revolution of intelligence, otherwise it’s stupidity trying to gage stupidity! We need to make a mark. We need money. We’re poorer than church mice. In fact, we owe the church mice money, at least they’ve got felt slippers. Any ideas?”

A few people looked disappointed, while some others simply mumbled, “Yeah”, in assent.

Andre kissed his teeth unconvincingly and whispered to the guy next to him, “She’s alright, doe, but I don’t normally do ginger.”

“But, we’re off-grid. Why do we need money? Why do you want to sell us out?” asked a boy who lived in his parents’ five-bedroom cottage in Chalfont.

“Calm down,” corrected Louise, “We’re not off-grid, are we? Most of you live at your families’ broadband-connected homes. Every aspect of your life is online apart from when you’re here. And when you leave home or school or college, you’ll have to be even more online to get by. We can change it. Build something long term. But we do need money.” Louise had little patience for rich anti-capitalists.

“How typical is that? The rich boy doesn’t care about money,” cooed a girl too beautiful to make eye contact with anyone. She had disliked this Chalfont guy ever since he had dared to assert that Christopher Hichens was overrated.

Every one of the fifty-two attendees that night looked blank following Louise's declaration. Soon afterwards, they went back to chattering amongst themselves.

Dylan's gaze met Louise's. He sheepishly looked away when she began narrowing her eyes like Clint Eastwood in a Yates's, seeing a so-called BFF wearing the same off-shoulder ASOS top.

"Alright?" Louise asked, continuing her Squint Eastwood-ing.

"Allro," Dylan stammered.

"Allro?"

"Yeah," he answered, "I was going to say alright like you did, but didn't want to come off like some Polly Parrot prick. So, I decided to go with a nice, old-fashioned hello, but it came out all allro. Now you think I'm special needs."

"Yeah", a smile crept over her lips, "*that's* why I think you're special needs. Nothing to do with your gormless expression and wearing a school jumper on a Sunday."

"Shabby chic, innit!" Dylan countered.

"Is it?"

"Is," said Dylan.

Louise became aware of Andre looking at them with his burnt holes-in-a-blanket eyes before she decided to walk away from the group.

"Five out of ten. Maybe," offered Andre in an unsolicited appraisal whilst punching the air with alternate, chubby fists and forcing the air from his Neanderthal nostrils.

"What?" Dylan asked, turning to Andre, although already knowing to whom he was referring.

"Her, innit!" screeched Andre, "You've got an in, but I wouldn't go there, get me? Skank. But then they all are, innit? Seriously, this is like a fitty famine, get me?" Andre had an aura of hospital gloom and spoke in a low monotone which he thought sounded like Tony Soprano. In fact, the sound was more that of a mentally ill man mumbling at a Lidl bag containing his favorite shoe. *And takes it up the arse, different coloured shoelaces…*

Dylan took a deep breath before responding, "Why do I get the feeling you've been reading the Lad's Bible?"

Andre looked vacantly at Dylan, preparing a witty one-liner which would trample this unexpected dissent. The silence persisted until, eventually, he hit upon, "You are well gay!"

"Fuck off," Dylan said, nodding and grinning enthusiastically as if he were agreeing with a lighthearted opinion about how goody goody gumdrops were.

"Who you telling to fuck off?" shouted Andrew.

"I'm Ronnie Pickering!" Elliot shouted back, interrupting.

"Shut your rasclart, Elliot," Andre said in sixty shades of Surrey, much too young and gangsta to know who Ronnie Pickering was. Andre shunted Dylan against the damp stone wall, drawing horrified glances from the others. These were teens, after all, who had been sent home from school for having unquartered grapes in their lunch boxes. *Choking hazard.*

Dylan was bored and tired and sick of everything turning shit. He looked back at Andre's stupid predictable face. *There'd always be an Andre,* he thought, *in every school and every work place. He was everything and everywhere. Wherever anything started to get cool, there'd be an Andre to make it less, make it small.*

Before Dylan knew what was happening, he'd clenched his teeth, stiffened his neck, and drawn his fist back, knuckles getting whiter and whiter. He punched Andre's cheekbone, which caused the recipient to fall into a disorientated spin and backwards stagger.

Nauseous and squeaky-voiced, Andre could only utter, "Wha? Wi? Cunt!" He was a wee bit sick over himself and his bowels had evacuated in the shock, which made the previously dominating damp stench a wistful nostalgia. "What was that for, prick?" he asked, as a few onlookers flinched and "oofed!" as though feeling the hit themselves.

"I'm just so bored!" Dylan narrowed his eyes and hissed the words with genuine venom, leaning into Andre's face as though searching for something he knew he wouldn't find. Reality caught up with him and Dylan touched his fist, surprised it hadn't hurt more. He watched as a bewildered Andre staggered away with shit-stained trousers, a swollen cheek, and vomit on his Stormzy T-shirt. Andrew could only manage to mutter idle threats as he proceeded on his way to give some other girl marks out of ten for prettiness.

The onlooking Offliners tittered amongst themselves, making generation-specific jokes. "That has totally triggered me!" and "That's totes a health and safety breach!" and "Come on, guys, lets hug this out. Cry if you need to!"

Dylan went off in the direction he'd last seen Louise go. He caught up with her and pulled the cuff of his jumper over his cherry-tinged knuckles. Louise was walking along a path in between a building housing an adventure playground and a poster for The Alpha Course.

"How you getting home?" he asked her.

"Bus to Charing Cross, then train to Penge."

"You'd be better going from Victoria," Dylan suggested, "They're replacing tracks due to damage and other problems with infrastructure and they're running a skeleton service."

Louise laughed uncontrollably at his use of the term skeleton service. “You seem to know a lot.”

“Yeah I’m –” he looked up for inspiration and found none, “– really boring.”

“What did you say?” she teased, “I lost interest halfway through.”

“Very funny,” he returned, “So, do you know Dave, then?”

“Dave?” Louise asked, “Who’s Dave?” She laughed again, this time finding the name Dave funny.

“Dave – Stewart, I think. 80s pop star or something. Beard, sunglasses, organiser of this – whatever this is. What is this exactly, by the way?”

“That’s rubbish!” countered Louise, “Someone here is a relative of his and all the little jaws started jabbering. It’s not him.”

“You do know him,” persisted Dylan, “That’s why you’re so sketchy!”

“Nah, ain’t him,” she said, “It’s some rave DJ from the 90s, I heard.”

“No way. They’re all busy with divorces or gender reassignment.”

“Well,” she wondered aloud, “how can we find out?”

“Dunno,” was all Dylan could offer.

The pair had wandered a good way off from the others. As it began to rain, Dylan pulled his jacket up and over both their heads. Being almost twice her height, Dylan made a good umbrella. Surrounded by nettles and ruins, it could have been a thousand years ago.

“Sky looks beautiful, doesn’t it?” Louise asked, gazing into the blue and pink backdrop which contained both sun and moon staring silently at each other – like a Relate counselling session. *We never see each other!*

"Yeah. Like, maybe, an oil painting." He thought that was the sort of thing he was supposed to say whenever anyone said something about the sky or clouds. "Who's that cock who keeps shadow boxing and walking in a circle?" he asked, hoping to shuffle away from his phony fey whimsy about sky and paint.

"Ah, Andre," said Louise, "Andrew, actually. Beta masquerading as an Alpha, probably. Presenting a heightened version of himself." To Dylan, Louise may as well have been speaking in tongues, or on Google Plus.

"Alpha?" Dylan nodded to the Alpha course poster.

"Oh, yeah," she said, bemused, "Dodgy, I think. Beta male theory?"

"You're just saying words now," he said, confused.

"Okay, so –"

"Oh, we're doing that now, are we?" teased Dylan.

"Doing what?"

"Starting sentences with 'so'. Like on 'Dragon's Den'. So, Dragons, we've invented an app that tells you where the nearest app is."

"Well," Louise sighed the word out in an exaggerated exhale, but failed for the moment to follow through.

"Yes?" encouraged Dylan, "Are you going to tell me about beta male theory or am I going to go to my silent tomb, nurturing a secret sorrow? C'mon. Let the dog see the euphemism."

"So," she snapped out of her brief reverie, "the theory goes that there were once alpha males, you know, when we lived in tribes and that – you understand the term alpha male, yes? The biggest, strongest, most protective? The one that wants to catch the most food and look after the group? “

Dylan responded by swinging on a branch and making monkey noises.

“But being the alpha is a short precarious life,” continued Louise, “They die young from heart problems. Because of all the adrenaline they’re constantly pumping. Or in battle or catching food and shit, so –”

“So –” he jibed, smiling.

“So, the alpha gets the first of the food and the sex. The rest are beta males and they huddle about. All they can do is wait for the moment when they can trick a female to the edge of the territory by hinting there’s some food. Or maybe they wait until two alphas are fighting over the female. Then the betas sneak up behind the females and boom!”

“Boom,” observed Dylan, “Quite literally, boom.”

“So –” she continued, undeterred.

“So –” he teased once more.

“So, the theory is that alpha males died out long ago and all that’s left is beta males being all sneaky. How many times have you heard people say that the world is run by corrupt little weasel men with their finger on the button and piles of money?”

“Not exactly those words,” said Dylan. “But continue.”

She did. “Because, the theory is we live in a beta world. Look around and everything is beta. All that’s left is a vague, inherited memory of an alpha that once looked after us. This explains why we love comics and superheroes. They tap into the ancestral DNA feeling that there once was a strong, kind, protective, and brave human that took care of things. This explains why men harass women in the street. Little men, shuffling along, making little mumbling noises. An alpha male never had to do that. It would be in the alpha interest to keep everyone feeling strong and healthy. Keep the team winning. All this explains the rise in trans issues too. Can't be the first sperm to penetrate the egg or even make the first twenty million? Just wear the egg! I am the egg! I win! Betas everywhere! Google any beautiful and famous woman right now, I guarantee you'll see threads and threads about how Megan Fox has man thumbs or Mila Kunis didn't have symmetrical eyebrows on Wednesday or Taylor Swift has circus ears –"

"Has what?" Dylan interrupted, befuddled.

"Well," she smiled. "maybe not that last one, but everything I said up to that point is true."

"And what even are man thumbs?"

Her grin broadened, "See how easily it draws you in?" The misty rain made Louise's paprika corkscrews separate even more around her body. She was a medieval maypole Medusa with asthma in a scalloped Bardot top by George at Asda.

"Life's so confusing," Dylan offered. He rubbed his brow, slightly disturbing his dark blonde hair which was fast fading back to ashy brown.

"Yeah, so when we go to the cinema and see Superman," posited Louise, "it's that recessive gene that we're seeing;"

"You asking me to the cinema?" Dylan clumsily blurted out. Louise ignored him and, in the ensuing awkward silence, he continued. "It's an interesting theory. I can't believe there are no alphas at all, though. Not one. Not even Caitlyn Jenner?"

"Perhaps they have recessive alpha traits, but they have to live in a beta world. It must be so frustrating,"

“Tell me about it,” Dylan said in a mock sigh.

“Maybe you *are* an alpha in a beta world,” suggested Louise.

“Yeah, I definitely think so, I mean, look! Man find food!” He produced half a Star Bar from his pocket.

“I love Star Bar!” she exclaimed, “Tastes like raw cake mixture.”

Dylan nodded, chewing the small piece of chocolate Louise handed back to him. “And Raw Cake Mixture is probably the name of a horrible K-pop band Simon Cowell would sign.” Dylan hoped he was creating a shared bond by being derisive about shallow, manufactured pop music, but he couldn’t read Louise’s reaction.

“Have you taken consent classes?” Louise made sure her question was moistened in mischief with its face rinsed in a ridicule rag.

“Well, I was away that day so, you know,” Dylan stammered, “I’ve got no way of knowing how to read signs. You’ll have to sue the Education Authority.”

“Because,” Louise stepped forward, “I might look like I’m interested in you, but it could be internalised misogyny or trauma-bonding or an expression of self-sabotage –”

Dylan kissed her hard enough to stop her talking. What followed was short and sweet and definitely did not contain any of the following words: “hungrily”, “explore”, “stood to attention”, “lioness”, “fully-sated”, “arched”, “teased” or “thrust”. It did contain these: “insecty”, “head-bangy”, “hamstring pain-y”, “clammy-y”, “dog piss”, “viscous”, “nettle rash”, and “postmodern”.

Afterwards, Dylan allowed a tiny gold-coloured spider to wander from hand to hand. Eventually, the rain’s persistence prompted him to hobble awkwardly away in his un-done jeans to place the spider safely in some ivy. He waved goodbye to the tiny arachnid as he had done only moments before with his virginity. Louise studied this expedition with bemused curiosity.

"What?" Dylan asked, suddenly aware she had been watching and squinting at the sunset through the ends of her hair.

"You're the nicest person I've met IRL," she abbreviated.

"YAT!" he blurted back.

"What?"

"You're - Alright - Too," he explained. Dylan realised that unlike the sun, moon, or sky he lied about earlier, Louise actually did look like an oil painting, a good one. Not one of those one's of Jesus with enormous ham feet, babies with old men's faces, or horses with tiny dog heads.

They eventually rejoined the group to find the others still discussing the raising of funds and Andre's busted cheekbone. It was the first time many of the Offliners had seen violence that wasn't a YouTube clip of a carpark brawl or avatar being navigated by their own fragile phalanges.

"Aloha, Snack bar Brosama Bin Laden!" Liam shouted in mock-jihadi, saluting the group. Immediately detecting Dylan's altered aura, he kicked him in the leg. "Alright?"

"Yeah?" Dylan smirked.

"You both look very flushed," observed Madison.

Someone always has to let you know that they know you've had sex, thought Louise.

Oblivious, Sophia wiped her glasses and continued taking things seriously. "Funding," she began.

Dylan was more determined than he'd ever been to think of something, anything, if only to impress Louise. Suddenly, he hit upon it. "That missing child woman! We could blackmail her!"

"Oh, that awful prick," Louise said, discouragingly, "Not even worth trolling. We need someone serious. Someone must have an idea." She sat down amongst some purple flowers, unconcerned with any lingering glances on her blushed skin and scratched limbs. She wasn't a businesswoman. She was a none-of-your-businesswoman.

Suddenly, Dylan had an epiphany. "Hey," he said, glancing at Louise and remembering, "you're –" The penny had dropped almost as fast as his Cheap Monday ink blue jeans had dropped just now. *It was her*, he thought, *Louise, the tempestuous Twitter troll that was winding up my old man's bit on the side.*

Dylan stopped short, however, from telling Louise. He didn't want to sound like a stalker. She might think he'd engineered this entire youth culture renaissance thing in an elaborate pick up scaffold. In fact, it had all been a happy coincidence.

"I'm what?" asked Louise.

"Never mind," returned Dylan.

"This is really confusing. Elaborate?" Louise asked as she rubbed Maybelline Baby Lips in Mexican Pig Plum – almost as hard to get now as Iced Miscarriage – over her skin where the nettles had branded her legs. This, of course, made it look much worse, like some war-time staphylococcus skin disease.

"Oh, come on," insisted Dylan, wild-eyed, "We'll pretend we're the kidnappers and demand a ransom. We can capitalise on someone else's idea. I mean, it's not evil, is it? It's handy. The work's already been done."

Sophia, in a half-yawn, half-laugh, said, "It's perverting the course of justice."

"It's interfering with an investigation," said Elliot, fiddling with a phone as usual, and then, added uncertainly, "Isn't it?"

"Nah, that's got more holes than a porcupine's blow-up doll," laughed Lenny, a boy with a 1970s face, name, and analogies.

A square-shaped boy named Isaac with a voice that sounded like bread – if bread could speak – asked, "The work's already been done?"

"That's beta cuck behaviour and I like it!" said Elliot to mostly confused faces, hiding his phone again. Silence ensued for what seemed like an eternity.

"You'll have to call from an anonymous, untraceable handset," Dylan proffered, "A nicked one, if possible. Ask Liam."

Louise's pirate smile morphed into a goblin grin. "If you disguise your voice, it could work. Probably not, but it could." Louise's goblin grin had something to do with the fact that she was sitting on something a million times better. For some time, she had had in her possession a series of dirtily dubious messages from a rising MP. She hadn't just screen-grabbed them, but, in case of a complete technology wipeout, had elected to have the messages printed out and stuck in a scrapbook from Poundland. The scrapbook featured cartoon penguins dancing with umbrellas on the front cover.

Louise had been just biding her time because The MP in question was relatively low-profile. His opinions generally were prescriptive. He had gone from university to Parliament to marriage to fatherhood. No wonder he felt an underlying need to send adolescent messages to someone like Louise. He had never gotten that out of his system and so, it would always be there. Call it a rite of passage, a learning curve. The trouble was, like many of his kind, he also needed comfort and security because he was a tremendous coward. Louise had been encouraging the MP to appear on a reality show to up his game. The politician generally found her lower-class expressions endearingly funny. "Up your game", "Smash it", "Hold it down, nuff paper". He often told her she made him feel alive or some such nonsense.

But her plan remained the same. As soon as he was a recognisable face, boom! she'd contact the papers. Or perhaps he could pay her directly and she could lift herself out of her physical and psychological hovel.

The rest of the group were still banging on about the ransom scheme. "They'll trace it straight away," derided Flynn,

"Not a Nokia 3210," corrected Liam.

"Retro," someone said, "Has it got Snake?"

"And Munkiki's Castle?" asked another.

"Whose castle?" asked a voice from the darkness.

Liam laughed, "Are you disrespecting the castle-dwelling legend that is Munkiki? "

This nostalgic bonding was suddenly interrupted by a Plan B from Dylan, "And if that fails, topless selfie for back up. Bad publicity or good, who knows. I'm not Rupert Murdoch, am I?"

Dylan pulled the picture of Stephanie Korovnik up on his phone. He only used his phone now for saving evidence which might be useful in potential blackmail situations. Dylan flashed the picture to the group. In the process, they all became like meerkats, up on their hind legs. Peerkats.

"Why've you got that? and also, that's the first time I've found her funny" squinted Elliot.

“Long story,” said Dylan, “Let’s just say my dad’s a dick and leave it at that.”

“My dad’s a dick and leave it at that!” repeated the group, beaming with joy at their impromptu coordination.

“And ironically,” added Lucas, “that was a total dad joke.”

A small crowd gathered to judge Stephanie Korovnik’s picture. “Urrrgh” was the collective cry of all, except for a solitary boy from Milton Keynes named Noah. He took himself off for a walk behind a tree.

Dylan was happy that Liam was now going to Offliner events as well. Things became familiar again. Dylan always knew when Liam had arrived. He had the smell of a school jumper that had been tumble-dried to death. A hot, woolen smell. Not unpleasant, just distinctive. Well, it was a bit unpleasant. Well, distracting. That smell had been embedded in Dylan’s psyche ever since infant school.

Of all the Offliners, Liam had the most lackadaisical approach to the whole thing. Arriving on his bike, eating an apple, Liam was as at home as he could be. This really wasn’t much of a novel experience for him. As a result, Liam had quickly established himself as a young Fagin who could get anything fellow Offliners wanted.

True to form, at the next meet, Dylan was presented with a Primark bag full of phones. "Take your pick,” Liam said, “but go somewhere random to make the call and then wipe it, throw it, and dip!"

“Kek!” Elliot squeaked. Five years out of date.

Chapter Twenty-Six

Dylan was living a twilight life – not the silly vampire series – a twilight life as in one that began at dusk. It was a dual existence. He fell asleep on the bus to school and was frequently awakened by Liam throwing Clingfilm wrapped sandwiches against the window Dylan's head was resting on. Fish paste on half-thawed-out bread makes a surprisingly loud thud.

Dylan had been sent home early again for drifting off in class. He picked up a magazine Grace had left on the sofa, one of those that thinks it's better than other women's magazines. The other women's magazines avoided it at parties and whispered its name disparagingly through pregnancy-ending fumes in North London nail bars. *Potential,* it was called.

It contained articles about how to take control of your life and embrace your curves or big nose. This was followed by no less than fifty back pages of cosmetic surgery adverts and appeals to join escort agencies with fully-vetted VIP clients and all-female run teams. The solicitations were written in swirly writing on pink backgrounds, presumably so the readers knew they were legitimate. Any business capable of mastering fonts like Kunstler Script must be above reproach. Dylan flicked through the pages and did a bit of content editing with a biro.

Coconut oil: Metabolism booster, antifungal supplement, miracle hair growth booster, magnetic portal into a higher dimensional time and space paradigm. He scrawled over one.

Thyroid disorders to really make your eyes pop, he wrote on another.

Six cute looks to continue to rock after you've realised you're just a vibrating, holographic illusion. Dylan scribbled mindlessly on the cover, going over and over in his mind how to successfully blackmail a dead-list comedian. *Aren't you supposed to put a sock over the mouthpiece when you ring to mask your identity? Or run a tap or maybe cut out some lettuce?* he wondered.

Dylan put off calling Stephanie Korovnik for a few days, but eventually decided to make the call from the school toilet. This way, it could be passed off as a light-hearted prank. Besides, there was strength in numbers.

The first few calls went straight to voicemail and he hung up each time. After this sixth attempt, however, a female voice on the other end answered, "Andrew? Is that you, Andy? I can't see you anymore. I already feel warped with guilt. Do I mean warped, racked, wrapped? Oh, I've had too much coffee." Stephanie Korovnik prattled on, unawares, "Why don't you say something?"

Dylan tried to deepen his voice, "Uh, we've got your daughter and –" suddenly it all came out at once, "we want fifty thousand quid," he exhaled.

"Excuse me?" Stephanie nearly laughed, "Very funny, Clive! I thought even you might draw the line at my missing child, but then, that's show business! Make 'em laugh, make 'em laugh," she burst into a snatch of *Singing in the Rain*, "Oh, I so should have got that part. I'm so Debbie Reynolds. Bloody Kelly Pearson, what a bloody little bastard. Oh, I've got a terminal disease, so I have to play bloody Kathy Selden because I might be dead in two years and it'll look good for the theatre bloody bastards, but never mind, make 'em laugh! Make 'em laugh!"

Dylan shook his head, confused by her bitter drama school reminiscences. "No. Listen, I'm a kidnapper. I don't know you. We have your daughter and we want fifty thousand quid."

Stephanie interrupted her reverie with a hint of feigned alacrity, "You're serious?" she asked, "How do I know? Prove it! Oh God, are you – are you a Jihaaardy?"

Dylan strained to remember the online conversation between Louise and Stephanie. "Look," he continued, "your daughter Molly says we have to ban lad's mags and some such thing." Dylan turned and shouted to empty space, "What's that, Molly? Oh, she says mummy is a funny lady and does jokes and wants a better world" he lied. *Thank fuck for over-sharing*, Dylan thought.

"Molly!" exclaimed Stephanie, "Oh, God, you're not hurting her, are you? Leave her face alone. She's on a waiting list for Little Gems models." A hint of suspicion crept into her voice, "By the way, you sound very. . . young."

"Your daughter is fine. Again, we want fifty grand. Anyway, we've got to go now," Dylan capitalised on his presumed menace and deepened his voice further whilst a student thumped on the cubicle door. "Fuck off," he whispered harshly to the student before turning his attention back to the phone, "We're off to Maghrib."

"Where shall I bring it?" asked Stephanie, "I do have Pilates at four and a meeting at seven with an important TV guy that I can't miss."

"Jesus, we've got your fucking child!"

"Shitty civilians," Stephanie mumbled under her breath. Anyone not involved in show businesses was a civilian. "Can you call me back after 8pm, by any chance?"

Exasperated, Dylan responded, "For fuck's sake, yes."

Later that night, at 20:03 to be precise, Dylan rang Stephanie back following a shot of vicious poitín he had procured from Liam to fortify him for the task. He was greeted with a cheerful "Hello!"

"Salam-alekum," Dylan's Asian accent was actually Asian by way of Liverpool, a refreshing anomaly of the usual Welsh cliché. "Got the money then?"

"Well," Stephanie said with a morbid positivity to her voice, "I was going to ask you about that. I was wondering if it would be terribly inconvenient if you, you know, held on to her for a few days or even a few weeks longer? Molly seems okay, yes? The thing is, I've just had this meeting and," she drew a deep and dramatic breath, "I'm going to be an ambassador for missing kids and 'This Morning' may have me as a guest on Friday. I can plug my new one-woman show 'Period Piece'. Oh! Thank God! You've reminded me I need to collect my boob dress from the dry cleaners. I was going to wear the yellow trouser suit, but Holly is wearing yellow! Not lemon yellow, actually, but banana. I don't want it to look like I've coordinated. Paul O'Grady might be cancelling. He's not well, apparently. Hope he gets better, obvs. And it would just be really, really helpful if Molly could, you know –" as the pitch to her voice increased, Stephanie morphed into a little girl lost herself – "stay kidnapped?"

At this point, Dylan wondered if someone had kidnapped Molly for her own good. "You're not human!" he exclaimed.

"I was actually going to put that on the posters for my next tour!" Stephanie prattled on, "Or something about finding a way to make damaged work for you in the world. What do you think? It's something my shrink said about me."

"I think you're a cunt," was all Dylan could say, "Goodbye."

"That was the name of Miles Fernbridge's 2005 tour," Stephanie continued, oblivious that Dylan had already rung off.

She didn't give a shit, Dylan painfully realised, *Where was the money going to come from?*

Chapter Twenty-Seven

Louise sat on the inflatable mattress in her damp B & B. There was only one place she could put the synthetic Lilo and this meant she was pushed up against a radiator which came on every morning at 6am and burnt her head sometime after the recurring dream of being enveloped by sea waves. The other end of the mattress was against a damp wall, which meant if she didn't want a burnt head, she could instead wake up sniffling amidst silverfish and flea bites. *Phoebe bloody Walnut Beaker should bloody well come and do posh one-liners from this stinking, shithole, piss parade*, she thought. It was so cold. Most of the time, Louise would be forced to run the hot tap or switch on the Baby Belling oven to warm the place up.

She sat with her legs bent at the knee and listened to the shouting next door. It was angry, intense, and threatening. This night it really sounded like someone was going to be murdered.

Louise needed to use the toilet down the hall, but last time she had gone in, someone had left pornography spread all over the floor. It was so toxic and disturbing - no one uses paper porn anymore. Not to mention, there was blood on the walls in splatters that she knew could only have come from someone banging up.

Every time she looked out of the window, the same three men in leather jackets and gold jewelry were standing in the betting shop doorway. They always interrupted their endless conversation to look up at her and wave. So, Louise couldn't even search the sky for escape.

Scabby, moth-eaten pigeons scrounged up old KFC on the pavement, like threadbare disabled cannibals intent on eating and fucking. Just like the humans ambling past, they were running on survival autopilot. But what for?

Louise suddenly jumped. Fingers shuffled under her door, making scuffling sounds. The hand went back just as suddenly. As predictable as ever, the owner of the hand lay his head down on the hallway floor and poked his tongue through the one-inch gap.

Louise had reported this activity to her key worker and could only sit nodding at the inevitable prognosis, which, of course, was bureaucratic disdain at Louise's lack of sympathy for her neighbor's mental illness. His supposed mental illness only encompassed making his poor scampering hand and tongue dance under the doors of young female tenants.

She grabbed the *Evening Standard* magazine and turned to an article entitled "Why Lily Warren-Paige Is Breaking the Mold". The piece had failed to convince Londoners that another actor's daughter, an actress herself, was really down-to-earth. *Some of her friends didn't go to university*, it read, trying to gloss over its own nepotism, I'm *very low-maintenance, I only use products by Sensai.* The entire back three pages should just be called *"Rock stars ugly daughters with expensive hair claim greasy spoon in Kilburn is their 'go to hub'"*

For Louise, the article would prove useful after all. She stuffed the pages under the door. leaving the poor old mentally-impaired dear to scrunch rather than wave his fingers about. Too bad the article couldn't do anything about the construction noise. The drilling in her street never seemed to end. She often felt she would be driven mad by noise.

Despite the towering odds against her and, almost to add a useless insult to a pointless injury, Louise's face was young, like a thing just hatched. It was something brought in from the forest, an incubating beauty that sugar and junk food only seemed to feed and enhance. Rather than doing the opposite, her highly-processed and empty calorie diet blackened her pupils, prickled her freckles, and lengthened her lashes. The result was a symmetrically intelligent beauty, all flowing from hormones and ovaries at the top of their game. Her beauty was something *in utero*, a supernatural science fiction that created patterns on itself that transmitted a code to the world. Hers was a self-perpetuating, sap-rising beauty that looked as though it was going to ooze out all over the place, perhaps too rich to be contained by mere skin and bones. Louise's looks were brief, bare-faced, bottle-fed, bread-and-butter. They were three summers' worth of beauty reserved only for the very, very piss-poor. She was PHAT.

The square of sky visible through her one window was grey. Doubly disappointing, the dull green energy-saving bulb made to cheer things up only made it worse. Everything in sight which was supposed to be a sign of prosperity just amplified the uselessness. The pastel dashes on the large white paper lamp shade, the WWF panda sticker peeling off the grubby pane, the poster inside the wardrobe door of a dimwitted cartoon elephant holding an umbrella with its trunk, all added to the hopelessness. The sickly-sweet smell of the cake mixture child's perfume she had stolen from Claire's Accessories was diluted by piss and old spunk and fresh shit from babies' nappies in the doorway. Every sign of life was a sign of death.

Louise stared straight ahead at the horrible material someone had nailed inexplicably to a wall instead of curtains. Festering pink and orange flowers printed on a yellow background that had once been white. It all left her feeling desolate. *Someone designed that*, she thought, *Why did people put flowers on things? What are they trying to say? What's it supposed to make you feel? What's the point? I bet whoever designed that pattern has a better life than me.*

Louise tipped out pennies from an ugly glass vase that came with the room. It had a swirly rose pattern incorporated into the glass. *I bet whoever designed that vase has* – she thought, before her attention was diverted by the television. The set was on mute, but Eddie Izzard's beret and earnest expression were loud enough that it was impossible to not get the gist of what he was saying. She jumped, startled as someone thumped on the walls three times.

Everybody, said Eddie silently, *Everybody can afford to give something. You can go without your Starbucks coffee tomorrow. You can bypass the gym for a week. You can afford to give something. We all have televisions and smartphones. Come on!"*

Louise looked at her pay-as-you-go smartphone. If she was lucky, it sometimes stayed on for longer than ten minutes without the battery dying. She had bought it for twenty quid at a dry cleaners/internet café/contact lens and pet shop.

She opened up Twitter.

@BarnabyJasparMP As a #feminist I completely support the removal of the Beach Babe poster from TFL. I'd like to think my daughter can grow up with positive images to support and inspire her

Louise next went to her photo album and found a screen shot of a message from the very same @BarnabyJasparMP

I would tie you up using your school tie and stuff my cock in your whore mouth until you're choking and crying:)

It was the emoji she found most offensive. *Did these middle-aged men use them as a form of grooming or was it how they really communicated?* she often wondered. And besides, she didn't have a school tie. Her Croydon comprehensive had banned them under health and safety regulations after thirteen pupils were hospitalised from being throttled in so-called 'peanutting' attacks. The school had tried velcro for a while, but students kept ripping apart the crunchy adhesive in class to drive the already heavily-medicated teachers over the edge. *Anyway,* thought Louise, *why on earth would I still have one now, four years later? Was I supposed to carry it around in case some Billy Bunter prick popped up in my mentions, in-between wanking over hair slides and the Clarks back to school catalogue?*

The right honourable Barnaby's message was followed by a few ridiculous anime pictures of strange prepubescent women in various states of bondage. These were captioned with cringe worthy babyish texts. *I'd really like to do this to you ;)*

Grow up, Louise thought, *I've had to. Why can't you?* These exchanges with a representative of Her Majesty's parliament had been initially interesting. It had been nice to talk to someone well read. She and Barnaby had both been on holiday to Devon as children and shared stories about the clean air and friendly people and Paignton Beach. Barnaby had also encouraged Louise with the course she wanted to do and that, of course, was a welcome novelty. But he had turned sexual very quickly and, in her position, she didn't feel she could afford to lose any contacts. Or rather, contact. Louise felt the heat rise in her body all the way up to her face. The bridge of her nose tightened and she thought for a moment that she might cry, but the urge was swallowed down by practical anger. *Good!* she thought. Rage, her one true and constant love, never duplicitous, never betraying. Always on time and always with her best interests at heart.

How to approach this? she wondered. Louise happened upon an app which did mock-up newspaper covers and quickly designed one using Barnaby's name and message. She couldn't include the emoji, which was a shame. It came out as the letter 'j' in the process. The headline looked convincing. That is, to one who had never seen a newspaper.

Delete, delete! she changed her mind, *just ask him for money? He's got three bloody houses, and something called a "pagida",*

Louise wrote a poisoned Snapchat message implying that a reporter was offering her "nuff paper" for her story and she didn't know what to do. She turned and stared while Izzard, surrounded by brown children who were justifiably trying to pull off his beret, implored incessantly, *We can all afford to give something.*

On the screen, a cockroach crawled over an African boy's foot, while in real life, a cockroach crawled over Louise's mattress. Louise's cockroach was lit up brightly by the B & B's television set. Hers jumped instead of scuttled. It was some new super-breed. She counted her blessings – one, two, three – tore open a sugar sachet, poured it into her entitled, Western mouth, and pressed send.

Chapter Twenty-Eight

Dylan was falling asleep on the bus to school when his eardrums rattled with the shrill screaming of the late Mabel's harassers. They had cranked up the volume to eleven and three quarters since becoming aware of the Offliners movement. It was all a bit *Whatever Happened to Baby Jane.* The bullies were in their death throes now and it all seemed terribly old-fashioned. Everything. Their look, their concerns, and even their version of *bad.*

This particular morning, they were in hysterics over a boy's Instagram picture. "He is chungting!" the girls argued between themselves. "He is so not chungting. Oh, my god!" "He's chungting, but not chungting. Get me?" "Grim, mank, fugly." "So not butterz?"

Dylan tuned out the Baby Bell-ows, occasionally picking up on their regularly repeated sentence starter: "So, me being me…." Often this served as the prelude to a series of fact-based instances showcasing that the narrator was well and truly *the* most event-prone person who ever goaded a child into suicide.

A girl from another school who resembled the offspring of Naomi Campbell and Cindy Crawford, if they had had, somehow had a baby in 2002, got up to walk down the stairs. The Mutley crew made barking sounds and said in voices loud enough to be heard but timid at the same time, "She finks she's pretty." This latter had to be the most inane insult ever. It was a Catch-22 with no exits. *How do you know someone finks they're pretty?* wondered Dylan, *And doesn't the fact that you fink they fink they're pretty mean that you fink they're pretty?*

"Excuse me, my friend wants to know why you're so butterz?" "Excuse me, my friend wants to know if you can smell fish" the brainless bunch taunted.

Dylan had heard all this before. It was their mundane method. It always began with an "Excuse me—", which was usually followed by some aquatic-based references to vaginas. Sometimes, by way of variation, they might begin, "Not being horrible but –"

Where did they learn it from, their Mums? he thought. Dylan stood up and turned to look at them. Of course, they all looked up instantly as well. He no longer felt any kind of threat from them. It was more of a dull pity. *Funny how getting a fuck helps you not to give one,* he smiled inwardly, thinking of Louise. It would have been a little dramatic to say he was channeling some higher power like those possessed with automatic writing, but Dylan really had no idea where his ensuing speech came from. If he had been Derek Acorah, he would have said that *The spirit moved through him. Mary loves Dick!*

"Thing is," he began, "you're all so boring, aren't you?"

A blonde corporate woman en route to work looked up with a smile at Dylan. Well, not so much a smile, rather an endorsement. Yes, it was definitely an endorsement. Dylan suddenly found he had allied forces as the bus drove past Allied Carpets.

"That's the most disappointing thing these days," he continued, "You're not even interesting enough to be evil. You're just provincial housewives, busybodies twitching net curtains and having an attack of the vapours because someone had the wrong colour hairband. You're all so old! You think as a unit. You can't function alone. You're such boring cowards! Look at your faces. Look at yourselves right now, looking at each other for direction. 'Oooh, what should we do about this situation?'" Dylan waved his hands in a cartoonish mockery, "Copying each other's facial expressions, prolonging the outrage. Murderers! Mabel's murderers! But incredibly dull ones. You've managed to make bad boring. Congratulations!"

For effect, Dylan slowly clapped his hands. Meanwhile, the corporate woman attempted to stifle a laugh by putting her chin down inside her mustard-coloured snood or scarf or whatever the fuck it was.

Dumbfounded, the fatuous five could only stare as Dylan descended the stairs of the bus. One of the group held up her phone to film him.

"Plug your chair in!" he half-shouted and half-laughed at the camera. He slung his duffle bag over his shoulder, feeling nothing but boredom.

Later in the day, he was called into the head of year's office. He had got the notification during the first five minutes of a highbrow classroom discussion entitled "What if Harry Potter Were Real?"

"Hi Dylan, sit down," said the administrator, "This is quite serious, actually." Her tone was entirely apathetic. The whole sentence came out pretty much as a sigh. "There was an incident on a bus this morning where you engaged in hate speech and misogyny."

"What?" Dylan could hardly believe his ears. This was going to be much worse than the Woody Allen line that had led to his psychiatric evaluation. "This is the same shower that made Mabel kill herself!" he exclaimed to the head of year. Upon this, Dylan suddenly felt a huge surge of freedom.

"Dylan," she said, the timbre of her voice matched Davina McCall meeting a recently bereaved survivor of a national disaster, one perhaps that had been diagnosed with a tumor and was plugging a new book about battling addiction. *Tune in Saturday evening after "Dogs Make You Laugh Out Loud"! "*Whenever something awful like Mabel's death happens, it's tempting to point fingers and find a scapegoat. It's a coping mechanism. Recriminations are common, but we counsel against giving into them."

"They had a Facebook page called Die Lizard Bitch," Dylan said, deserting diplomacy. "You know the expression 'smoking gun'? I mean, this would be like if Princess Di had left a note saying *my husband is planning to have me killed in a car accident,* oh, wait. I mean, the gun isn't just smoking. It's covered in Nicorette patches and on the NHS waiting list for a new lung."

"Enough Dylan" the administrator flew into a calm.

"You're just afraid of how this reflects on the school. It's all politics, admit it!"

"I can assure you that's not true," she said, "We have a long history of dealing effectively with bullying. In fact, we pioneered the monitor programme which has been copied all over the country."

"Oh yeah," Dylan scoffed, "the monitor programme. Who do you think volunteers to be a bullying monitor?"

She ignored the question. "How are you sleeping?"

"Like this," He opened his mouth, closed his eyes, stood up and skipped around in circles, shrieking, "I'm asleep! I'm asleep!"

"Any worries on your mind?" she continued, undeterred.

" No," he said.

"Would you say you identified more with the male gender spectrum or the female gender spectrum?"

"I identify as a bored person," he returned.

"I'd like you to attend a course at a pupil referral unit. Anger management."

"The sin bin!" Dylan exclaimed.

"You'll have the opportunity to gain additional training in managing your behaviour and resolving conflict effectively. And that can, in turn, benefit the whole school."

Dylan squinted at her, "Are you a robot?"

"I beg your pardon?" she asked.

Fearing reprisal, he obfuscated, "Do you know Robert?"

"Get back to class and we'll connect again next week," the administrator concluded. She had to bring this spectacle to an end.

"Connect - later – week," Dylan muttered in an impression of a robot. The administrator missed this, however, as she'd begun spraying her territory by smothering her hands in Neroli Emulsion from Neal's Yard before turning to her Frida Kahlo colouring book.

Chapter Twenty-Nine

Barnaby Jaspar was at a "Green Fish Farming after Brexit" meeting in Islington when he received Louise's message. He had been fish-farmed, alright. Done up like a sustainably-sourced kipper, ironic, since a salmon is a slang word for an older, predatory man punching above his weight, i.e., swimming upstream. Upon reading it, Barnaby heard his heart thumping in his head and the tinnitus he'd developed at Cambridge during his final exams returned like a lonely jazz percussionist wandering the streets for twenty years looking for a head to play in. *Puh-wahh-sssss, Puh-wah-ssssss.*

She wouldn't really go to the red tops! Barnaby wondered in terror, *How would she even know how to do that? Fuck! I haven't even met her in person, have I? It could be anyone.*

The right honourable member looked around the beige community hall. Heather Cartenhorse, Conservative MP from Old Bexley and Sidcup, smirked at him and looked at the floor. Barnaby then looked to his left to see Michael Flowers - Captain Cardboard, and the Friends for the Abolition of Tuesday party - Camden. Flowers nodded and tapped his head with a Dora the Explorer pen. Barnaby's pulse raced as he headed for the door. Jackie, the tea lady, raised a paper cup. *Was that a wink?*

"And on 'Question Time' tonight, we have June Sarpong, Eddie Izzard, Julia Hartley-Brewer, Barnaby Jaspar, and Katie Hopkins," announced David Dimbleby in an unreasonably optimistic tone. "We'll be broaching the subjects of Corbyn's corporation tax proposal, anonymity for those accused in sexual assault cases, gender-neutral toilets and – you won't be watching this on Iplayer – the Offliners!" A smattering of forced laughter and applause followed.

And then the questions began. "The gentleman right there," Dimbleby kicked off, "No, second row, glasses."

A sickly-looking man with bulging eyes began his 80 seconds of fame in the high-pitched and frightened tone of a ten-year-old reading a school assembly piece. "Many people are expressing concern about the amount of young people attending Offliner events and a resurgence of Covid-19 –" he was interrupted by a round of applause. The man waited until that had died down before continuing, " – and MPs don't seem to be doing anything about it, I mean –" another applause break followed, "—I mean, if anyone can explain why nothing's being done, then I, for one, would be very interested and I'm sure a lot of other people would be, too."

The applause grew exceedingly wild at this point before finally dying down. "June Sarpong," Dimbleby directed.

"Yeah," began June, "I think that this is a very good opportunity for everyone to just get together and begin a dialogue about mental health." This was met with even more raucous applause.

"I'm sorry. What does this have to do with – "Barnaby began before Sarpong held her hand up to his face.

"Can I finish what I was trying to say, please, about mental health?" she huffed, "Because I was listening the other day to a counselor who visits schools and colleges and they said -- can I finish? – they said that all of the behaviours consistent with the Offliners are also consistent with – can I finish? – the symptoms of depression. And I don't know why it's not being dealt with. I mean, I haven't heard it discussed at PMQs. I don't know if you know any young teenagers, but let me tell you, these are worrying, worrying times."

Dimbleby proceeded, "The lady with the shaved head and large earring. Oh, it's a hearing aid? My apologies. I'll get back to you in a moment. Meanwhile, Barnaby Jaspar, go ahead."

"Firstly," began Barnaby, "I think there's a lot of misunderstanding about these young people. And we're not giving them anywhere near the credit they deserve. Young people are much maligned these days and they're often unfairly branded as either criminals or snowflakes or just lazy and feckless. And when a movement like this comes along, they're denigrated for it! I think it's a bright, inventive, and creative venture with lots of potential to galvanise communities and youth groups all over the country. And, there hasn't been a single case of Covid-19 among these gatherings and attendees and perhaps we should stop looking for the negative and give these bright young things a little encouragement for a change!" A smattering of claps and a sprinkling of cheers followed this assessment.

"Julia Hartley-Brewer," directed Dimbleby

"As usual," said Hartley-Brewer, "the Lib-Dems have not done their homework." To this, the crowd booed vehemently. "So, I'll fill you in, shall I? Do the hard work for you? I don't mind," the boos now morphed into a smattering of laughter, "Statistics show that 97 or 98 percent of these children – and they are children – are having problems at home, which we need to address."

Katie Hopkins interjected, "What I don't understand is why we're even having this discussion. Surely, it's the parent's responsibility to –" here, the crowd clapped and yelled furiously, "– to know where their children are and to get their own houses in order before they –" the audience was now baying for blood, "– go running to the government for help."

"Barnaby," said Dimbleby, "Please, go ahead."

"I agree," concurred the right honourable member, "parents need to be aware of what's going on and where their children are spending their time and that it's being spent in a productive way. And that's why I'm pioneering a new scheme to work with the Offliners to promote, support, and encourage their talents, their ideas, and their energy!"

"Who's going to be paying for all of this?" lisped Hopkins.

"We've applied for a grant," said Barnaby, "and one million –" this was greeted with a collective gasp, "– one million, for a start, will be spent on planning for spaces, safe spaces, and a digital health service so that for these young people can develop their skills."

Sarpong was livid, "But unsupervised, and digital health service, for Offline kids, the clue is in the name" she observed. The crowd, for the most part, agreed with her. So much so that Barnaby had to really shout to be heard.

"Look," he shouted, "we expect young people to be able to join the army, fight, and get killed for us. To deal with an avalanche of material at their fingertips, navigate extremist websites and YouTube streams. They can go on highly emotional reality shows and talent contests, but we don't trust them to have their own spaces without killing each other? I suggest they just might do a damned sight better than we've been doing. And, if we stand back, we might even learn a thing or two!" His effort garnered him the most riotous applause of the night thus far.

When Barnaby checked his phone in the green room afterwards, a huge yellow thumbs up from Louise greeted him. Relief flooded over Barnaby. *She isn't about to fuck me over into another shamed MP,* he smiled to himself, she's *probably a dopey heart-in-the-right-place activist type, doing anything she could for The Movement! She isn't about to sell me down the river for a few quid. It's political agency that she wants. Well, I can do that without compromising my beliefs. Christ, it could even put my name on the map!*

Before leaving the studio, however, Barnaby thought it better to play things safe. *Sod it*, he decided, *I'll send her a few quid just in case.*

Barnaby had an appearance on "Celebrity Come Dine with Me" lined up. Louise had encouraged him to do it. "Reach out to a wider audience," she had admonished him. Perhaps she was right. It was useful to have the eyes and ears of the common man and woman at the tap of a – Whatsname?

The MP congratulated his daughter Audrey over Instant Messenger for nailing a speaking part in an assembly. He then drove over to W2 for a loose-lipped blowjob from a prostituted woman on Bayswater basic meth with a Bayswater basic black eye. He needed the stress relief. As an ambassador for three women's and girls' organisations in the charity sector, he felt it would be grubby to complain about the poor customer service.

Chapter Thirty

Miles Fernbridge hadn't kidnapped Molly Korovnik in the strictest definition of the word. "Kidnap" was an ugly word, a 70s word full of paedophilic connotations. Besides, the offer from the government department that had protected him during a spate of death threats at the height of his unpopularity was too good to turn down. The plan was simple: Stage a kidnapping and help usher in the new microchipping legislation.

The government had tried to get a higher-profile target, but they had to weigh that against better security and private detectives. It had been decided that Molly was the perfect guinea pig and Stephanie Korovnik's drama school background would "lens well" for the appeals.

Miles had wanted to let her in on it, but the government spooks thought Stephanie's natural reactions would work better. Plus, Stephanie owed Miles anyway. Miles was almost family, an uncle even. No, that sounded wrong, too. Miles was a guardian, that's it. He had supervised Molly when Stephanie had supported him at a huge stadium gig. Anyway, Miles was simply borrowing Molly. He had pretty much launched Stephanie's entire career. So, if it hadn't been for him, Molly wouldn't have even existed, because Stephanie couldn't have afforded a child.

Stephanie had no other work experience. It had been all luvvie stuff, tutus, tap shoes, and walk-ons in "The Bill". Miles, on the other hand, when it was all over, could waltz onto Piers Morgan's programme like Rolf Harris had done and cry selfish tears. He would let Stephanie know in advance, of course. *In fact*, wondered Miles, *it would be a funny misunderstanding. Perhaps we could turn it into a play and get some publicity out of it.* "*Molly Good Show*!" *we could call it. Or what about "Miles Away"?*

Molly wandered into Miles' living room.

“Nesquick?” he offered Molly, “Everyone likes strawberry Nesquick!” Mile’s fat, pink, placid face tried to look friendly.

“Has it got monoglycerides in it?” said the precocious young girl, “Because I’m allergic.”

Miles ignored her, getting distracted by “Question Time”. He immediately whipped out his phone. Thinking aloud, he stuttered, “Nigel Farage looks like – a frog. No! Boring. Looks like – a tadpole being anally raped by a –”

“Oh, I know what you’re doing,” said Molly, “Mum does this. She has a formula.”

His ears perked up, “What did you say? What’s the formula? Quick! Quick! This is time-sensitive!” Miles produced a pad and pen as if plucking it from the air.

“Ok. It’s current event plus sex thing,” Molly giggled, “plus oppressed minority equals punch line.”

“Right,” Miles scribbled furiously and then looked at his watch. “Oh, come on, ‘Question Time’ will be over soon. Think! Think!” He suddenly hit upon something, “Extinction Rebellion should wear a Nigella Lawson mask and put baby powder round their noses to look like cocaine and people might care a bit more about . . .?”

“That’s only one out of three,” Molly scolded.

“It’s bloody not,” contradicted Miles, “Nigella Lawson is in the news this week. It’s two out of three, smartarse.” Molly was unmoved, so Miles took another crack, “Nigel Farage looks like an amoeba who’s so racist that it fucked its own – no, no – Nigel Farage is what happens when a drunk otter fucks a racist tortoise!”

“Where’s the current event?” Molly demanded in the manner of a 52-year-old managing director.

"Farage!" he screamed impetuously at her unflickering face, "Farage is the current event!!"

"Perhaps five years ago. You're not very funny, are you?" she looked at him disappointedly.

Molly had committed the unforgiveable sin as she soon found out from Miles' ensuing tirade, "I am! I am funny! I am fucking funny! What do you know, you ugly little freak? Have you got any idea how important I am? How important my role is? I'm the archetypal trickster, the bubble burster, the mediator between this world and the underworld!"

He opened the cupboard under the sink and rattled around until he pulled out a roll of masking tape. He then grabbed Molly by the arm, almost dislocating her shoulder in the process, and began hitting her with her own hand, "Stop hitting yourself! Stop hitting yourself!"

"Grow up," she said, unaffected. Molly was used to dealing with overdramatic and needy adults.

"Grow up?" echoed Miles. "Sit down, you retard."

"Who says 'retard' anymore!?", sighed Molly, "Uh, 1992 called and they want their insults back."

She smirked as Miles put her in a chair facing the television. He flipped from "Question Time" to a "Live at The Apollo" repeat he had compered five years ago. Spitting bubbling froth through the slit in his face masquerading as a mouth, Miles resembled an angry glove puppet. He cracked Molly hard on the back of her head, calcified with indignant ire. "Silence is golden. Duct tape is silver."

As his rage abated, he unclenched his fists and returned to his bedroom. There, he changed into the Sheer Peach satin-look Janet Reger nightdress he kept on a special hanger and Pretty Polly gloss tights in Royal Blue – a baffling clash of colour choices and rocked himself to tear-sodden, ego-clutching sleep, whimpering, "I hate myself; I hate myself!" Before completely slipping into oblivion, he managed to write a note to remind himself to replace "Farage" with "Trump" and "tortoise" with "orangutan" but could also switch it to Dianne Abbott or Bernie Saunders should the landscape change.

Chapter Thirty-One

"We need to talk about Dylan," said his mum.

Dylan's dad was mugged by the 'joke' one cold kitchen morning. "Do we?" he was scrolling and twitching, twitching and scrolling.

"He left an hour earlier again," mum persisted, "He walks all the way to school, reading a book. Jacinta and the girls saw him. When he's here, he sits reading. I've tagged him in 37 photos since September and he hasn't commented once."

"Probably a phase," Dylan's dad guessed, "I experimented at his age, too. Look at this cat's reaction to his owner faking his death."

Dylan's mum peered over Dylan's dad's shoulder, "Who posted that? Is that Rob from uni? I should be following him."

Lost in the hilarity, she forgot her parental concerns until later that day. Coming home on the train, she saw several children of Dylan's age also reading books. The children appeared old-fashioned. They had wild hair and no gadgets. *Eerie*, she had thought. By the time the train reached Clapham Junction, Dylan's mum's carriage contained seven teens burying their noses in literature, spines straight as the books they were reading, whilst all around them, adults scrolled and twitched, LOL-d and bitched. And they weren't just reading the classics. One little rascal was reading something about an anthropomorphic bicycle. The whole spectacle gave her the creeps. It was *Children of the Corn* with paperbacks.

Offliner events were growing and becoming more coordinated across the country. There were rumours of Offliner gatherings in New York and Paris, but they were only rumours. Nothing online could really ever be trusted. It would have been easy to Photoshop oneself into an Offliners backdrop, grinning and throwing gang signs around like a domesticated indoor cat with its claws removed. There had been a few attempts at a hijack by people still online, who would show up, furtively looking around, and nervously reaching for their carefully concealed phone every few seconds. Invariably, they would prove unable to resist the "like" potential. Some would even take a selfie and post it to their platform with the caption: *Me at an Offliners event.* One would think the irony was obvious, but. . .nah.

The real world had come alive again. The currency in fake IDs was hectic. Children travelled on their own or with older siblings. Ten-year olds were gaining the confidence to go up to fathers in playgrounds who regularly hogged the equipment.

"Can I use it please?" an Offliner named Tyler had asked a lycra-clad man-baby, who responded by slinking away, mumbling into his jowl-disguising beard, and updating his status to complain about the chav who was in his 'best tracksuit'.

All the mums and dads continued to swipe away, plugged into the heavily-censored matrix, unable to have an opinion straying from the #hashtag of the day or inspirational meme. Meanwhile, their successors did the only thing they could possibly do at this point. They rejected the lot. More and more young people were joining them by the week. It was IRL as class warfare. Guerilla Offlining.

This all culminated in a *Daily Mail* article. Of course.

IS YOUR CHILD AN OFFLINER?

Offliners, the worrying new trend amongst British teens, sees families shattered as more and more youngsters appear to reject online life and mainstream entertainment in favour of gathering at secretive meetings in forests, rejecting their prescribed medication, and attempting to have deep conversations with their distraught parents.

In the wake of widespread concern, the government has joined forces with major internet companies and appointed a group of top scientists to examine the situation and formulate a plan to address it.

Labelled the "The New Ferals", the team of psychologists assigned to study them have compiled a checklist for parents to help them identify if their child has fallen under the dark spell of the Offliners.

14 SIGNS YOUR CHILD MIGHT BE INVOLVED WITH THE OFFLINERS

1. *Have they stopped taking selfies?*
2. *Are they reluctant to take their prescribed medication and occasionally questioning the diagnosis?*
3. *Is there a dip in their level of online activity? For example, they don't like your posts on Facebook?*
4. *Are they spending more undocumented time away from the family?*
5. *Have they shown an interest in unusual or obscure topics and hobbies? For example, woodwork or playing the recorder*
6. *Are they no longer communicating in emojiis and instead using unusual words or phrases? Are they making eye contact when they speak?*
7. *Do they forget to take their phones with them from time to time?*
8. *Do they seem less bothered about their physical appearance?*
9. *Have they stopped playing computer games? Do they appear more interested in the natural world?*
10. *If obese, have they lost weight? If anorexic, have they gained weight?*
11. *Have they been playing old music such as David Bowie albums or cassette tapes?*
12. *Do their clothes smell of bonfire or are their shoes covered in mud?*

13. *Have you found materials in their room such as candles, cash boxes, food, or burnt photographs of celebrities?*
14. *Number 13 is a trick – this is NOT a sign of being an Offliner.*

The article was preceded by a picture of some male model the editors had put in charity shop clothes with what looked like a Pritstick in his hair. The model stared defiantly at the camera, holding a book by Emil Cioran in one hand and a bottle of gin in the other.

Following the article, though, was a medical piece asserting that young people had a huge deficiency in Vitamin B6 and the government would soon impose a legal requirement to have injections. A tiny article on the subsequent page boasted that knife crime had fallen by twenty-five percent over the last three months.

Dylan sneered at the paper. *Where did they get the idea Offliners drank gin and put spunk in their hair?* he wondered, *That was only on Wednesdays.*

The Offliners had mostly adopted a style which looked like they had walked into a Salvation Army clothes bank and put on the first things they had seen. They were young and pretty enough to carry it off. This, of course, was very rebellious in an age of people as old as twenty-five being taken to see Top Shop-style advisors by their mothers. Or those who followed "how to take the perfect selfie" tutorials sponsored by Kourtney Kardashian's airbrush foundation. There was a formula behind the Offliner's disheveledness and this was annoying a lot of older people.

Despite procuring from charity shops, the Offliners tried mostly to go for classic clothes, grown up wear. They wanted to avoid the giant toddler, puffer jacket, sexless, shapeless, and genderless look. But they weren't going to adopt the "Love Island" sleeve-tattooed, eyebrow stenciled, over styled, groomed to death look either. If anything, they were after a mixture of a *Boys Own* adventure, Jolly Hockey Sticks, and Jolly Rogers. *Infidels against*

Infantilisation! Apaches against Apathy! Pirates against Pococurantism! Blackmailing Bandits! Radio Rebels! Demagogue Dissidents! Malcontent Mutineers! Out-a-lot Outlaws!

Ian Farringdon usually began his shows with the same boring, current events monologue. And today was no exception.

My kids don't understand me. That is the cry across the nation. They sneak out alone. They disengage from social media. They fiercely pursue so-called real-life experiences. They talk of resilience and robust adventure. But what can we do? What's the answer? At the risk of being a party pooper, in my uni days I remember we used to have some cider. And we would make crop circles in a nearby field. Great days, those were. In fact, we also used to smoke some very funny stuff. It never affected my grades either. And my girlfriend at the time –

Over the last several months, a small faction of Offliners were starting to appreciate the idea that the only way left to rebel was to be a legitimately good person. Hard-headed cheerfulness was very subversive in a culture obsessed with itself. One that was perpetually diagnosing, medicating, and oversharing, wearing its mental illness like a fashionable coat. Bedecked with social anxiety earrings, bipolar cufflinks, and a jaunty Asperger's hat.

Chapter Thirty-Two

Late October in a Buckinghamshire wood, Dylan weaved through the trees as tinny cassette music and voices got louder. The air had the science fiction greeny tinge it gets in films just before a storm. Shouts were muffled by the thick foliage and smoke crept in between the branches. A child in half-falling-off pyjamas was spinning round and around in a rubber tire whilst an older teen swung on a rope, just skimming a bonfire. Dylan's eyes darted at a billion gigabytes per second. They were suburban refugees, greenbelt gangsters, and Greater London Luddites.

Covering yourself in dirt and branches and then jumping out at others was still a novelty. A few times, someone's dad had tried to join in, hoping to hijack the tiny window of youth which had at one time been an unquestioned rite of passage.

But parents were banned from Offliner events with no compromise. The participants wanted undocumented mucking about and unstructured play. They fought. They broke limbs and health and safety rules. They fell in love, fell off things, fell foul, felled trees - they didn't do that one - they kept secrets, went helmet-less, and ate unquartered grapes.

They were lost in the moment, never to be seen again. They were the living embodiment of mischief, spontaneity, and existing in the spur-of-the-moment. They were, in short, Offline.

Dylan looked up and saw Andre shrink away as a glass bottle spun over his head and hit a tree. Liquid and glass rained down in shards and flames just as the skies cracked open and clapped with thunder.

The Offliners scattered throughout the brilliantly bright burning woods. Dylan herded a small group to a country road and, eventually, to a bus stop.

A single decker bus of orange and blue arrived. Dylan caught a glimpse of himself in the window as he chose his seat from the many empty ones. Breathing deeply, he reflected that the air smelled fresh with no hint of death. His cheeks were flushed and eyes bright. The blood pumped through his veins. A shard of glass had cut his forehead, but it felt good. For once his clothes seemed to fit. He'd grown into his face. His bones fitted his flesh. The planets had aligned and the universe had thrown him a cheeky wink. *Wink!*

He felt alive.

Alive.

Alive.

Dylan's mum being Dylan's mum, was one of the first to book him an appointment for the government-imposed B6 shot. He hadn't wanted to go, obviously, but she managed to dupe him with the promise of an increased allowance.

The procedure took much longer than Dylan had expected. Afterwards, his wrist swelled up a little. This was odd since the solution was supposed to have gone into his forearm. It was only when Dylan's scratching led to bleeding that his mum felt cornered into telling him the truth. She had given his GP the green light to install a microchip in him. A signature had been all that was required.

“Smaller than a grain of rice!" she enthused to Dylan, thrilled to bits with the idea of technology enabling the upgrade of her cyber-family. What was really clever, though, was that the authorities didn't refer to it as a microchip. They called it by the brand name Anemone. They did this because Anemone means protection from evil. And, as luck would have it, the procedure also left a prickly flower pattern at the injection site. The five-page pamphlet featuring a cartoon family of non-specific races and genders – or even species – failed to mention the word Anemone also meant “Dying Hope”.

"Fuck!" erupted Dylan upon hearing the news.

"No need for that language, mate!"

He hated his mum calling him "mate". "You chipped me?" he said, dumbfounded, "But, I had no say! Are you an idiot?"

"You'd have created a fuss," she said, not exactly missing the truth. "You read all those daft blogs and with all the weird cults cropping up and that latest firebomb incident or whatever it was, I worry."

Dylan would have continued arguing, but suddenly he felt overwhelmingly tired and went upstairs to crash out on his bed. "Chipped!" he said to himself, "Like a pet rapist or a serial rabbit."

Over the next few days, the tiredness consumed him. He couldn't quite put his finger on what was happening to him physically, mostly because his deep tendon reflexes and motor skills were severely impaired. He could still walk, talk, and go to the toilet. It was a foggy-headedness and a heavy-footedness. A General Malaise, cousin of Colonel Apathy.

Consequently, Dylan missed the next seven Offliners events. It was only when Liam dropped off a flyer that he felt galvanised enough to go. The latest flyer featured tiny maggots with the faces of various television personalities crawling around the mass of the exposed brains of Mark Zuckerberg. Hand-drawn, mind you. The lady at the library had complimented the creativity as the designated Offliner artist hijacked the printer for over an hour.
Unfortunately, the image was marred by the presence in the far-left corner of a corporate logo followed by the words: *Sadiq Khan Investing in Youth*

The government funding had finally trickled down and the Offliners had been granted independence. Well, somewhat. Now a few miles outside of London, the unruly ferals could make as much noise as they liked. Within reason.

The deal was ostensibly simple. The Offliners had only to comply with the Government sponsorship requirements. Which meant they had to fill certain diversity quotas, monitor minor health and safety requirements, and, of course, think about allowing people who were still online to attend events – lest they be marginalised. The first plans were drawn up by councils who used some of the money to build facilities to enable the supposed freedom of the Offliners.

In the midst of these changes, more articles had begun to appear: "Internet Use in Adults Rises to Almost Twice That of Their Children", "A Generation Shuns the Technology their Parents Crave", and "Via the Mediums of Gifs and Emojis Read How Parents Claim Their Children Don't Understand Them".

The Offliner movement was dirty and refreshing, a theatre of ideas, a new enlightenment. The online world began to feel like a faint echo in a shallow plastic pond.

"But in all fairness, we must take responsibility for the times we live in," June Sarpong had said in a recent "Question Time. "It's very dangerous out there. These teens are steeped in a culture of violence, as last month's firebomb attack shows. And we live in a highly-sexualised society. And it's just not safe to let these children be having these clandestine meetings."

Sarpong's analysis was met with half-hearted claps and a solitary individual shouting, "Spoilsport!"

Chapter Thirty-Three

Dylan, now consuming up to four Mountain Dews a day in order to counteract the stupor he had felt ever since his body was violated, turned a corner near his school and saw Kieran, a confirmed Casanova from his year.

Dylan witnessed Kieran force - *faux* force – Malika, a girl from another school, against the wall. Malika let her bag fall on the ground and played into Kieran's shove, smiling corpulently. "Add me. We can WhatsApp, innit!" Kieran suggested lasciviously. Grinning in her face, he pushed his lower body against hers.

"WhatsApp?" she responded, pulling a face like a vegan doing a bush tucker trial. "Literally *no-one* WhatsApps anymore!"

Dylan continued down the road to see a street trader touting his tat. "I'm an #Offliner" T-shirts, "Offline Forever" mouse mats, "Don't Ring, I'm Offlining" holographic phone covers, and" Offliner" posters featuring wild children with dirty hair and crazy eyes swinging in rubber tires. Further down the street were posters for weekenders in Canvey Island hosted by DJ Offline. Meanwhile, the newspaper racks revealed *Evening Standard's* headline yet again was "Offline Craze Goes Global".

Page seven of the *Metro* contained a photo of Andre pulling a sad face and pointing to his grazed cheekbone. This appeared above a whinging article claiming that after attending a meeting in the hopes of "making friends", Andre was bullied by a survivalist underground gang of hackers with stockpiled weapons and plans to bring down the government.

Buzzfeed, on the other hand, ran a piece on how to be a modified version of an Offliner.

1. *Keep your Facebook friend list to less than 2500*
2. *Limit selfies to 20 a day*

3. *Avoid high street or designer clothes (Superdry now have an Offliner range which is based on clothes you might just stumble across in a thrift store. Prices start at around £80)*
4. *Take only 15 minutes of every day to browse emails or catch up on missed calls*
5. *Get someone to take your picture in a park or on a swing. You could just pass for an Offliner!*

The writer of the above piece was subsequently barred from Offline events. He had been caught gatecrashing in order to furtively film for research. Within a month, Buzzfeed doubled down by publishing an article entitled, "Why Being Offline is Culturally Problematic and What You Can Do About It".

Dylan's dad excitedly unwrapped his parcel of cycling gear from Svelte, complete with Hawaiian arm warmers and reflective heritage cap. He admired himself in the mirror and took several selfies, splattering them all over Instagram with hashtags like *#bike, #cycle, #road, #outdoors, #paleo,* and *#mamil*. To Dylan's dad's line of thinking, if one acknowledges one is a middle-aged man in Lycra, absolution for being a dickhead is shortly to follow.

Dylan's dad mounted his Trek Madone and cycled all along St Margaret's, Chiswick bridge, Hammersmith, Putney, and Putney Graveyard, where some of *The Omen* was filmed and the peasants revolted.

There, smoking a Marlboro on the tombstone of Eileen Fogharty - *born 1943, fell asleep 1997, loved by family and friends and always alive in our hearts* - was Stephanie Korovnik. A Mamil and a MILF, two mythical woodland beings, surrounded by the rotting corpses of bygone Londoners who didn't grumble and ate up all their pie.

"Hello, sailor," Stephanie thought this greeting was enigmatic.

"Hello, you," Dylan's dad responded.

"Does your wife know you've gone out like that?" asked Stephanie. She always liked to mention his wife. She liked the fact that he was married, she didn't even fancy Dylan's dad that much, just liked the idea that someone liked her enough to take the risk. It boosted her confidence. Her psychotherapist had told her that because she had had parents who spoiled her, it had given her an inferiority complex about whether she deserved praise. Stephanie was a brave little soldier, really, to make it through some afternoons. Additionally, she also liked the look of guilt on Dylan's dad's face when his wife or family was mentioned. The look of slight sadness made her feel like she had a magic light she could flick on or off at a whim.

"You look nice," he said by way of reply. Stephanie was wearing a beige skirt just above knee length.

Her legs were slightly apart, not in a sexual way, but like an apathetic teenage boy flicking ash on someone's tombstone. "Can I touch your helmet?" she asked.

"It's not a helmet," he corrected, "It's a heritage cap. I have got a helmet. It's a specialized aligned helmet with micro-adjust dial for secure and accurate fit."

Without warning, Stephanie grabbed him by the cock. Mechanically, Dylan's dad responded by kissing her. Stephanie could feel the coldness. "What's the matter?"

"Any news about Molly?"

She tutted. "Yes, came back two hours ago," Stephanie said in an attempt at dark humour, "I just didn't think I'd mention it."

"Sorry, that was a stupid question," he responded, acknowledging the sarcasm, "How are you, by the way?" he asked, making one-sided eye contact.

She stared ahead and continued to smoke, "Horny."

“Any gigs?”

“Preston, Dartford, Billericay,” she said as if rattling off the locations by rote. There followed a pregnant pause with varicose veins and a craving for wall plaster. “Look, can we just fuck?”

“Here?” asked Dylan’s dad, waving towards the graves.

“Yes, your silly bastard,” snapped Stephanie, “that is, if you can climb out of your leotard.”

“Actually, I don’t think I can. Any chance we can we just chat?”

She closed her legs, sighed contemptuously, and stubbed out her cigarette on a fresh bouquet of lilies someone had left in remembrance of their dead child. “I suppose.”

“So,” he offered, “must be strange with Molly gone.”

“Not that” Stephanie took a swig from a small bottle of Evian, gulped down a Menoforce tablet and willed a tiny blackbird to fly off to the right of her eye line giving her an excuse to look away.

“By the way,” he continued, searching for a neutral subject, “what do you think about all those kids not being online? Personally, I can’t see my kids getting into it. What do you reckon they do at these events?”

“Oh, it’s probably manufactured by a production team,” surmised Stephanie, “They can’t possibly be doing it without wanting recognition. When does anyone do anything anymore without wanting positive feedback? I should know, I’m the queen of positive feedback. My therapist says it’s my Mana, my Prana, and my –”

“Banana?” he teased.

“That’s why I’m the comedian, not you.” she snidely responded.

“I just wondered,” continued Dylan’s dad, “you know, if we’re all being brainwashed.”

"Steady on, David Icke."

"I had this dream the other night," he said in a rare excursion into self-reflection.

"Oh yes?" Stephanie asked in a camp voice like Alison Steadman in *Abigail's Party* or Marlene Boyce from "Only Fools and Horses".

"Yeah," he said, "I dreamt that it was about 1999 or 1998. I don't know when exactly."

Stephanie stifled a yawn and gave her phone a covetous look.

Dylan's dad continued, unabated, "And I had no worries. I felt free. And there was no internet and no mobile phones. Well, there were, of course, but not really. And when I woke up, I felt happy."

"That's because you didn't have a wife and family," she cynically conjectured.

"It was more than that," he said wistfully, "I can't explain really. It was a deep feeling. A feeling of relief. Freshness."

"Calm down Captain Cave-in, listen," she exhaled, "I know a very good shrink. He's brilliant, in fact. Let me send you his number and we'll hook up when you're feeling more up for it. Remember when you were up for it?"

"Sorry," Dylan's dad apologised sheepishly.

"S'ok." Stephanie arose and kissed him on the cheek, looking for the nearest exit. "I'm going to pop by Hammersmith Apollo. Ross Noble's there. He's a friend!" She walked off, tap-tapping away, chin spreading onto neck, and neck melting onto chest.

Dylan's dad sat on the grass, careful to avoid anyone's grave, and stared ahead of him. *Who am I?* he wondered; *I am a person doing an impression of a person.* He breathed in the raw air. It smelled fresh with a slight tinge of nettles, a pissy smell of weeds and nettles. And, appropriately, a fair amount of sap.

He looked around at all the inscriptions on the headstones. All the men who had died at war, all the women who had died widows of men who had died at war. There were tiny baby graves covered in teddy bears and butterfly mobiles. *What have I become?* he thought, *I have stopped feeling, haven't I? I've stopped thinking about the deeper things.*

Dylan's dad felt as though that crazy weekend at uni, smoking half a weak spliff, and pondering whether everything was just a dream might not have been enough. He apprehended that he hadn't, as he'd previously believed, walked on the philosophical wild side and managed to get everything out of his system. *Maybe I am just playing a role,* he wondered, *Maybe my life has just run along tramlines at the whim of the culture around me. I'm a pubic hair wafting around in the winds of fate, a prisoner of the zeitgeist. Do I even know what I like? I mean, did I actually like* Lord of the Rings? *What about shitake mushrooms on sprouted pumpkin bread? Or Strawfest?* Strawfest was a music festival geared towards parents and dominated by children, replete with face painting and puppet shows.

His internal monologue continued to bubble over, *Do I really find "Comedy Scamps", BBC1's latest primitive primetime? Do I really fancy Scarlett Johansson? Well, obviously, yes. But perhaps I'm only doing an impression of the sort of person who likes all those things?*

The penny suddenly dropped so loudly it knocked him out of his pretentious reverie. "Woah, that was deep!" Dylan's dad exclaimed. To capture the raw feeling, he took a selfie exactly as he was at that moment. He then logged into Facebook, uploaded the photo, and captioned it: *Just sitting in the sun pondering the meaning of life...*

Dylan's dad felt pleased with himself. He had often wondered how he could make his online activity more organic by raising his authenticity game. *This was it*, he grinned to himself, *feel a feeling and immediately document it. Reach out and start a conversation and all those sorts of terms.*

He cycled home in a jovial mood and spent the afternoon scrolling the feedback on his upgraded cyber-self. Later, he shared a couple of powerful memes about how one should spend more time having real conversations with real people. To top the day off, he liked a funny post someone had written about how boring it is when people photographed their dinner. It had been bitter and angry, a proper *rant!* The post felt anarchic and exciting to his fat suburban mind. This was the new rebellion. The prisoners were rattling their plates in advance of a potential breakout.

And then, realising the house was empty, he pushed all thoughts of revolution out of his head for the time being and logged into Redtube.

Yes. Licorice hair and caramac bodies.

Chapter Thirty-Four

Louise had only taken a couple of escorting jobs, not including the Steven Starkey diversion. The attempt had been a stupid, spur of the moment thing. She had reached a desperate state of mind, one so topsy-turvy that she actually felt like an imbecile for *not* being an escort.

With her trusty fake ID, she had uploaded her picture to the agency website with more speed than she had used to open her Spotify account. With cold detachment, she allowed the avatar in her mind to go through the motions as the real Louise banked the spoils. To her reckoning, she'd feel nothing. *Of course, I can do this,* she calculated, *It wouldn't be me. I'd have to feel like this anyway doing tele sales. Maybe I can make it an out-of-body experience, split myself in half. It's not me they're swearing at, insulting.*

When Louise worked at a regular job, she had received so much harassment that she convinced herself she might as well be properly paid for being harassed. *It's the smart thing to do, isn't it?* she had thought, *Who was the real idiot, after all? Life was always going to be shit, so, why not make some money?* It had been one of those three in the morning, piss-poor, no hope, no chances, got to get out of this, cool chick in a Hollywood film moments. After all, who wants to be the mousey wife or clingy ex in the film? There's always an independent 'sex worker' with smart one-liners and more self-possession than a bailiff who owes himself money. *Pull yourself up by your bootstraps*, she had justified the venture to herself, *like that song by Bobby Gentry. Maybe I can end up in an elegant town house like those lyrics promised or be taken to the opera like Julia Roberts.*

Louise hadn't ended up at the opera but there was a *soap* opera playing in the bedsit of the mentally ill – or, in his own words, "I've got mental health" – beetle-bodied man in Crystal Palace. This was convenient because it allowed her to focus on Gail Rodwell's long-suffering face while her first client awkwardly approximated a vague shadow of a memory of doing sex on a lady. The only drawback was that she could never watch "Coronation Street" again.

This experience hadn't been as bad as she'd expected, mostly because it hadn't felt like sex. The mentally ill man was like an angry child acting out his own physical exorcism whilst she was. . . nearby. Granted, at some intervals, she was nearby enough to get bodily fluids on her, but that's what soap and water was for. And besides, Louise could've been superseded with a pot plant wearing a necklace. So, the entire experience felt far from personal.

The icing on the fat, lumbering baby's cake was when the kitchen door opened. The client's carer had come out and offered to give Louise a £20 tip. When Louise refused, thinking the carer was trying for a threesome, he informed her that she may as well take the money as it was the local authority's cash. It was part of a new scheme to provide sexual relief for the mentally ill, or the mentally fragile, or anybody else at risk of being on the bipolar spectrum or, presumably, anyone vaguely miffed. Not that Louise was complaining, but she did wonder that if sexual activity and body image positivity seemed to be a human right which should be catered to and funded, then why didn't the same hold for university degrees? *Why couldn't one go to the doctor and complain, 'Doctor, I feel stupid, can I do a course in astrophysics, please?* 'she imagined, *Surely, this was a statement of preference. Brawn over brain. Sex over sense. Oh, well. Just hope for a fortunate rebirth.*

Her subsequent client had been a South London ex-boxer who had taken so much cocaine he was incapable of getting an erection. Eventually, after pacing around, punching the wall, watching *The Smurfs* and *The Smurfs 2*, the Bermondsey Brawler told Louise he was bipolar, asked her to put lip gloss on him and call him "Stacey". Her L'Oréal Mercury Crystal conflicted with his colouring quite alarmingly, so she promised to give him a full makeover the following week.

Right now, though, it was beginning to get dark and Louise's stomach was panging. She popped out with a handful of tuppences to see if she could make a meal. More *Quel Dommage* than *Belle De Jour.*

"Where are you from?" demanded a foreign man with an ant's head and a long leather jacket.

"England," sighed Louise.

"Finland?" he misheard.

"England."

"Finland?" he persisted.

"Here," she snapped, "I am from here."

"No, you are not."

"Why not?"

With a crooked smile, he opined, "English people are not friendly."

"I'm not friendly," she said.

"Yes, you are."

"No, I'm not," Louise insisted.

"I think you are very friendly," he continued.

"You are mistaken."

He went in for the kill, "Come to casino with me."

"Nah, s'alright."

"Why not?" he was taken aback, "You are not very friendly!"

"You just said I was!" she sighed in dreary deadpan.

She rattled her keys in the front door of her B&B and made her way in. Negotiating the pile of pushchairs that always helpfully blocked the entrance in case of a fire, she noticed something that had fallen down the back of the hallway radiator along with a Pimlico Plumbers' leaflet.

It was a letter addressed to her. That usually didn't happen. Only brown envelopes from case workers and social services ever arrived. Louise tore through the envelope as she ran up the stairs. Once in her bedsit, she sat cross-legged on the lumpy, veiny mattress. Almost shredding it in her urgency, she produced a cheque from Barnaby Jaspar for £50,000.

The MP had big, square handwriting, just like his big square head. The amount, it was specified, was to pay for any courses she may want to do along with a deposit for a flat. Or, as Barnaby himself put it before the closing smiley face, *Have a break in Devon.*

Louise screamed in joy and leapt in the air several times, shaking her arms and legs. The elation was too much for her small frame to contain. Things like this never happened to people like her. After processing the fortunate turn of events and calming down enough to function, she began searching Gumtree for decent accommodation. *Devon can wait.*

Chapter Thirty-Five

Monday morning, Dylan kept falling asleep during yet another special assembly about the Offliners.

"So, there will be some posters around the place with some websites you can visit to learn what to do if you find a flyer, and an App you can download and share any information about this growing menace" the head teacher, Mrs. Devaney-Cox, said to the students, "They look like this. Does that make sense?" Devaney-Cox had wanted to keep her maiden name along with her married one in order to be taken seriously - as a woman. She held up an Offliners flyer which none of the students could possibly see from that distance. "And what you can do if someone approaches you about attending one of their so-called events. It might seem like fun, but police are gathering increasing amounts of intelligence that they are highly dangerous. Not to mention the health and safety issues, a reemergence of Covid-19, for one. Remember, we are putting the older generations and minorities at risk, we are all in this together and have a duty to protect society as a whole. So, what we are asking you to do is to cooperate with us and, in so doing, you'll be helping yourselves, the school, and your community. Does that make sense? Now, on to other news. Some of you are still turning up with whole grapes in your lunchboxes. Grapes must be cut in half and, if possible, quartered. Please tell your parents. Also, running in the playground. It continues. We've had awareness sessions. We've sent emails. We've hired lunchtime stewards." She enunciated the following for effect: "No. Running. Inside. The. School. At. Any. Time. Is this clear?"

As if personally affected, a 15-year-old burst into tears and was quickly taken away with a teacher's comforting arms around him.

Sleeping in the main hall, Dylan suddenly jerked awake in time to hear the final insult.

"Ooh, I almost forgot," said Devaney-Cox like an excitable YouTube influencer demonstrating how to make slime from contact lens solution and not the educator she was supposed to be, "my daughter Millie is entering a poetry competition and her entry is on this webpage. DiVerseCity.com. She's done extremely well so far and we're all really proud of her. If you'd like to go and give your support by liking the page and voting for her, then that would be super-duper cool."

I don't get it, thought Dylan, *What's the "Di" in DiVerseCity for? It doesn't work as a pun or anything. Why didn't she ask if that made sense?*

Dylan decided to bunk off school to sit in the park and listen to his battery-operated radio in the sunshine.

Offliners, began Ian Farrington, *What are they? A new species? A rebellious breed of feral youth? Just a bunch of nice kids who like a good old knees-up? Whatever they are, they're becoming impossible to ignore. Bob Dylan once sang "your sons and your daughters are beyond your command" and it appears, for the first time in what seems like a revolution famine, it's true. Call me if you are an Offliner. Presumably, you can still use telephones. You're not Luddites, are you? Or orthodox Jews on the Sabbath? Also, I'll be speaking with a real-life Offliner, Elliot, a bit later on. That is, if he can get here without Google Maps! If you call right now, you'll get to speak to Master Farrington, who's here on work experience. Chip off the old block, he is! And if you're still here at four, we'll be pondering the recent news that knife crime has declined to 1992 levels. What's the cause? Are young people just. . . tired?*

Dylan frowned at hearing Elliot's name, but fell asleep with a contented excitement about life. Something was happening. Whatever else might be going on, there was something at last. At long, long, bastard last.

Dylan had been attending almost every Offliner event he could. This involved an exhausting degree of lying and subterfuge. It was very hard to avoid the internet at school, so he would feign illness or eye pain and be allowed to go outside and get some air. At home, Dylan's dad would sometimes torture him by calling him over to look at something on the laptop. To Dylan, computers had begun to look and feel so small and plastic and worthless. Computers were now nagging, know-it-all parasites that were always vying for attention.

Dylan, on the other hand, was reading five books a week. His vocabulary had changed. He was ticking every box on the *Daily Mail's* Offliner checklist. There was a chance that this generation was going to arrest the steady fall in IQ since 1998 and stave off a further predicted decline of 1.3 points by 2050.

It could all be reversed. The Offliners still accessed data, but they printed it out or managed to get other people to print it out. Reams and reams of articles were at their disposal free from all the unnecessary clickbait down the sides like: *You won't believe these 20 child stars who now make porn.*

On his way to the latest event, Dylan heard faint music getting louder along with a low murmur of voices. Soon, he was able to pick out individual laughs and screams. Dylan crossed over the road, smelling the suburban summer night air of Chinese food and Sports Centre chlorine.

"Dylan!" a boy shouted, running whilst dodging traffic. The boy held the hand of a beautiful girl in a purple dress. As they approached Dylan, the girl's lilac perfume mixed with all the other small-town smells of Lynx, bonfire, takeaways, fresh sweat, and frustration. Eventually, even this was subsumed by the car exhaust fumes as the couple walked ahead of him en route to the event.

Dylan grinned, nodding in recognition. He picked his pace up into a half-run, half-walk. He soon merged with a huge group, all of whom were marching in the same direction. The night was alive again as it had once been a long, lost time ago.

Passing the barriers was becoming a tiresome affair, but Dylan's recognisable face as a founding Offliner was a backstage pass. A five-person deep ring of photographers and other Nosy Parkers was blocking the gates to paradise, but Dylan made it through.

It felt like two separate dimensions existed in and outside the barriers. It was like one of those dystopian films, but with the ferals inside and the rest of the world captive outside. The government-funded Offliner enclosure was still in the process of being built. In the interim, hastily-thrown together music bands thrashed out their offerings. On site, there were compounds of interconnecting log cabins that made the members feel as though they were part of the woods. A huge billboard greeted the participants as they entered. *Barnaby Jaspar Housing Project*: *Proud to be Investing in Youth.* The government logo could be seen at the bottom of the billboard. Someone had graffitied over it, however, in thick, black spray paint: *Unsafe Space.*

Dylan suddenly recalled the salacious messages from Barnaby that Louise had shown him a few weeks earlier. *He'd been Investing in youth, all right*, he thought.

Walking towards the music, Dylan was hit hard in the shoulder by a boy running as fast as his fat legs could carry him – which was not very. The boy was wearing an #Offliners T-shirt and live-streaming his activities.

"Got one!" shouted a teenage sentinel. The battle cry made everyone within ear shot turn around to look for the dirty infiltrator.

"Oh, come on," pleaded Elliot, "we have to have a few for diversity." He defended the interloper and was backed up in his plea for mercy by Madison, Kaia, and several others. Numbers prevailed and they were allowed to remain.

Dylan looked around the scene. Record companies wanted to harvest the sounds they made. Food manufacturers wanted to know what they were eating. Clothing companies wanted to copy their peculiar rags. Everything moved faster in the offline world. There were no loops to get stuck in, no body dysmorphia, no gender issues, no hashtags, no sitting and scrolling, and no binary thinking. The medium was the message and the medium was instantaneous fun. "You thought it and you did it," was the unwritten credo, "right there and then, in real life IRL."

They were bringing sexy back.

Chapter Thirty-Six

It was at this apex of offline activity that, for the only time in its nine-month incubation, a police siren was heard. What should have been its birth was about to become a messy abortion performed with the rusty coat hanger of bureaucracy.

The appearance of the first black helicopter on the horizon at first seemed an anomaly.

"Probably on its way back to MI6," Flynn speculated hopefully, yet his lingering gaze into the sky was a Saturday morning giveaway. The first chopper was followed by another, then three more, then eight, all of them hovering around like flies on a child's spilt ice cream in the sand.

A voice boomed over a loudspeaker, informing the Offliners that they were taking part in an unauthorised event.

"We should run, now!" exclaimed Madison, suddenly. In her fear, she looked five-years-old. In fact, they all did.

"Nah, trust me," disagreed Elliot, "I've been kettled *hundreds* of times. Running is what they want you to do. Honestly, stay still and it'll be over soon." His khaki parka with the A for Anarchy on the back commanded at least a modicum of credence.

"No!" shouted Owen, "It was all getting better!" He pounded his head with clenched fists before plunging a knife into the side of a bright young aspiring footballer and fellow Offliner named Aaron. The knife's handle was brightly coloured in red and yellow swirls which stood out from the wooden surface and gave it texture.

Looks Mexican. Someone designed that, Aaron thought, awe-stricken with the colourful tool that had been plunged into his flesh. He was vaguely aware that the pocket of his Nike cagoule was damp with his own blood. As "Sympathy for the Devil" blasted from an old cassette player, Aaron grimly realised he was being served up as a human sacrifice at his own Altamont. The good spirits at discovering they were in possession of some Kettle Chips whilst being kettled was a short-lived novelty for the Offliners. A novelty which could not sustain them for the five hours they were trapped inside a ring of riot police. Not to mention, the whole murder-in-cold-blood thing.

The Offliners were slowly filtered through the hi-vis funnel, one by one, their microchips scanned, their location and participation duly noted. Those without a chip were quickly ushered off to a mobile unit and helpfully zapped by navy blue cardigan wearing NHS volunteers – all solid and plodding and biscuits and talking about summer holidays.

Dylan had been among a subset of Offliners to defy Elliot's advice and run before the ring of steel. Consequently, Dylan was surprised when a friendly community policeman shone a torch at him in the alleyway near Chicken Cottage. The community officer had been looking on a Satnav device. From beneath his recently assigned gender-neutral cap, he looked like a child's drawing of a policeman. The officer was all deflated as if he were supposed to be fat but someone had pulled a stopper and all the air had come out. Children drew Father Christmas much the same way. Someone should really teach children how to illustrate weight distribution. It would be a kindness.

"Dylan Curtis?" asked the officer.

How the fuck did he know my name? wondered Dylan.

"Well, it says it's you," continued the officer, "Unless there's a microchipped cat down here named Dylan Curtis. I wouldn't be surprised. People give their pets all kinds of bizarre names these days." The officer was gentle and jolly and showed Dylan the data he held on him as if the officer were an interested sociology teacher. "There you are," he pointed, "look, that's you. And if I click on here – hold on – it's still got a few teething problems – there! Your medical records." The officer tapped and scrolled, scrolled and tapped. "Ah, not much here yet. Yours is a skeleton file, but it'll build. Here's mine, look." He then held a scanner to his wrist and the screen before them was filled with a picture of the Canadian rock band Rush. "My wallpaper," he exclaimed and happily hummed "Tom Sawyer", his data-accessing song. "There's my profile," he continued, "Job, national insurance, allergies, family members, bank details, Amazon purchases." The officer was genuinely thrilled about it all." Look," he scanned his own chip again and touched the screen several more times. "It tells me my friend Carole lives 7.4 kilometers away and that she's in right now, but she's watching Ant and Dec's – well, 'Dec's Takeaway', so not an appropriate time to call. There's a gourmet burger stand here and it closes in 27 minutes. That must be because it knows I had a gourmet burger two weeks ago. Have you had one? Not sure what the difference is really. Quite gristly. My medical records, Covid clearance and blood donor details, in case anything happens to me. Which is why your mum and dad had the good sense to give you one, too. You're a lucky lad. They obviously care very much."

Chapter Thirty-Seven

It was day five of Dylan being grounded following the police raid on the Offliners.

"It was for your own good, mate," said Dylan's mum, "Those unauthorised events are death traps and we're so close to the official one anyway. We can all go as a family!" She tried her best to talk her son around.

Dylan was being kept off school. Sitting in front of the TV in his Dad's *Star Wars* dressing gown, his thumb twitched on an invisible phone. Dylan's phone had fallen between two cushions, one with an Aztec pattern and one bearing the words "Keep Calm, Seriously? In This House?"

The programmes screamed at him in bright colours and hysterical bursts. There was no point going out anyway. There were no genuine Offliner events anymore. Most Offliners had also received a microchip along with their B6 shot. Many of them had gone back online, blogging and vlogging about their short adventure. Of course, there were also many who hadn't been there, blogging and vlogging about their short adventure. It was similar to all the people who claimed to have been at The Screen on the Green in Islington in 1977 to see Roger Decourcy and Nookie Bear.

Many teens were also reporting the B6 overdose was giving them vivid dreams, along with a noxious and luminous lime-coloured piss. Owen, however, wasn't doing any of these things as he'd been arrested the night of the raid. He had been kettled and connected with eighteen stabbings during the nine months of the Offliners existence. Also, the Duchess of Cambridge attended SportAid in a tailored beige coat and fitted black trousers.

Meanwhile, closer to nature, birds tweeted like they always had and a breeze ran through Liam's poker-straight, not quite brown, and not quite blonde, hair. He rode round the abandoned official Offliner site in his school jumper on a Saturday. He fed half his sandwich to a family of foxes now living in the unfinished interconnected log cabins. Above the derelict enclosure hung a huge billboard bearing the name of a private corporation.

Heroin addicts shot up in a bricked-off square which had once contained a fire, gloriously burning all that was stagnant. Onesies and giant animal slippers, adult colouring books, and wicker hearts.

Luckily for him, Liam did not get a microchip. He wasn't registered with a doctor and happened to be off school the day the nurse came in to administer it to anyone the national round-up might have missed. Besides, his Nan didn't agree with it in principle, said it was "Against God's plan" Liam cycled faster as his cousin Seany caught up on his Apollo Envy Junior, a bike which Seany was far too big for. Liam looked back, taking huge bites of his apple and then throwing the core at Seany's spokes. He flicked his fringe from his eyes which creased at the sides with laughter. A fox poked its head out and licked its mangy coat.

Liam's life had not changed at all.

Chapter Thirty-Eight

"It was a proper cheque," pleaded a worried Louise, "made out to me. I deposited it in person. Can you look? Just check? Check the cheque? Ha ha. Does it sometimes take longer than three working days? I mean, isn't it breaking the law or something?" The advisor at Barclays Bank was starting to give sideways glances to his colleague. Meanwhile, the security guard was pacing closer and closer. "Oh look," she said dismissively, "here comes the cavalry."

"It hasn't cleared," said the Barclays advisor, "and I'm afraid we're limited in what we can do at this end. Does that make sense? I suggest you speak to the account holder." The member of staff spoke to her as though she were stupid yet dangerous.

Louise was sure the phrase "does that make sense?" would be coming around again soon if she persisted. She felt slightly shaky. Part of her ached for something she was so close to she could almost taste and part of her relaxed because things were back to normal. A sadly resigned segment of Louise sighed with a fatalistic relief. Things were as they had always been and always would be: Shit.

The pink drained from her cheeks and her brow furrowed. *Well*, she concluded, *that was that.* Her brief butterfly summer had flown away with flea-bitten wings and a £1.50 deficit on its Oyster Card. Further depressing matters, she returned home to discover her room had been trashed. Her scrapbooks had been taken and phone wiped except for a new message escorting job at the address of an M. Fernbridge '*bring tights'* This just as Barnaby Jaspar had - alongside a member of the Royal Family - been appointed advisor to a government initiative offering support to sexually abused teens - #handsoff they had named it.

In forums, some ex-Offliners swore blind they could dream themselves into Offliner events. They offered up pages of data concerning B6 increasing dream recall and intensity. Lucid dreaming, they reckoned. The dreamers would oversleep, trying to keep the nocturnal event going, if only in their minds. And, for their efforts, they would be diagnosed as depressed and put on pills which made them depressed. This made them want to escape by sleeping. It was similar to *Nightmare on Elm Street*, but in this version, Freddy Krueger existed in the waking hours. Freddy was Facebook and Instagram and daytime television. Freddy was a dad dressed in Lycra on a Saturday morning. Freddy was a Mum typing seventy-five paragraphs on a Positive Parenting thread about how her kids have gone off Shreddies and sometimes tapped their feet when they talked.

Freddy was the reality show contestant named Raymond, a personality substituted with sleeve tattoos and an exotic pet. Freddy was the not-quite-a-bully who hovered around the real bullies because anything is better than not joining in. He was the 50-year-old man, logging in to write a status about how he had just performed an anonymous act of random kindness. He was the passive-aggressive meme of a girl in denim shorts in a field with the weasely caption "I will not apologise for evolving past your comfort level". Freddy was the guy in the park filming his dog chasing a stick repeatedly, until the canine's activity was deemed screen-worthy. The poor dog looking up patiently as his companion watched each frame, carefully assessing the like potential. Freddy was the viral poem about how we all need to look up from our phones. The one that everyone shared on their phones. The YouTuber community, evangelical about free speech, neurotically obsessing over views and subs, blocking people over imagined slights, playing to the gallery with what their patrons wanted, flipping on a dime for popularity, and saying anything to avoid a job requiring leaving the house or mixing with the drab mundanity of a real life they were too fragile to navigate. The 'culture wars' Ex-Leftists fighting their own shadow selves. The internet had

PWNED them all. No selfies of them next to a surfboard or in a bar with a pint was going to make amends. It was everywhere and everything.

Families attended the brilliantly stupid Online Offline events with full security and stewards and Facebook groups. Profits were up on all platforms and log-ins were climbing by the minute. Live-streaming devolved into 90s Dirty Sanchez-style desperation. *I'm an Offliner, dude!* Short films were being blogged and re-blogged about being free and re-discovering life away from the internet. Grown men set fire to their beards or squirted petrol up their arses. Jugglers, baby lambs, and people meditating in India with little night lights and poems about authenticity and touching base with humanity – all of these went viral.

Several weeks passed by for Dylan in a fog of sleep, carbs and *Grand Theft Auto*. He caught a glimpse of himself in a mirror. His face was softening around the edges and he could no longer do up the zip on his jeans. He was apathetic, immobile, a castrated hamster in a tank. His skin was yellow-tinged and his piss fluorescent. He was becoming a plump, dimwitted emoji, the one that signifies "I give up".

There had been three more suicides at Dylan's school. There were hints, rumours actually, that the victims had been bullied both face-to-face and online. All this information had led to was opening up a dialogue about mental health and the pressures that young people face in a complicated digital age.

"I fink that Layla struggled with self-esteem and that we can all feel like we have to be perfect sometimes, but it's good to just let the pressure off from time to time and be aware that we all have these feelings. I mean, it's like with a broken leg. Everyone can see that you have an injury but –" Dylan's classmate Chloe performed before a nodding panel of pop star, politician, and cookery show presenter. This awareness event, incidentally, took place three weeks after Chloe had Snapchatted Layla to tell her that everyone hated her and she should probably kill herself because she was too much of a disgusting skank to live.

The photo of the mental health event that appeared in the local paper was a huge hit. The school was thrilled with the publicity. The sanctimonious image featured Chloe's head on one side, iron-on eyebrows, and boil-in-the-bag charisma. She grinned widely and held a piece of card which read *#mentalhealthawareness #speakup*. Next to her, the politician made a heart shape with his clumsy, hammy fists.

Catching up with the present, Dylan groped around until he had his phone finally back in his hand. He tapped on Twitter. *#ripStevenStarkey* was trending.

OMG, tweeted Stephanie Korovnik, *they're saying he scheduled tweets to go out after he died, anyone know about it? so sad.* She had added a sad face emoji in case there was any doubt. *I LOVED his last book 'My Bicycle My Guru.'* she persisted as she closed Starkey's Wiki page on her laptop. *I hope no one thinks this is insensitive, but if anyone had him booked for interviews this week, I'm available. I'm pretty sure it's what he would have wanted, we were friends for 40 years*, she said of the deceased 38-year-old author.

Dylan vegetated as reality shows flashed between ads. There was "Where there's a Will, There's a Gay", a self-explanatory legal half-hour with Judge Rinder. Also, there was "1940s Woman", an excruciating hour-long comedy featuring a horse-faced, drama school Emma Thompson substitute pretending to be a woman from the 1940s in different modern settings. The ingénue carried on with a cheery, wartime, sleeves-rolled-up Blitz spirit. If these didn't suit, there was a new programme, "Offline and Sinker", which cashed in on the now-defunct and shortest-lived youth movement ever. Italia Conte kids pretended to be offline, simulating sex with furniture. They were all sleeve tattoos and ambiguous sexuality.

A live panel of experts appeared in between prerecorded footage to discuss the dynamics. Stephanie Korovnik had a regular gig there, now reunited, as she was, with Molly. Miles Fernbridge was on the panel as well. He had confessed to kidnapping, but to ameliorate his crime, had also confessed to a life-long history of depression. According to Miles, he had always felt that he had to cover up his emotions with barbed dictums and heartless conduct, but inside he was crying for help. When he had finished reading his publicist's statement, he was embraced, once more, by the public. Additionally, he was given regular slots on chin-stroking magazine-type shows. This was a boon for him since he felt too old for stand-up comedy/had run out of people to steal lines from/was addicted to masturbating in pre-worn 10 denier tights - which requires a lot of time on eBay. And was, almost *elaborately,* unfunny.

Chapter Thirty-Nine

Dylan flicked through channels, squinting at Television X before his Mum seized the remote from him and turned it back to "Country File" with an agonising "boys will be boys" look. Dylan had been sure that one of the babes had looked exactly like Louise if she had had her long red ringlets butchered into a straightened, deep brown liquorice iron curtain. Whoever she was, she had been doing that shaking the phone thing, riding an invisible aardvark, and trying to keep up the manic QVC facial expressions in the process.

It wasn't Louise. Louise was drinking Buckfast - the discerning tramp's choice - with her super-naturally beautiful girlfriend, Simone - a high waisted waster who looked like she'd stepped off the set of an 80's pop video - Whitesnake or Cameo - not Half Man Half Biscuit or The Cardiacs. It appeared the three-magpie prophecy had come to pass. She licked the *Sexy Mother Pucker White Chocolate, Rose Petal and raspberry After Glow Pixie Lip Butter* that Simone's tongue had left on her teeth in a frenzied celebratory kiss - like a forklift truck, struck upon a porn star.

They'd met on the mid-wifery course forming an umbilical bond, no awkward, boring weeks of testing each other's friendship potential. They knew. Quitting the course together during the second module when the teacher began referring to people as 'cis-gendered' and 'chest feeders' they realised there were other things they wanted to bring kicking and screaming into the world besides the next generation of box ticking shadows of a memory of humanity.

Louise wasn't a complete idiot. Of course, she had backed up all of the dirty data from the dishonorable member and bypassed blackmail going straight to the papers giving her 'nuff paper' herself, spookily enough, fifty thousand pounds. Karma is a beach, Praia Formosa beach in Madeira to be exact which is where they were headed.

Their first kiss had Louise briskly up against the wall of Simone's Stratford flat, the happy drunken maneuver broken by Simone laughingly wiping Louise's face which had Clinique Black Honey lipstick – a hundred percent deserving of its cult status - smeared all over her white silk stocking skin, "I'm not a dyke" Simone made clear, holding Louise's face in front of her make-up smudged Betty Boop mirror and contradicting the electrical storm happening in her body and brain which pissed all over anything a boring boy had ever made her feel. "Neither am I!" Louise insisted, and with that misunderstanding cleared up, they continued not being dykes for the next two weeks before they threw their phones in the Thames – no more open portals to perversely puerile politicians or crossly cross-dressing comedians - jumped on a plane in a real girls adventure story that Adam Lastname's red raw from Redtube, eyes would never get to see. The world was their Oyster and not just the kind that gets you to Peckham on a Friday night.

"I think maybe I should try some sort of medication again," Dylan pliantly muttered. His eyes were black holes and he could not move his mouth fast enough for the words. Consequently, spit came out instead of sound. He didn't even notice as his mum wiped his face, just like when he was a toddler.

"Oh love," said his mum, "I'm so pleased to hear that, mate. It's not a sign of weakness. You know, it's actually a sign that you've been strong for too long." Her enthusiasm emanated through Manuka Doctor Bee Venom Plumped Lips. *A duckbilled platitude.* "I'll make you an appointment for tomorrow and we'll see if they can recommend some sort of serotonin re-uptake inhibitor. Duloxetine is a good one."

Dylan felt his insides cave in. It was a long, dark, aching echo of hollow nothingness. He sobbed uncontrollably.

"Oh, it's okay," she cooed, "Come on, now." Dylan's mum rubbed her son's back. "Look, I know I'm just your mum and I'm profoundly uncool and everything and I've got no idea what it's like to be a teenager these days. I mean, Karen Yate's Harmony hair-sprayed crimp going up in smoke on the bus when someone lit up a cigarette was all we had to worry about. But I do care and – oh, I don't know! It's all insane, isn't it." Looking away from Dylan, she frowned in concentration.

"How'd you mean?" asked Dylan. He began to see his mum as a human being for the first-time in . . . well, ever.

"I mean, this," she said, picking up her phone with careless contempt and then instantly slamming it down again. "This isn't what I signed up for. I mean, I have noticed how everything's been hijacked. I'd sometimes just like to kick back and listen to a mix tape and not worry that I haven't replied to a bloody email or wished someone I haven't seen for 25 years a happy birthday on Facebook. It's bullshit, isn't it, to a degree?"

Dylan nodded slowly with wide and red-rimmed eyes. *What a selfish prick I've been*, he thought, *Of course, everyone felt the same. There was nothing special about the Offliners. Everyone else knew it all, too. They were just getting on with things. Perhaps that was a bigger sacrifice. Perhaps they were the ones buckling down to make lives, homes, and memories. And it would have been the same when books were invented, wouldn't it? And telephones and televisions and* – he reached the grim conclusion – *it was time for me to grow up. I'm twice as big as my mum and it was time I acted like it.*

Dylan sniffed into his mum's hair and gave her shoulder a reassuring squeeze, blinking away his blurry tears. He tried to control his throbbing head as something was flying around in the corner of his eye. Not the black floaters he used to get from too much screen time. These were yellow.

The emojis floated up like Safe Space Invaders across Dylan's mum's laptop. It was her friends' reactions to their mum-and-son interaction.

"What're you doing?" Dylan squinted with sideways eyes and pointed to the computer with his little finger.

"Live streaming on E-moat," she beamed, "It's for special moments. 'Emotion' and 'Moat', because the community forms a moat around you. A moat of mental health and well-being and support."

A shiver traversed Dylan's spine as if someone had unplugged the cord. With that, one last spark of hope escaped, crackled, and died.

Lovin your interaction, keep the channels of self-expression open! #Motherandson #heart2heart #Emoat #Anemone

Chapter Forty

Welcome back to 'Offline and Sinker'! When we left, Tasha and Hunter were getting it on!

Woooooooooooo! chimed the audience in unison as though there could be anything sexually stimulating about the announcement – trying, as it was, to drag out a tired old rag of an idea of sexually stimulating. The "Wooooos" were led by Stephanie Korovnik and an "Offline and Sinker" contestant who had been voted out. Miles Fernbridge was there, too, shamelessly advertising the faddish blue health drink he remembered to keep within eye shot on the desk. He attempted every now and then to inject dark cynicism into the proceedings, but his efforts were empty. The fact that he was there negated anything dark or cynical.

"Just when you thought it couldn't get any more exciting," Miles monotonously droned, trying to build a knowing sense of sceptic connection with the viewers. His eyes were redder and deader than Chairman Mao's ghost, dressed as Santa, to give out gifts for all the kids. A prospect that Chairman Mao himself would *hate.*

Dylan's mum tweeted *Can't believe I'm watching this rot, do quite like Olivia tho!*

Grace checked what everyone else was saying and responded in kind, *Can't stand Lacey!* She left that tweet up until public consensus suddenly shifted, *Can't stand Tasha!*

In the studio audience, unbeknownst to each other, Adam Lastname and Amy, in separate sections, stalked each other's profiles. They tweeted along with *#Offliners*. Amy had been forgiven by the online community for her act of animal cruelty when she had come out as bipolar. Of course.

Dylan's dad's intern Shane updated his status like everyone else. *OMG! how much fake tan is Chloe wearing?! what a SLAG! Quite fancy Hunter though.* This effort was liked by his straight colleagues who would have harshly judged another straight man or even woman for saying the equivalent, but his workmates needed people to know they were not homophobes.

For the protected classes, it would forever be 1985 politically. Profile pictures, happy and robust, human selves rotting, desperate eyes searching and grasping and forever missing something they couldn't put their fingers on.

Let's have a sneaky look at what they've been doing in the pirate castle of love! a black-market Bobbie Norris enthused, grabbing the tits of his co-presenter and managing to skillfully cram the visual portrayal of *look at me being heterosexual – isn't it sexy? Oh no, I actually find you repugnant* – into a three-second, peevish gurn.

The theme tune to "Offline and Sinker" brayed like a hyperactive three-year-old with its face stuffed with fizzy strawberry shoelaces and caffeine. The ident of a pirate ship sinking with cartoon teens in bikinis flashed in a brutal, primary-coloured, frontal lobe epilepsy attack.

And if you want to interact with "Offline and Sinker", you can Snapchat us, follow us on Instagram, or I'll be live on Facebook in 5, 4, 3, 2, --

Underneath the live stream, the comments arose. *I think Harry and Siobhan are SOOO well suited!*

Totally despise that skank Lola

Bring back Rylan, this guy's a fucktard

Angie is fit

Nah she ain't she looks like a fucking vampire rat

Too much make-up

Woman shouldn't wear make-up, all the woman on this show are such ugly skanks

Grow up idiot, typical, union jack in bio! Lol

*Aw, sorry snowflake *meme of Boris Johnson with the caption I AM YOUR PRIME MINISTER**

The grass grew outside, and the sun made unique patterns on the trees, never to be repeated in exactly the same way, pets went unappreciated and books went unread. Some of these people were 50-years-old.

Dylan scowled at the comments on his phone as they appeared and disappeared like sneering Cheshire cats. He put it down and looked up at the TV through dark and hollow eyes. Now that he looked at it objectively, in the cold bright light of day, he could see everything with a crystal clarity. There was no prejudice remaining. It all now made perfect sense. The scales had fallen from his eyes and this sheeple had finally woken up. *Angie was an ugly vampire rat with too much make-up!* he thought, *What a skank. What a stupid bitch! What an attention whore, going on reality TV, begging to be liked. How desperate can you get?* Dylan picked up his phone again and fumbled around. His fingers were out of practice and slow, nevertheless, he managed to tap out lethargically, one letter at a time: *Fuck off and die Angie!*

LOL the flurry of responses began.

Innit!

#fuckoffanddieAngie let's get this trending!

The replies gave Dylan a boost and he smiled, ever so slight, a mere fraction at the corner of his chocolate-encrusted mouth. His fingers limbered up and, like riding a bike, it all came back.

Kill the weasel face! Kill it with fire! Dylan typed with one hand at a mighty speed. Meanwhile, his other hand remained upturned on the sofa in-between his bulging gut and McDonald's chocolate milkshake his dad had picked up for him.

Lol

This is why you take a bitch swimming on the first date

To see if it's a weasel?

Nah! see how much make-up it's wearing!

LOL

Chapter Forty-One

"So," the company man began, "going forward, if we compare the fourth quarter financial highlights, share amounts, revenue, operating margin, and daily active user count going forward, we can see that there is a £48-57 billion cumulative increase ever since our data scientists implemented Operation Famine by expanding and utilising the growing Offliner trend. So, as our analysis team predicted, going forward, this has acted as a shot in the arm to the temporary slump brought on by users reaching an inspirational plateau in 2019. So, on average, users who partook in Operation Famine rebounded with an increased data usage of 70%. So, going forward, here are some more figures from monthly active users. Before, during and – this spike represents the improvement immediately following – the decimation of their offline activity, there was much to E-moat about, clearly. Now, on to our next project, Nano particle smart dust."

The corporate heads had gone so far *forward* that they had changed time zones.

The thirteen men and women, along with the diversity officer - an unspecified neurotic named Abigail, they/them/him/her/me/him/who/where/now/then/cheech/cheong/ laughed into their non plastic cups and cardboard cut-out copycat beards around the large glass table. They were a corporate hoody-wearing Last Supper, breaking ciabatta and drinking vanilla cashew milks and ginseng waters. The team assessed the figures, happily anticipating their well-earned bonuses.

Head of Strategy and Business Development Robin Chapman glanced at his Apple watch while his advisor and eldest son Elliot sucked iced coconut and mango from a hazelnut, cacao, and agave sugar straw. Elliot's fuck hair was now gone, the remnants combed forward over his alabaster forehead in a fluffy, third eye venetian blind. And his skinny black jeans' regulation symmetrical rips in both knees were slimy, slitty smirks.

Elliot's activist clothes were dug out again in time for him to livestream the Arcelormittal Orbit Offline celebration party. Che Guevara's beret was now faded, rendering the image nothing more than eyes, mouth, and flowing locks. An intern, not recognising the communist icon, asked him where he got his Rita Ora merch.

Elliot even had the audacity to carry a placard reading "Freedom for Offliners!" All the while, notifications pinged across his iPhone X, likes and comments for his latest post - a photo of him in front of a sunset with the caption *gratuitous and indulgent selfie!* When Elliot had the time, he would update his brand content.

#Lovin the latest #OFFLINE 3 game on Xbox. Like this post or upload a #selfie to get a #bankholiday #discount with #TheCheekyDancingMonkeyCompany #workhard #playhard #lovinglife #blessed #amazing #Anemone

Dylan's mum uploaded a picture of her son to the comments section of Elliot's post. His soppy blank eyes and half smile from a mouth that he'd either chewed until it bled or applied dark cherry lip gloss to, were sunken into a borderless porridge face. A triumph of hormone blockers, serotonin re-uptake inhibitors, digital implantation and social media addiction which had out-wrestled any dregs of primordial soup left in him into dull, stupid compliance. He was nothing more than a device through which his sexless, brainless, feedback addicted parents could feel they existed.

Gen Xrs. They were never going to be David Bowie or Courtney Love, now. And Tim Curry's *be it, don't dream it*, from Rocky Horror was a ship that sailed while they were smoking squidgy black, watching Eurotrash with one of those dancing flowers; reading Loaded, and moving in with the girlfriend/boyfriend they're in love with because he/she laughs at Newman and Baddiel just as much they do. But no one, but *no one,* was going to tell them that they couldn't have a sad cyborg son on a spectrum. They'd found their alternative lifestyle after all these years - an indie identity in the Chart Show smugly squashed between Lush and The Pixies. And therein lay their glimmer of glamour. Their fifteen minutes of same. Their Salvation to The Faithfully Departed.

Had an #amazing #interaction #therapy #session with my #Dylan. Feeling very #blessed and looking forward to having them home for as long as it takes #selfcare #emoat #mentalhealth #awareness #anemone"

Liked by Dylan Curtis.

Printed in Poland
by Amazon Fulfillment
Poland Sp. z o.o., Wrocław

58774066R00139